LIONS OF JUDEA

BOOK 1

eBookPro Publishing
www.ebook-pro.com

The Rise of the Maccabees
Lions of Judea - Book 1
Amit Arad

Translation: Jonathan Boxman
Contact: amitarad@013.net

ISBN: 9781091425422

LIONS OF JUDEA

THE RISE OF THE
MACCABEES

AMIT ARAD

PROLOGUE
Judean Mountains, 166 BCE

Dramatis Personae

Bold = main character

* = historical figure

- Apollonius*—Meridarch (governor) of Samaria
- Helena—Mistress of Apollonius
- Helios—Coachman of Apollonius
- **Tario**—Commander of the Seleucid garrison in the meridarchy of Samaria
- Nexus—Commander of an infantry company in the Samaria garrison
- **Phryne**—A Jewish slave girl of Apollonius
- **Judah***—Commander of the Jewish rebels

In spite of the parched air, beads of sweat poured down Helios' skin with the effort of keeping focused on driving the carriage. He constantly shifted his position, trying to evade the attentions of the woman who tantalized him with her feminine wiles, trying to entice him into handing her the reins of the horses.

In the interior of the wagon, a powerfully built man dozed, his hands behind his head serving as an improvised pillow.

He could hear the whispers and giggles of Helena, seemingly always tipsy, and smiled at the thought of his loyal driver and the effort he must be making to concentrate on the path before him. He opened his eyes and glanced at the corner of the wagon, where a young woman was curled up. She lay on her stomach, covered with a thin sheet. In his imagination he pulled the sheet away, fantasizing about the sight which would be revealed beneath it. Her darkly tanned skin, testimony to the long and warm summer, sharply contrasted with her white linen nightgown, which revealed more than it concealed. Her wavy brown hair was bound in a thick braid from the middle of her back downwards, but remained unbound further up, spreading like a fan across her bare shoulders.

Phryne. Just thinking of her name aroused him. He had yet to try her out. His wife was used to the comely slave girls he surrounded himself with, and knew that he slaked his lusts with some of them. And yet, this Jewish maid aroused her resistance. His wife warned him not to bed her, for this would be unwise given his intention of crushing the Judean revolt. Apollonius suspected that the true reason for her interference was her jealousy of the comely maiden, but was forced to accept her reasoning. As a small compensation, and as a petty revenge against his jealous wife, he had decided to take the Jewish slave girl with him to Jerusalem, intending to use her presence as a symbol of his triumph over the Judean rebels.

In the front seat of the wagon, Helena and Helios heard the clanking of metal from within the wagon, testimony to their master awakening and donning his arms and armor. Helena immediately stopped her flirting and sat down besides Helios. "Behave yourself," she said with facile seriousness, "Do you dare to lust after the companion of the Governor of Samaria?!"

Helios' face reddened, and he angrily stared straight ahead. Helena choked down her provocative laughter as the awning of the wagon was drawn aside and Apollonius exited to stand beside the pair.

"Get inside woman! You've harassed him enough."

Helios glanced gratefully at his master.

The governor stared forward. A broad-shouldered horseman broke off from the convoy's vanguard and cantered towards the carriage. It was Tario, the commander of Samaria's regular garrison. "The ravine is right ahead of us, Governor," reported Tario as he rode alongside the carriage, "We will not be able to cross it before sundown."

Apollonius' forehead crinkled. The mountain highway on which his force advanced crossed the land from north to south, mostly following the ridges of the central mountain spine connecting rebellious southern Judea with his home province of Samaria to the north. It was a largely convenient and secure road, but in the section just before them it descended into a deep ravine formed by a stream, which was narrow and winding. This was the only section of the road considered hazardous, given its vulnerability to ambush and bandit attacks. Apollonius gestured, and a servant hurried from behind the carriage, leading the governor's horse.

"Prepare yourself and the wagon," Apollonius commanded as he mounted his horse from the slowly moving carriage.

Helios stared at his master in astonishment, "Bandits would never dare attack us, master."

"We are not facing bandits but priests—never underestimate the enemy," replied Apollonius, and turning his attention to Tario, he continued "from what we know of the leader of the rebels, he is taking up the torch lit by his father the priest. I have no intention of providing him with his first great victory."

"What do you want us to do?" asked Tario, "Should we set up our night camp here, north of the ravine crossing?"

"If we do that, they can organize during the night and prepare a deadlier ambush for us tomorrow. No. We cross today, even if we have to complete the crossing in the dark. Ensure that everyone is prepared for fighting, even if the esteemed gentlemen think we are just out on a field trip," Apollonius said, jerking his head back at his force—at the Hellene citizens. The force he commanded included six hundred warriors and many clerks and slaves. Two hundred regular garrison troops, two hundred local Samaritan auxiliaries, and a similar number of Hellene citizens—Greco-Macedonian-descended residents of Samaria who were recognized citizens of the polis of Samaria. The Greco-Macedonian citizens showed conspicuous lack of discipline. They did not maintain formation, conversed loudly, and laughed at the top of their lungs. Beside them walked their slaves, carrying their personal equipment, weapons, and shields.

Tario smiled, "When push comes to shove, we can rely on them more than on all the others. They were all veteran soldiers before they were settled in Samaria."

"Yes, yes," grumbled the governor, unconvinced, "take your citizens, cavalry, and infantry, and advance before us in the vanguard. If you run into an ambush, show me your mettle and fight as you know so well."

Apollonius fell silent for a moment and inspected Tario. The man was an extremely experienced warrior. He would not let him down. With his veteran soldiers he could overcome any ambush.

"Concentrate the wagon train in the back and secure it with a detachment of infantry," Apollonius continued to outline the plan, "I, together with the rest of the force, will advance behind you. If there are no other surprises, we will continue advancing until we ascend from the ravine, and that is where we will camp for the night. Send all of your officers and commanders to me; we hold council. The field trip is over; we are now entering enemy territory."

Tario rode to the vanguard of the column's cavalry screen and gestured at them to advance. As soon as they broke away from the column, he ordered an increase of the pace. Tario wanted to make it through the ravine before darkness descended. The infantry company also advanced rapidly, just behind the cavalry screen in a measured trot, trying to keep up with the cavalry preceding them. The path wound down the mountains into the deep and winding ravine, clinging to the mountain slope. Sometimes the road rose as if it was trying to climb the mountain, and sometimes it descended once again, clinging to the route of the dry streambed. Here and there small pools of stagnant water still lurked, evidence of the water that had flowed in the stream in the winter.

The many winding and twisting turns of the path troubled him—they blocked his field of view and provided many possible ambush sites. The possibility of a surprise attack on them from the top of the mountain endangered them and further complicated the situation. Apollonius was right to send part of the force ahead, he thought. They approached another sharp leftwards turn in the ravine. The ravine had now become deep and narrow. His danger sense sent a prickle down his spine, and he slowed his horse down. He inspected every rock on the steep slope to his left and shifted his balance on the horse as he momentarily raised his shield arm. He passed the curve in the ravine and immediately halted, tensely observing the narrow ravine before him. A large pile of rocks blocked the path ahead of them, exactly at the point where the ravine began twisting again in a manner which could serve as a perfect spot for an ambush party. The mountain slope to the left of the narrowing path rose into a steep cliff.

The sensation of danger constricted his lungs, making it difficult to breathe. There was no room for doubt, he reflected; the rock pile blocking the path was clearly manmade. It would be only an hour's work to dismantle it—but the men dismantling it, and the entire column, would be hideously vulnerable to an ambush from above in the meantime. He cast his eyes upwards, trying to look through the mountainside with his gaze, imaging in his mind's eye the rebels hiding away, silently prepared, just waiting for him and his troops to ride into the trap. We were saved by pure luck, just because I chose this place to halt, he thought, angry at himself. I should have sent a scouting party ahead of us. He turned his horse around and instructed the nearby horsemen to head back. The force obediently and rapidly followed his orders and turned back the way they came.

Nexus, the commander of the infantry company that followed in the footsteps of the cavalry, noticed the cavalry turning back and ordered his infantry to halt. The infantry halted at a place where the road converged with the ravine into a small valley, wide enough to enable the soldiers to spread across it. The cavalry arrived at a light canter and took up positions alongside them.

Tario intently scanned the ridge of the mountain overlooking them. The small valley where they had stopped was far safer than the narrow path ahead where they had nearly fallen prey to an ambush, but they still held an inferior position against any force which might assault them from the ground overlooking them. The sun was about to set. Within a short period Apollonius would arrive with the entire column and then the valley would be clogged up with hundreds of people. If the entire expedition were clogged into the small valley, they would place themselves in incredible peril in the case of an enemy attack.

Nexus approached him. "Tario, we need to act quickly!"

"What do you propose?" asked Tario, happy to share the responsibility.

"The slope is not incredibly steep", Nexus pointed at the top of the mountain. "I will take some of the men with me and secure the high ground. Then you can advance and break up the barrier down below."

Tario considered the possibilities facing them. "I'm joining you," he said, without giving Nexus the opportunity to express opposition.

The climb was more difficult than expected. Tario stopped for a moment to catch his breath, feeling the blood pound in his temples. The sun was setting, and the sky had begun to redden. Behind him, fifty warriors were trying to keep up with his pace. Nexus, leading twenty especially fit warriors, was in front. They were climbing the mountain at a near run, grabbing on to rocks and bushes with their bare hands.

Suddenly, Nexus's voice rose loud and clear: "Enemy straight ahead!"

Nexus and his men had already deployed in a combat formation on the mountainside by the time Tario and the other warriors had reached them, huffing and puffing with the effort. About two hundred paces ahead of them, roughly above where the ravine had been blocked by the rock barrier, were fifty or so armed men, some standing and some hiding behind the rocks. The ambushers were shouting and arguing amongst themselves, gesticulating wildly. It was clear that they had made no preparation for their intended victims climbing up the mountain to their ambush position.

Tario took his place at the head of the force. Three lines of warriors advanced in perfect form up the mountain, their swords drawn and their tower shields concealing almost all of their bodies. The rebels continued to argue amongst themselves and could not make up their mind on how to conduct themselves— and then some of them began to flee.

Tario and his men increased their pace to a steady run. The final rebels, those brave enough to still hold the ridgeline, scattered in all direction in the face of the advancing professional soldiers. Some disappeared over the ridge, others ran back along the side of the mountain. The more heavily armed and armored soldiers chased the fleeing rebels, hurling jeers and curses at their backs for a while, and then halted, gasping for air and smiling.

Apollonius was well satisfied with the developments, and ordered the establishment of a camp to pass the night in the valley before the makeshift barrier established by the rebels and dismantled by Tario's men. Soon, the din of organization filled the locale. Tree branches were rapidly gathered, and torches and bonfires were lit all over and around the camp. The dignitaries reclined in the tents put up for them, while the slaves labored at preparing a meal. The small valley was too narrow to hold all of them, so some of the soldiers spread out down the ravine. Apollonius gathered all of his officers and praised Tario to them, while giving him full credit for the detection and defeat of the rebel ambush.

"My lord, it is all thanks to Nexus," protested Tario humbly, "it was his idea to scale the mountain."

"You both have my full appreciation," responded Apollonius. "Let the men eat and rest. The rebels will not trouble us further tonight."

"It appears that the only thing they are good at is assaults on civilians and ambushes," said Tario. "They didn't really have any intention of fighting us."

"That is probably it," said Apollonius dismissively. "We will have to give some thought about how to capture and eliminate them, but we will cross that bridge when we reach it. Eat well; you deserve it."

Phryne curled up in a blanket in the back corner of the governor's wagon, leaning from without on the canvas of the wagon. The camp had darkened as the fires slowly died down. Most of the soldiers had fallen asleep, full of a generously portioned supper and exhausted from the day-long march in the heavy heat. To her rear, between the campfires of the clerks and staff of the governor, faint conversations could be heard between those who were still awake. Within the wagon, Helena slept peacefully, her breath rising and lowering at a steady pace. The night was cold, sharply contrasting with the oppressive heat during the day. From time to time the chirps and calls of night birds could be heard. Phryne raised her eyes up to the stars, imagining herself spreading wings and flying towards them, to the heavenly dome above.

Sad thoughts rose up within her, mixing past, present, and future. She was sold as a slave when she was too young to know her parents. The only thing she was told about them was that they were poor Jews. Her new name was granted to her by her new masters, who, impressed with her beauty, named her for a famous Athenian hetaira. Legend had it that she was so beautiful that she served as the model for the statue of Aphrodite, the Hellene goddess of love and beauty. As a child-slave in the home of the governor of the Samaria province, she had spent most of her time in the kitchen and in various cleaning duties. Sometimes she was sent to the market or to various stores in the city, which is how she'd had the chance to wander the streets of the city. She walked barefoot, her brown hair sliding down her shoulders, drawing the attention of her male peers. When she grew from a girl into a young woman she began drawing more and more compliments and stares from the older merchants in the market, until they became a major annoyance. It was at that time that the attitude of the women of the household towards her changed and became chilly and hostile.

Her beauty also drew the attention of the governor, who proved unable to ignore the attractive slave girl who had blossomed in his household. It was not long before she was assigned to the personal service of the governor and his household. Everyone in the governor's house knew that only particularly attractive young women served in this capacity—and that they were required to provide special services to the master of the household. Phryne was all too aware of the way the governor gazed upon her body every time she was in his presence. When she found out that the governor had ordered her and his mistress Helena to join him in his expedition to Jerusalem, she fearfully understood what she could expect once they arrived.

A prolonged howl from the other side of the ravine returned her back to reality. A howl immediately rose in response from her side of the ravine. Phryne shook and felt shivers run down her spine. The night suddenly seemed alive with all manners of sounds and for a moment it seemed to her that the very mountains overlooking the camp had begun to rumble and growl. A luminescent light of an unfamiliar character descended from the overlooking mountains into the ravine, accompanied by a growing thunderous rumble. As the rumbling sound grew so did the intensity of the light. Phryne wanted to scream and wake up Helena, but fear paralyzed her, and she could not speak, let alone move. Around her, people woke up from the noise and began to shout in panic, waking up their still-slumbering comrades. Within seconds, the situation became clear, but too late for anyone to react. Massive balls of fire hurled down the mountain slopes into the camp, rolling with incredible speed into the ravine, some of them collapsing into piles of burning brambles and thorns, while others continued to roll intact through the camp, crushing and burning everything in their path—men, equipment, and wagons alike. More and more fireballs continued to roll down the mountainside, leaving destruction, panic, and death in their wake.

Within seconds the camp was gripped by chaos. The tethered horses and mules panicked, and those who managed to break free of their tethers rampaged throughout the camp in all directions, trampling and injuring both soldiers and slaves. Some of the beasts were injured when they stumbled over rocks, breaking their legs and collapsing, their cries of pain adding to the cacophony and panic. Flames lit up the entire camp, consuming everything around them.

And then the arrows began to fall on the camp. One moment there was the distant buzz of an unleashed bee-swarm, and immediately thereafter the night was pierced with sharp whistles, some of which ended with cries of terror from the injured. A rain of cruel arrows sought and found their targets, as if they had a malignant consciousness directing their paths.

Then, suddenly, there was silence. The mountains ceased raining down destruction on the valley below and seemed to pause to observe the result of their handiwork. Apollonius, bare-chested, his body glistening with cold sweat, arrived at a run from his flame-enshrouded tent, taking shelter behind his wagon. He stood by Phryne, not noticing her existence. He held a drawn sword in his hand, his eyes scurrying from side to side in horror. His men—soldiers, clerks, and slaves—were fleeing in all directions up and down the ravine, consumed with fear and with no thought but flight on their minds. There were also some who took shelter, using their shields, hiding in between the rocks or behind a rare unburnt wagon. The injured and the dead lay scattered across the camp, their wounds bleeding and arrows protruding from their bodies. Arrows from the mountain slope once again fell on the camp, but this time not in dense volleys, but as single, carefully aimed shots, each arrow directed at a single target. Occasionally a heavy javelin was hurled from above as well, causing horrific wounds and instilling terror even when it missed its mark.

From her shelter at the flanks of the wagon, Phryne was the first to see the approaching figures. Under the cover of darkness, they were nearly invisible. The first figures were nearly at the camp before Apollonius noticed them. A cry of helpless rage rose from him as four groups of rebels charged down the lower slopes of the mountains, advancing into the ravine, directly at the governor's wagon, which had miraculously remained whole throughout the assault. The warriors of the first group wielded spears. Those in the front rank aimed them forward, whereas the others aimed them diagonally upwards in order to avoid harming their comrades. It was hardly a Macedonian phalanx, but it was still a surprising display of military organization from what Apollonius had imagined to be no more than a band of ragtag rebels. Two particularly muscular warriors led them, each wielding a sword in one hand and a tower shield in the other.

Night seemed to fall once more on the ravine, and an odd moment of silence occurred as the cries of the wounded stilled. The four groups of the attacking force converged in front of the governor's wagon and then split, each to its assigned task. The first, headed by the two Herculean rebels, surrounded the governor's wagon in an arc. The second and third groups began to advance in parallel up the ravine. A fourth group stood ready at the downstream side of the ravine but did not advance.

Phryne glanced from side to side in trepidation. What had been, until a short time ago, the night camp of a well-ordered military force, was now no more than a chaotic scene of injured and dead men, scattered equipment, and fires run rampant. The lightly injured and a few lucky souls who were spared injury and had not taken the opportunity to flee were trying to aid their wounded comrades. Down the ravine, some soldiers were trying to gather arms and shields and organize into a fighting formation, intending to come to the aid of the governor, or perhaps just to prepare for the upcoming enemy attack. Regardless, the aimed arrow fire made it more difficult for them to do so.

The two Herculean warriors leading the force surrounding the governor's wagon strode forward and halted in front of Apollonius. Phryne stared at them, feeling somehow both connected to these rebels and distant from them, as if in a dream. She felt no fear; in fact, she barely felt anything. In the distance she heard Tario calling out the governor's name. The warrior closer to Apollonius aimed his sword at the governor's chest. He displayed none of the warrior's battlefield fury Phryne had expected. His stance and expression revealed nothing but self-confident power.

Apollonius, her master and the governor of Samaria, stood only an arm's length away from her, with his back to her. His body slackened, his shoulders stooped, and he pointed his sword at the ground.

"Judah," Apollonius slowly pronounced the name, his voice heavy with defeat. The Herculean warrior nodded without saying a word and lightly gestured at Apollonius, inviting him to attack and permitting him to make the first move. In spite of the darkness, Phryne thought that she noticed a sparkle of pleasure in his eyes, though his expression remained serious.

Loyal to the warrior's code on which he was raised, Apollonius accepted the offered opportunity with a certain relief. It was better to die in battle with a sword in hand. Phryne could no longer see Apollonius' face, but by the way he drew up and raised his head, she could sense his determined expression. He charged rapidly forward, extending his sword. His opponent responded immediately, taking a rapid diagonal half step forward, keeping his tower shield close, and extending his sword hand forward.

The exchange was so swift that Phryne could barely take it in. She choked down a whimper when she suddenly realized a blade was sticking out of the governor's bent back. She covered her mouth with both hands in terror. Apollonius stood for another moment and then the man who slew him pulled out his sword with a jerk and Apollonius collapsed in place, lifeless.

Judah sheathed his sword and bent over to retrieve the sword of the deceased Governor of Samaria, raising it high above his head in victory.

The few soldiers who yet remained fit and were attempting to form up into a fighting formation under Tario's command observed the occurrences from the distance. They turned away and clustered together, having lost the will to fight after the death of their governor.

Before he turned away, the eyes of the rebel leader and the Jewish slave girl met. She gasped, overcome by fear. She noticed his eyes widening in surprise. But then he nodded at her, as if in greeting. Phryne could swear that he even flashed a smile in her direction. For a moment time stood still: a battle raged around them, people were shouting and crying out, but Phryne knew that no harm would befall her. She smiled back in relief.

The commander of the rebels turned around, barked a short order, and began to advance down the ravine, his men at his back. Phryne plunged back into reality: it was the middle of the night in a dry wilderness streambed, and she was watching a battle in which the men of the group she had been a part of up until that time were being slaughtered by the rebels—her people and coreligionists.

The rebels advanced down the ravine, striking down soldiers too wounded to flee but who still wielded weapons. Their comrades continued to fire arrows from above. They met no real opposition. The army of the Governor of Samaria had been routed and was unable to resist.

Historical Background

In the late second millennium BCE, the Children of Israel were divided into tribes, each tribe residing primarily on part of the Land of Canaan. The Tribes lived under the pressure of common external enemies such as the Sea Peoples, the Philistines, the Midianites, other nations and tribes (Amon, Moab, Edom, Aram) on the outskirts of Canaan, and the Egyptians to the South. To face these threats, some of the tribes would occasionally join forces under the authority of a single leader, whose influence would sometimes include more than one tribe. Gradually, throughout this period, a belief in one supreme God grew, alongside belief and worship in other gods. One possible explanation for this phenomenon is a belief in the creation of a supreme god heading the divine hierarchy but ruling over many servitor and subject gods.

At some point, in the face of the growing power of the Philistine kingdoms and their cooperation in the struggle against the Tribes of Israel, voices within the Tribes supporting unity under a single king grew. Saul of the Tribe of Benjamin was anointed to be the first king of the Tribes of Israel. He was followed by King David, of the Tribe of Judah, the largest and apparently strongest of the Tribes of Israel. King David solidified his rule over all the Tribes of Israel and extended his writ throughout the entire Land of Israel — and beyond. As part of the process of the unification of the Tribes into a single kingdom, Jerusalem was established as the Capital. King Solomon, David's heir, established the Temple in Jerusalem, which was declared to be the sole center of worship in the kingdom, with other centers of worship being forbidden. The High Priesthood was awarded to the priest Zadok, a longstanding loyalist of both David and Solomon.

The United Kingdom of Israel lasted no more than seventy years. Immediately following the death of King Solomon in the ninth century BCE, the kingdom split into the Kingdom of Judah under the rule of the house of David (who, aside from the Tribe of Judah, only ruled over the Tribe of Binyamin), and the Kingdom of Israel, which incorporated all the rest of the tribes under the rule of kings from a variety of dynasties.

The Kingdom of Israel was destroyed in 722 BCE by the then-dominant regional superpower, the Neo-Assyrian Empire. A significant portion of its population was exiled to the Assyrian heartland in northern Iraq, and vanished from known history. Some of those who remained in the land were assimilated by the tribe of Judah; others apparently merged into the populations settled in the former Kingdom of Israel by the Assyrians and formed the basis for the Samaritan faith which is similar to that of Judaism.

The Kingdom of Judah was led by two dynasties throughout its existence: the House of David and the House of Zadok. The House of David was the royal dynasty which formally managed the kingdom. Under its purview were foreign policy, the military, tax collection, and so forth. The House of Zadok provided spiritual and religious leadership. From time to time a prophet would arise amongst the people, take center stage, and influence the kingdom through charismatic leadership and the strength of his personality—as well, of course, as his faith in bearing the word of God and ability to sway his audience to accept this certainty.

In the early sixth century BCE, the Kingdom of Judah came into conflict with the new regional superpower, Babylon. As a result, the First Temple was destroyed and the political, economic, cultural, and spiritual elite of the Kingdom of Judah were exiled to Babylon. From this time onwards, the royal dynasty was shunted aside and never again took center stage in Jewish history.

In Babylon, the exiles encountered an extraordinarily powerful and wealthy culture which constructed vast monuments and temples that dwarfed the destroyed Temple in Jerusalem. Under the shock of their seeming insignificance, the exiles reforged their faith anew as a clearly defined monotheistic faith. Rather than losing their faith in the God of Israel and disappearing from history, as occurred with the Tribes of Israel exiled by the Assyrians (and many other nations who suffered the same fate under both the Neo-Assyrian and Neo-Babylonian Empires), the Jewish Exiles defined their God as a God holding dominion over all nations, including their conquerors, and their exile as an expression of divine punishment for their failure to adhere fully to his will.

A few decades passed, and Babylon fell in turn to the Persian Empire, which established a vast empire stretching across the known world from India to Kush (modern Sudan) and into the outskirts of Europe. The Persian self-perception was of themselves as kings of kings, and they permitted a wide-ranging level of autonomy to the kingdoms under their rule, as well as displaying religious tolerance towards all those who were loyal to their rule.

The Persian Empire found the exiled Jews, who were relatively literate and highly skilled but who lacked national ambitions or military power, to be reliable subjects. Persian rulers recruited Jews into both their military and civil administrations and permitted the Jews to maintain and establish communal cultural and religious institutions, which managed many aspects of Jewish life in the Persian Empire. Jews who so desired were permitted to return from Babylon to the Land of Israel and re-establish their Temple in Jerusalem.

Following the return to Zion and the establishment of the Second Temple, the Zadok dynasty was left in an exclusive leadership position over the Jewish People in the Land of Israel. The High Priest became their spiritual and national leader, a supreme and decisive authority in all fields of life, and the representative of the Jewish People towards external rulers and Jewish communities throughout the world.

In 334 BCE, Alexander of Macedon launched his campaign against the far larger Persian Empire; within a few years, he brought about the collapse of Persia and the establishment of a Hellenistic Empire in its place. The Land of Israel was conquered by Alexander in 332 BCE and became part of the new Hellenistic world order.

Following the death of Alexander the Great, his Empire collapsed into rival Hellenistic kingdoms ruled by his former generals. The leading kingdoms were Seleucia (centered on Syria and Mesopotamia, and, at its height, the Iranian Plateau), Macedonia, and Egypt. The Seleucid Empire and Egypt battled for control over Coele-Syria and Phoenicia (known today as Israel and part of Lebanon) for over a century and a half—wars which were named the Coele-Syria wars. In 202 BCE, during the fifth Coele-Syria war, the Seleucid king Antiochus the Third, also known as "the great", captured the Land of Israel from Egypt. The events described in the historical novel Lions of Judea occur during this period, when the Land of Israel is under the Seleucid rule of the sons and heirs of Antiochus III.

The Hellenistic age brought with it a widespread immigration of "Greeks" (residents of Greece proper, Macedon, Epirus, Thessaly, Thrace, and Asia Minor who shared the Hellenistic culture were perceived by the people of the East as "Greeks") throughout the ancient East. These "Greeks" brought with them their customs and culture, established polis cities upon the same pattern as polis in the Greek homeland, and formed islands of Hellenistic culture and influence. Throughout the conquered territories in the East, a three-layered social hierarchy formed. The highest was held by "Hellenes", which included people who immigrated to the East from Hellas and its proximate neighbors. The second was that of Hellenizers, locals who adopted Hellenistic culture. The third was that of locals who remained loyal to their original cultures, including language, faith and tradition, customs, and lifestyles. An unusual and fourth component of this hierarchy were the Jews, who had, due to prior exiles under force and voluntary migration, formed Jewish communities throughout the East where they safeguarded separate customs, lifestyles, and cultures, though they interacted freely with their gentile surroundings in secular aspects of life.

In Judea, the heartland of the Land of Israel and the ancient kingdom of Judah, the High Priests of the house of Zadok continued to lead the Jewish People. Alongside the High Priest existed the great Knesset (assembly) institution, which was made up of elders and notables. However, this was apparently a body that lacked any real authority and which was largely under the influence and perhaps even control of the High Priest. Over time, social and economic shifts took place amongst the Jews in the Land of Israel and abroad. Central among such shifts were (a) Hellenization; (b) the development of the scholastic sages in the Land of Israel; and (c) the growth of local leadership in the Jewish communities around the world, which ceased to be based on the priesthood. These trends undermined the status of the ruling priestly family in Judea.

The status of priests in general, and especially that of the high priesthood in Jerusalem, gradually declined into an open struggle for power between the priests of the house of Zadok and the Hellenizers, with the sages seeking to establish their new authority in this context. This struggle reached its peak during the period described in this book.

180 BCE—Games of War

Dramatis Personae
Bold = main character
* = historical figure

- *Kratos*—*A Greek tutor*
- *Tiamos*—*A highborn Syrio-Macedonian boy from Antioch*
- *Hercules*—*Tiamos' dog*
- *Judah**—*A Jewish boy from a traditionalist priestly family; the son of Matityahu*
- *Plutades*—*A Macedonian noble from Antioch; Tiamos' father*
- *Elianus*—*A Jewish boy from a Hellenizer family*
- *David*—*A traditionalist Jewish boy from Judah's gang*
- *Grandfather Yohanan**—*A traditionalist Jewish priest; father of Matityahu and grandfather of Judah*
- *Matityahu**—*Son of Yohanan and father of Judah*
- *Glitarius*—*A Roman boy from a patrician family*

Kratos examined the boy standing by his side with affection. Tiamos, he thought, is wise beyond his years. It is a pleasure to teach such a student. When you are educating highborn sons such as this one, you are shaping the future with your own two hands. When they grow up they will lead and influence the world.

Kratos was not a typical tutor. He did not lecture them much, preferring to teach in the Socratic method, asking them question after question. I am not as wise as Socrates and I will never be as famous as Plato, he would typically say, but I am a Helene tutor and I will proudly follow in their path.

Tiamos was deep in thought, his mind hard at work seeking to answer the riddle his tutor had asked him. They were walking in the hills not far from his home. He was in the habit of observing these hills, in which Jewish youth often played, from the gates of his home. Today as well, not far from where they stood, there was a group of Jewish youth engaged in target practice with their slings.

At Tiamos' side was Hercules, a massive and intimidating war dog. The easy life in Tiamos' family home had softened the aggressive nature of the hound, and transformed him into a relatively friendly family dog, but at need he was quite capable of tearing apart any enemy who dared to threaten his master. The Canaanite sheep dogs who were common in the area kept their distance, and he in turn treated them with highly conspicuous condescension. Both sides, however, knew that as a pack the Canaanites made a worthy and dangerous opponent.

The Jewish youths cheered out loud. A moment later, a dead bird landed not far from where the Greek tutor and his student stood. Near the bird landed a round stone, almost at their feet. Hercules approached the bird and sniffed at it, but rapidly lost interest and lay down by its side.

Tiamos cast a questioning gaze at his tutor.

"A sling," explained the tutor, "It is quite difficult to hit a bird in flight. Whoever struck it is extremely skilled, but rash. This stone could have easily landed on someone's head. Ours, for instance."

Tiamos smiled, but his eyes remained serious. These youths seemed to be near his own age. Jerusalem was a forsaken, peripheral city as far as the court and high society in Antioch were concerned. It did not have the stature and constitution of a Hellenistic polis, as other important cities in the Seleucid kingdom did, nor did it have many Greek families with youths his own age. Although his father had brought a private tutor with them from Antioch, to instill in Tiamos a proper Hellenistic education, Tiamos yearned for friends his own age with whom he could laugh and play. He was jealous of the youths, observing them from the distance.

The youths noticed that the bird had landed at the feet of a Hellene highborn lad and were afraid of approaching. Nonetheless, one of them broke away from the group and began marching towards them. His gait was loose and released, and at the same time characterized by catlike dexterity. He seemed to be around the same age as Tiamos, who had turned thirteen the past summer. From behind, some of the boys began calling at him in a language which Tiamos could not understand, but from the laughter of the others, he understood that they were teasing their friend.

The local lad, in the meantime, had approached them swiftly enough to raise the suspicions of Hercules. The dog advanced in his direction, prepared to attack should the lad turn out to be a threat. Tiamos wished to call back Hercules, but Kratos placed his hand on his shoulder and held him back. He was curious to see how the boy would act when faced with the threatening dog. The lad halted a few steps away from the dog and began to speak to the two Hellenes. He spoke in Aramaic, a language which neither Kratos nor Tiamos understood, although it was not difficult to comprehend that he wanted them to hand over the bird his sling had brought down, especially given that the lad pointed in its direction while he was speaking.

Kratos liked his body language and expression. They expressed self-confidence, a zest for life and leadership. However, his movements also indicated disguised alertness and caution—to be expected in an encounter with the Hellene ruling caste of Judea and the Seleucid Kingdom.

Tiamos glanced at Kratos, a silent question in his eyes. When Kratos nodded in approval, he replied to the Jewish youth in Koine Greek[1]. Pointing at the dead bird, he told the boy to take it. The local lad smiled and stepped forward, passing by Hercules and absent-mindedly petting his head. Kratos was amused at the awkwardness of the massive war dog at the confident behavior of the lad.

The youth stood for a moment by the downed bird, and to the surprise of Kratos and Tiamos stroked it gently for a moment, as though apologizing for slaying it. Then he approached them and picked up his sling stone from the ground by their feet. He showed them the stone, smiling and speaking once again in Aramaic.

"Notice how round it is," said Kratos to Tiamos, "It is like a little ball. This is a pebble from a streambed, but someone invested considerable time and effort in carving it into a perfect circle. This sling is a weapon for all intents and purposes, and this lad, like any professional solider should be, is not prepared to leave good ammunition behind."

Tiamos stretched out his hand and the local lad placed the

---

1   Koine was a dialect which the Macedonian and Greek settlers in the lands conquered by Alexander the Great developed. A composite of the different dialects of the Hellene homeland, it became the new lingua franca of the Hellenistic world.

stone in his palm, permitting him to feel its smoothness. They looked into each other's eyes. In spite of their vastly different backgrounds and not understanding each other's languages, this was enough to form a bond between them. The local youth pointed at himself with his thumb and spoke his name. Judah. Tiamos did the same, introducing himself. Judah drew his sling from the cord which served as his belt and placed the stone within it. He then handed it over to Tiamos, inviting him to try it out, and explaining, with broad gestures, how to operate the deceptively simple weapon.

Kratos had no choice but to release Tiamos from his lessons for the rest of the day and permit him to join the local youths. Tiamos and Hercules walked with Judah back to his friends, and Judah introduced them. The locals were awkward at first, not sure how to speak to the Hellene nobleman who could not speak their language. However, within a short time, they found common ground, and the sounds of their laughter, accompanied by the thunderous barking of Hercules, echoed in the distance.

In the evening, Tiamos shared his experiences during that day with his father, Plutades. He had a talent for describing events in a colorful way that both brought life to the words and was amusing to the listener. Plutades listened with interest to the events his son related, and occasionally laughed at his descriptions, particularly the part Hercules played in the story. He knew that his son yearned for company, and so consented to permit him to take part in the activities of the local youth, provided that this would not be at the expense of his studies.

The next day, around the same time when he had met the local boys on the previous day, Tiamos urged Kratos to head out to the hills. To his disappointment, his new friends did not arrive. He did see a local boy roughly his own age in the distance;

however, that youth was busy herding a small flock of goats on the slopes of the hill, and showed no interest in approaching the strangers or their huge dog. Tiamos saw no sign of Judah and his friends on the hills for the next two days. Tiamos was frustrated by their absence and even suggested that they enter the city to seek them out; however, Kratos ruled this idea out immediately—Jerusalem was crowded and honeycombed with many small and crooked alleys where tens of thousands of people lived, and thousands of others passed through every day.

On the fourth day, Tiamos received Kratos with a surly expression when he arrived at the family home to tutor him. Kratos, understanding that he would have little success in beating wisdom into the boy in this state, required him only to read the works of Homer independently. Suddenly, the home echoed with the barking of Hercules, rising up from the grounds. Tiamos leapt to his feet, ran outside, and climbed onto the wall surrounding the estate to observe the hills. A cry of joy escaped his lips. "They are back!" he cried out in excitement to Kratos, and did not wait even an instant before leaping to the other side of the wall, disappearing behind it.

He ran rapidly to the top of the hill. Judah was indeed there with his friends—but they were not alone. Facing them was another group of youths, and it was clear that a conflict was developing between the two groups. Tiamos slowed down, feeling the tension in the air as he approached. The youths of the second group were also local, but they dressed and carried themselves differently than Judah and his friends. They had the look of Hellene youth, and, oddly, they all held long sticks in their hands, as if they were phalanx formation warriors carrying Sarissas[2].

Tiamos dove into the huddled mass of youths, making his way into the fray. Some of the friends he had made a few days ago noticed him and smiled at him hesitantly. At the center of the fray stood Judah and the leader of the Hellene-style dressed boys. He was a solidly built and heavily muscled lad, his dark hair oiled back on his scalp. The body language and gestures of the second youth made it clear that he was demanding that Judah and his friends get off the hill. Tiamos felt rage rising from within him. He counted Judah and his group as his friends and he intended to stand by them. Tiamos halted by Judah's side. He felt relieved when he realized that Judah, unlike his friends, remained calm and smiling, and even winked at him as he approached.

The youth confronting Judah was surprised with the arrival of Tiamos, but being self-absorbed, did not realize that Tiamos knew Judah.

"I am Elianus," he told Tiamos, speaking to him in Greek. "My friends and I are Hellene, just like you. It is good that you came; we were just about to send these boys away."

A short and skinny boy who stood behind Judah and was proficient in both languages, Aramaic and Greek, translated the words of Elianus in a low voice, almost a whisper.

"And I am Tiamos, son of the king's representative Plutades. This hill faces **my** home. Who are you to drive away **my friends**?!"

---

2   **Phalanx**—A dense infantry formation. Its striking power is based on spears, which present their opponents with a dense, hedgehog-like barrier. The Macedonian army of Alexander the Great and his father Phillip improved upon the Greek phalanx by doubling the length of those spears, naming the 4-6 meter pikes **Sarissas.**

Elianus's mouth gaped open in amazement. He never imagined that the Greek nobleman's son would choose Judah and his friends over him. He glanced back at his own friends, but they all seemed just as nonplussed as he was.

"David, translate my words," said Judah in Aramaic to the wiry boy behind him, "so that our friend Tiamos will understand them. I propose we resolve this issue in combat—sporting combat, with proper rules."

Elianus smirked dismissively, but kept a civil tongue, now that he understood that Tiamos opposed him.

"Sure, just say which rules you prefer. I will face you in whatever style you wish. Boxing, wrestling, free-style blows, whatever you like."

Elianus was a solid looking and muscular fellow, as were most of his friends. The Hellene lifestyle they had adopted emphasized the cultivation of the physique and training in boxing and wrestling.

"Oh, I suggest that everyone fights. Me and my friends against yours," answered Judah. His proposal led his friends to cringe in horror and the boys of the opposing group to guffaw. Elianus and his muscular, stick-wielding friends were certain who would win the type of contest Judah had proposed.

"Here are the rules: you can fight however, and with whatever weapon, you wish, but you cannot hit the head, maim your opponent, or strike at anyone who surrenders. Since we are probably the weaker side, we will defend this hill. You will descend to the bottom and then try to take it from us."

"Agreed!" answered Elianus as his friends broke out in laughter and cries of exuberance, eager to do battle with their weaker opponents. Their conduct indicated they had no intention of respecting the laws they had just agreed upon. "We are going down," said Elianus, "Signal us when you think you are ready. Beforehand, to improve the contest, let each side name itself. We will be the Seleucid army, commanded by the **Great Antiochus**. Who will **you** be?"

"We are the Jews," answered Judah and smiled serenely.

"No, that's no good. You must understand that after we defeat you the entire city will be abuzz. You know how… sensitive matters are. It wouldn't do for Seleucids to harm Jews. Pick another title. Perhaps the Parthians, or the Persians?" Elianus concluded sardonically.

"Well, if you insist, we will be the army of Hannibal of Carthage," answered Judah.

"Who?! Where is Carthage anyway? Well, never mind, so long as you aren't contesting us as Jews," replied Elianus dismissively, and turned away, walking down the hill with his group.

As Elianus and his group walked away, the Jewish youth surrounded Judah, everyone speaking at once. Even though Tiamos did not understand their language, it was clear to him that they were not pleased, and opposed the fight Judah had gotten them into, fearing defeat. Judah remained at the center of the storm, calm, collected, reflective, as if he were all alone on top of the hill. After a moment his friends fell silent, and then Judah spoke. He spoke fluently, with passion, his eyes sparkling with laughter, managing to both relieve his friends of their anxiety and instill confidence in them. Gradually, he brought his friends around, convincing them of his plan's prospects for success.

Tiamos stood at the sidelines. He would have rather been on the Seleucid side of the battle, but Hannibal was also considered a hero and an ally in Antioch, capital of the Seleucid Kingdom. Judah was handing out orders to his friends, detailing his plan into operational stages. One of the boys asked who Hannibal was. Judah replied briefly that Hannibal had defeated mighty, far off Rome in several battles. He himself knew no more than that. He then approached Tiamos and told him what he wished him to do. David translated his words, and Tiamos smiled and nodded in agreement.

At the edge of the hill, Kratos, who had hurried out of the house after his student, began to approach the rival youths, accompanied by Hercules. He'd noticed from afar that the two groups were in the midst of a confrontation and saw Tiamos enter into the midst of the fray. He did not like that, not at all. Should anything happen to his student, he knew that Tiamos' father would hold him responsible.

Elianus' group ordered themselves into a three rank formation, each of them three boys wide. The youth of the first rank inclined their wooden poles so that they faced forward, whereas the youths in the rear ranks inclined their poles upwards. They rapidly strode up the hill, acting the part of the phalanx warriors of the great Antiochus. In the center of the first rank strode Elianus, chest flung out, a self-important look on his face. He was imagining the satisfaction on the faces of his father and friends, the older generation of Hellenizers, when they heard the tale of this 'battle.'

About twenty steps below the crest of the hill stood Judah and Tiamos, at the head of their own group. Kratos watched events unfold from the distance, gripping the collar of Hercules in his hand. He had briefly considered intervening and dragging Tiamos out of the conflict, but curiosity overcame his concerns, and he decided to permit matters to progress.

The phalanx formation of Antiochus III advanced on the warriors of Hannibal of Carthage. Unlike Hannibal's fabled victories over the Roman armies, the boys behind Judah and

Tiamos panicked and began to flee to the rear and flanks of their own formation. Judah turned at them and called them to return, but they continued to speed away, some of them scaling the top of the hill and disappearing behind its crest. Judah, Tiamos, and David were the only ones to stand their ground; they looked at each other, and then turned back towards the phalanx and held their positions.

Down the hill, Elianus and his friends saw the 'Carthaginians' scatter, and broke forward at a run, raising cries of victory. The three youths who had held their ground under the crest of the hill now began to hesitantly retreat backwards, trying to preserve a modicum of their dignity. When Elianus and his friends came within twenty paces of their uncertain position, however, the three turned tail and fled before them.

Elianus and his friends were panting from the exertion of running up the hill. They slowed down to a walk, happy in their victory, barely able to speak, let alone release exultant cries of triumph.

At that moment Elianus realized that Judah, Tiamos, and David had halted at the crest of the hill, facing him. At their side suddenly appeared another two Jewish youths. All of them, aside for Tiamos, drew slings and began spinning them over their heads. In a moment all of the would-be phalanx warriors were stung by sling-hurled pebbles. The pebbles hurled into them from all directions as the remaining members of Judah's band, who had fooled them into believing they had fled, now appeared at their flanks.

Elianus and his friends realized that they had fallen into a trap. Judah and his friends had them surrounded, and held the higher ground to boot, raining sling stone crossfire down on them with the precision of professionals. Nearly every projectile hit its mark, and the blows they delivered were both painful and horrifying. The 'Carthaginians,' to their credit, upheld the rules of the contest and aimed only at the body, but Elianus and his cronies, who had never intended to observe the rules themselves, were struck by panic. They turned tail and began fleeing back down the hill, with the sling projectiles continuing to deliver their stinging punishment at their backs. The skilled slingers continued to snipe at the retreating 'Seleucids,' even when they had reached the bottom of the hill. Indeed, the farther they fled the more difficult the slingers found it to aim accurately, and a number of pebbles struck the heads of the Hellenized youths.

Kratos now released Hercules. The intelligent war dog correctly sensed what was going on and which side was the foe. The dog chased after Elianus and his cronies, driving them before him and snapping at their heels. Kratos was enchanted by the misdirection and the trap that the local Jewish youth had set, as well as by their skill with the sling. It was clear to him that the Jewish youth who had approached him and Tiamos was the individual responsible for this 'great victory.' As far as he was concerned, what he had just seen was a living demonstration of all the qualities which made a general great.

Kratos had toyed with the idea of teaching several boys from different backgrounds together in the past few months. A Roman citizen had arrived in Jerusalem several months ago with his family. He had a son called Glitarius who was the same age of Tiamos, and his father was seeking a Greek tutor for him. No one knew what a Roman was doing in such a peripheral area of the Seleucid Kingdom, but after it turned out that he was embarking on prolonged expeditions towards the great Eastern Desert beyond the Jordan River, rumors spread that his presence had something to do with trade, or perhaps even diplomatic contacts with the Nabatean kingdoms or other Arab tribes beyond them. Kratos knew that Plutades, the father of Tiamos, was involved in such endeavors, and thought that Plutades and the Roman might even be rivals in their secret activity, but he saw no reason why he should not suggest that their sons get together to study under him. He wondered if he could get the Jewish youth to join them as well, so that he might teach the children of three nations together.

Kratos consulted with Hellene friends whom he had known since he had arrived in Jerusalem. Unlike him, they had made Jerusalem their home many years ago and were familiar with the customs of the locals. He found out, much to his surprise, that Jewish male children from traditional families were not unlettered, but were taught to read in their ancient language— Hebrew, in which their holy books were written—as well as to read and write in Aramaic. They studied in the mornings, in small classes composed of children of different ages, all of them relatives or neighbors.

Kratos understood that he would have a hard time extracting Judah from the traditional curriculum of his family and his people; he concluded that he would probably have to be flexible in the schedules of the joint classes he wished to establish. But even that would not secure Judah's participation without the approval of his family. He decided to approach the highest authority in Judah's family: the father of his father. Tiamos knew that Judah's grandfather was a venerable and highly respected priest by the name of Yohanan. Equipped with this information, Kratos used a Jewish contact, a resident of the city, to coordinate a meeting.

Several days later, Kratos found himself lost in the maze of alleyways which honeycombed the city, searching in vain for the home of Judah's family. His contact had told him that he should go down the main route descending from the Temple and ask along the way for Yohanan the priest. However, when he did, Kratos discovered that it was impossible to identify any Jew in Jerusalem without referencing the name of his father. "Yohanan son of whom?" he was repeatedly asked by Greek-speaking Jews whom he met along the way. "He is a priest and has a grandson named Judah," he told them, but his words were received with outbursts of laughter. "There are dozens of priests named Yohanan in the city," he was told, "and each and every one of them has many grandchildren. Judah is also a common name. You will never find him this way."

Kratos tried his luck amongst the alleys. Most of the Jerusalemites he met were traditionalists who spoke only Aramaic and were therefore no help at all. He walked for a long hour through the endless alleys, gradually abandoning hope of reaching his meeting with Yohanan at the appointed time. Gradually, he began to show an interest in his surroundings. The streets were very narrow and densely packed, but were characterized by a warm and cheerful atmosphere. The doors of most homes were wide open, and people came and went, entering each other's homes and greeting each other with loud declarations of "peace be upon you" and "upon you be peace." The odors of cooking and spices rose up from the homes to the street, together with the sounds of laughter and joy from both children and adults. In these streets there were no oil lamps such as those installed in the main streets of the city, but the sense of security was powerful and clear.

He heard a voice call his name. It was his contact, accompanied by several youths, among them Judah, who had gone searching for him when he did not arrive at the meeting on time. They led him in a veritable entourage to Yohanan's household. His contact person told him that a jocular rumor had spread across the streets about a Hellene looking for Yohanan the grandfather of Judah, which is how they had found out that he was lost.

They led him to the family home. As with many of the other homes in the city, the front of the home was in fact a small store, which was now closed. Kratos wondered what was being sold in the store, but before he could ask his escorts they hurried him into the house.

Kratos followed his escorts into the house. The home was humble, simply furnished, and yet imbued with a welcoming atmosphere. The room he entered was relatively large and served as a living room, a reception area, and a kitchen in one. An elderly man was waiting for him there, casually reclined on a couch looking at Kratos with kindly eyes. He gestured at Kratos to enter and to seat himself. Kratos assumed this was Yohanan, the grandfather of Judah. Beside him sat, in silence, a tall and bearded man who approved, with a single meaningful glance, while at the same time warning Kratos. The children obediently disappeared into the interior of their home, and Yohanan spoke.

"Welcome be to the gates of our humble abode," said Yohanan in Aramaic, and the translator, Kratos' contact person, translated his words to Greek. "This is my eldest son, Matityahu, the father of the boy that you have encountered. We are happy to host you and look forward to hearing your words."

Judah's mother served them water, a loaf of bread, olives, goat cheese, and fresh fruit. Kratos got the impression that she had a cheerful, good-natured demeanor, but also that she was troubled by his presence.

"Honored priest, I thank you for your hospitality. My name is

Kratos and I am a Greek tutor. It is my duty to provide highborn sons with the tools they will use throughout life to shape their character into achieving great deeds. Such has been the custom in the cities of Greece since time immemorial, and such is the custom in the cities of the kingdom where Hellene citizens live. A number of affluent people from amongst your people, who have adopted many of our customs, have approached me and asked me to tutor their sons as well. It is your grandson, however, whom I wish to tutor, both because I am favorably impressed by him, and because he is a member of a traditional Jewish family."

"Why should you desire to tutor a boy from a traditional family which has not adopted your customs?" wondered Yohanan. "Do you wish to make him like you?!"

Matityahu, coiled like a spring, seemed like he was about to breech the traditional customs of hospitality and throw himself at Kratos.

"Absolutely not! As Zeus is my witness," cried out the flustered Kratos, "I have no such intention. I am doing this so that my charge, Tiamos, may become familiar with the customs of your people and the wisdom of your religion. I myself have studied and am somewhat familiar with your religion and customs, for I have studied Greek translations of your holy scrolls. Indeed, I hold the wisdom within them in high esteem. Though you may be unaware of this, there are many Hellenes in Antioch, Alexandria, and other cities where your people dwell who have been exposed to your customs and traditional wisdom. Some have studied them more deeply, and a few have even drawn close to your faith in one God. That is one reason I wish the boy I am tutoring to study with, and grow familiar with, your son and grandson," said Kratos, nodding at Judah's father and Grandfather in turn. "Nor do I desire any payment for the tutoring of your grandson, though I am certain that he too will benefit from acquainting himself with the customs of the Hellenes."

A thundering silence filled the room as Yohanan considered the various issues at stake. He had long been troubled by the thought that an abyss was widening between the traditional Jewish families, who were turning inwards; and the Hellenizers, who shared common speech and customs with the representatives of the Seleucid regime, the citizens of the various Polis of the kingdom, and even with Jews who were residents of other lands. His five grandsons by his eldest son were a source of pride to him, and Judah was dearest to him of them all. His tall, erect posture, his athletic build, and his incredible charisma almost seemed destined for greatness.

When the old priest finally spoke, Kratos could barely believe the translator's interpretation of his words. Not only did Yohanan agree to his proposal, he had further asked if Kratos' students could also be trained to fight.

"Fight with what?" wondered Kratos, "They are too young to train with weapons."

"Then without weapons," answered the grandfather, a twinkle in his eye.

A powerful feeling of affection towards the old priest overwhelmed Kratos for a moment. "This is a very wise idea, sir. I will be delighted to search among the Hellenes of the city for a man skilled with wrestling, boxing, or the pankration. The final style is the best as it combines wrestling, boxing, and kicking as well."

179 BCE—Miriam

Dramatis Personae
Bold = main character
* = historical figure

- **Kratos**—*A Greek tutor*
- **Tiamos**—*A Macedonian-descended son of a highborn Antioch family*
- **Glitarius**—*A Roman boy from a patrician family.*
- **Eupolemus***—*A Jewish boy from a priestly family, son of Yohanan ben Hakotz*
- **Grandfather Yohanan***—*A traditionalist Jewish priest; father of Matityahu*
- **Matityahu***—*Son of Yohanan*
- **Rebecca**—*Wife of Matityahu*
- **Yohanan***, **Simon***, **Judah***, **Hannah***, **Eleazar*** and **Jonathan***—*The children of Matityahu and Rebecca by age (the eldest, Yohanan, is named after their grandfather, Yohanan the priest)*
- **Hunio***—*Zadokite High Priest*
- **Tuvia clan***—*Rich and influential Hellenizer family*
- Simon the Merchant—*A wealthy Jewish Jerusalemite*
- **Miriam**—*A Jewish girl from Alexandria*
- Maluma—*The wife of Simon the Merchant*
- **Elianus**, Menachamus and Xenophon—*Hellenizer youths*
- **Joseph**—*Brother of Matityahu*

Kratos pretended to go through his notes as he glanced out of the corner of his eye at the four youths who sat silently in the room. This was probably the first time four such youths had been gathered in the same room. Tiamos represented Hellene civilization, although his family had lived in Syria for several generations. Glitarius represented Rome, and Judah the traditional Jews. The fourth youth was Eupolemus, the youngest son of a high-stature line of priests. His father—Yohanan, son of Hakotz—had won fame as the man who negotiated with King Antiochus the Great, father of the current Seleucid King, after he had conquered Coele-Syria and Phoenicia[3] from the Egyptian Ptolemy Dynasty, and even managed to secure extensive privileges for the Jews from him. In spite of being priests, the family maintained extensive trade relations and had adopted the Hellene life style. After considering the matter, Kratos had agreed to accept Eupolemus into his class as a representative of the Hellenized Jews.

This was the first lesson of the multicultural class he had established, and he decided to leave them be for a time without intervening, trusting in their natural abilities to bridge gaps and make friends. Tiamos and Judah had already become close friends in the past weeks, especially after they had learned that they were about to study together in the same class. They had developed their own language, based on agreed upon signs and words that they had taught each other. They both now glanced suspiciously at Glitarius, the Roman youth who had joined them, and who spoke in a foreign language that only Kratos could understand. Glitarius, for his part, donned the severe

---

3   The area wrested from the Ptolemy dynasty by Antiochus III: Southern Syria, Lebanon, Transjordan, and the Land of Israel.

expression he thought suited a Roman, as he sought to suppress his frustration at his father's decision to send him to study with the sons of lesser nations. Eupolemus smiled at everyone, trying to break the ice.

Tiamos, whose home was the assembly place for the class, played host. He rose and pointed with a hesitant smile at a plate of fresh dates that had been placed on the table gesturing at Glitarius to help himself. Glitarius initially shook his head, but seeing the insulted expression on Tiamos' face, smiled lightly in thanks and pointed at the clay water jug to the side of the dates, speaking a word in his language. Tiamos' face lit up and he repeated the word, first in Glitarius' own language and then in Greek. Suddenly Judah laughed, rose and stood by the table, and, pointing at the water jug, spoke the word in Aramaic. Within a moment the youths were swept into mutual study of the three languages, laughing excitedly. The youths took turns pointing at various objects, stating their name in their respective languages, as the other youths repeated the word, and then spoke it in their own language. Kratos was wise enough not to interfere in their bonding.

Several days later, Kratos informed the boys that they would soon begin pankration training as part of their education.

That night, Judah was so excited at the initiation of the pankration training that he could not sleep. Thoughts of the combat training filled his mind and kept sleep from him. He imagined himself in a stadium in Antioch, competing with opponents from all over the kingdom. The crowd cheered for him as he defeated his opponents, one after the other. A mission of Jews from Judaea had arrived at the competitions especially on his account and watched him, together with many of the Jews of Antioch, compete and win. The King granted him the victor's trophy to the sounds of the applause of the crowd. Victory led to his inclusion in the Olympic team of the athletes of Antioch at the Olympic Games in the Greek homeland, where he would fight opponents from all over the Hellenistic world—Alexandria, Macedonia, and all of the city states of Greece. Should he win there as well, he would win vast rewards upon his return.

The next morning, Judah could remember almost nothing of the dreams of the previous night. He barely woke up, and was very nearly late to his regular lessons. It was only during those lessons that he recalled that the pankration training would be beginning that afternoon, and a wave of excitement almost overcame him. He spent the rest of the day in anxious anticipation, attending the lessons in body but not in spirit, hearing but not really listening.

At noon, when he concluded his lessons, he hurried to his parent's store, where he found his mother Rebecca standing amidst a wide variety of scarves, fabrics, and pillows. Rebecca had a sharp eye and a refined aesthetic sense and knew how to use them to purchase special fabric products for the store, both from itinerant merchants and local women who sold their handiwork to the discerning.

"Hello mother, where is father?"

"He went to the Temple with grandfather and your uncles. Hunio has summoned them to him. Are you hungry?"

"No. Why has the high priest summoned grandfather?"

"They say that Hunio is summoning all of the priestly families to him."

"The Tuvia clan is stirring the pot again?"

"Apparently. They and the extreme Hellenizers are making Hunio's life miserable again; this time the issue is the city market, but that is only an excuse. They will not rest until Jerusalem is a Hellene Polis. But this is nothing you should trouble yourself with—your time has not yet come. Enjoy your childhood."

She reached out to stroke her son's cheek. "You are beginning your pankration training today. Are you excited?"

She didn't need to hear his response in order to sense her son's heart stirring.

"Ask your father in the evening about events in the Temple. In the meantime, take this package to the home of Simon the trader and then go to the home of your Hellene friend."

Rebecca provided Judah with a small loaf of bread and a skin of water, embraced him warmly, and sent him on his way.

Simon lived outside the city walls, in the same hills overlooking the city from the West where Tiamos' home was located. He was one of the great magnates of the city. He traded in carpets, perfumes, and other merchandise from all over the known world. He had a number of stores scattered throughout the city, but his carpet shop was the most famous. One could find carpets from far-off Persia, Egypt, Rhodes, Greece, and every other location in the known world. His clientele included the wealthy of Jerusalem and Judea, the meridarchies of Samaria and Idumea, and the lands beyond the Jordan River. Visitors to Jerusalem, pilgrims, traders, and official envoys made a habit of purchasing at his shop and taking the carpets back to their countries. His clients included quite a few Seleucid administration members.

This was not the first time that Judah had performed an errand to the trader. However, in the past he had visited his carpet shop rather than his home. He climbed up the narrow street leading to it. On both sides of the street lay storefronts with homes above and behind them. The people living in the narrow homes had a similar economic status to his own family. They included traders and professionals from a number of different fields, including sandal-makers, tailors, and carpenters. Judah knew most of them, and in some cases knew their children as well.

Outside the city walls, the streets were much wider. The area where Simon lived was considered to be the high-class quarter of the city. Gentiles such as the families of Tiamos and Glitarius lived there, as well as wealthy Jews such as Simon, who could afford to live in such splendid houses. The home of the merchant was surrounded by a tall wall. He rang the bell and waited. A dark-skinned servant opened the courtyard gate for him. His hair was dark and slightly curled. His forehead was marked by a geometric scar pattern with the figure of a snake like animal which Judah was not familiar with.

"I have come from the store of Matityahu the priest," he said, suddenly realizing that he did not in fact know whom the package was intended for. He had assumed that the package was intended for Simon, but if it were, then he would surely have been sent to the store of the trader as he had been in the past.

"The lady is waiting for you," said the servant in broken Greek in a foreign accent that Judah was unfamiliar with.

The courtyard of the house was wide and spacious. Between the gate and the house was a garden with trees, statues, vases of flowers, and shrubbery. Between the vegetation were small ponds. The house was tall and impressive, with a wide door in the center of its facade and elongated windows along its walls. The servant showed him in and spoke in an unfamiliar tongue to another servant with a similar appearance. They were both dark-skinned and wore similar brown-hued clothing. They also both wore copper bracelets and simple earrings. A sense of foreignness filled him, as if he had entered a distant, exotic land the moment he had stepped into the house.

The female servant led him to the private quarters of the

household. She halted before a large, light-hued wooden door and knocked softly at it.

A young girl opened the door. She was darker skinned than Judah but not nearly as much as the two servants. Her eyelids were made up in green makeup which emphasized her pretty brown eyes. Her lips were dyed in crimson, and lustrous black hair framed her face and descended, unbound, to the middle of her back. The handmaiden told her something in a language Judah did not understand, and the girl glanced at him, her eyes twinkling with a mischievous glint.

"I, ah, brought a package," stuttered Judah, embarrassed at the sight of the girl and the feelings she raised in him.

The girl smiled, revealing two lines of perfect pearly teeth, glittering on the backdrop of her crimson lips. "Come, enter."

She too had a foreign accent, but different than that of the servants. He entered the room. It was a large bedroom, dominated by a large and sumptuous bed in the center. At the rear of the room, behind a dark curtain, was another door which led to a porch. The girl lightly touched his shoulder and pointed at the porch. She stood close to him. The smell of perfume filled his nostrils. He felt his mouth go dry and his body stirred, his blood pounding in his veins.

Thick and soft carpets were spread across the floor of the balcony, with large sitting cushion scattered across them, and a breathtaking panorama of the mountains of Jerusalem before them. To their left spread out the City of Jerusalem itself, surrounded by its walls, and the Temple rising above it.

"Incredible, isn't it?" He heard a feminine voice to his right.

He swiftly spun towards the voice, remembering at once where he was. A beautiful and impressive woman was comfortably seated on a chair, a baby in her lap. She smiled at him warmly, as if they were long acquaintances.

The woman gestured at the girl, who approached and picked up the baby gently. Judah could not prevent himself from staring at her, his eyes clinging to her flowing raven locks. The girl noticed him staring and smiled at him again. He swiftly turned his eyes away, ashamed for being caught staring, and realized that the older woman was examining him as well, a light smile on her lips.

"So, you are the son of Rebecca?"

"Yes, madam. She sent you this package," he answered, handing the package over to her.

"A wonderful woman, your mother. I am very fond of her."

His expression revealed surprise.

"Your mother hasn't spoken of me to you? My name is Maluma; I am the wife of Simon."

Judah thought that her accent was similar to that of the girl.

"I am relatively new to the city," continued Maluma. "I married Simon two years ago, but I arrived with my servants from Alexandria only a few months ago. The first place I wished to visit was the Temple. Your mother was there as well. When she saw me with my servants, she assumed that we were gentiles sight-seeing at the Temple. However, when she saw that I had left my servants in the Court of Gentiles, and entered the Court of Women, she understood that I was a Jewess and guessed that I knew no one in Jerusalem. She approached me and offered to instruct me in the customs of worship in the Temple. Ever since then she has been my best friend in Jerusalem."

"So your servants are from Egypt?"

"Are you interested in the servants, or one particular servant?"

Judah reddened in embarrassment and glanced aside.

She placed her hand softly on his arm. "I am sorry; I simply could not help myself. Feel at ease; you are among friends. Miriam is an Elephantine Jewess, like myself. She is not a servant, but the daughter of my sister. She assists me with my child and keeps me company."

Judah felt relieved. He was beginning to like Maluma. "Elephantine?"

"The island of Elephantine lies in the far South of Egypt. When the Persian Empire ruled Egypt, before the conquests of Alexander the Great, they established there a military colony of Jewish warriors, who were tasked with safeguarding the southern marches of the Persian Empire. Since that time the Jews of Elephantine have gradually moved to Alexandria, but we remain proud of our origins and our legacy as warriors."

"I have heard Alexandria is a vast city."

"It is indeed immeasurably larger than Jerusalem."

"I hope to visit it one day."

"There is no reason why you shouldn't. One can travel anywhere in the world these days without any difficulty."

Although the woman was kind and pleasant to speak with, his mind and heart were occupied elsewhere. From the corner of his eye, he searched for the girl.

"Your mother speaks of you much. The truth is, stories seem to spring up around you. The son of a priest who is studying with a Greek teacher, together with highborn Roman, Hellene, and Hellenizer scions. Fluent with the holy tongue, Aramaic, Greek, and Latin."

"I can speak only a little Greek, and only a few words in Latin, and Kratos is not my tutor. It is more like we are learning from one another. I teach them about our ways, those of traditional Jews, and they teach me about their own ways. They respect me as a Jew... that does not make me into a Hellenizer!" emphasized

Judah, his face darkening.

"Of course, I never thought differently," smiled Maluma pleasantly, trying to appease the lad.

"Do you think it is a mistake to study with them?"

"Learning is never a mistake. Amongst us Jews, every child with a father studies. In Syria, Egypt, and Macedonia—even the city states of Greece—only the rich and the highborn study."

"My grandfather says that ordinary Jews began to learn how to read the Torah during the Babylonian exile, and that that is why the tribe of Judah survived, unlike the ten northern tribes exiled by the Assyrians earlier."

"And what does your Greek teacher say about that?"

"Kratos knows and respects our faith in the one God. He has also read the scrolls of the Torah, translated into Greek of course. We frequently discuss our respective customs, and Kratos asks us questions about them and draws comparisons. Sometimes I get the impression that he does not believe in Zeus and the other Hellene Gods—or perhaps in any gods at all. But regarding the scrolls, he merely says that one should distinguish between the writings of historians who record the past, and records made by the authorities that are intended to nurture certain opinions and beliefs."

Maluma wrinkled her forehead, not fully understanding the words of the tutor. "I have heard he is a wise teacher," she said doubtfully. "Can you wait for me? I wish to prepare something for your mother."

Maluma entered the home, leaving Judah alone on the porch, Miriam on his mind. He walked to the edge of the balcony, looking down on the inner courtyard of the house. His breath was taken by the sight which greeted his eyes. In the shaded edge of the courtyard sat the girl, her upper body unclad, playing with the baby within a shallow tub—holding him in her arms, dipping him in the water and then raising him to her and kissing him. The skin of the girl was smooth and dark, sparkling from the water dripping off her. She was laughing together with the baby, and he was gurgling happily and waving his hands up and down in excitement. There was something natural, joyful, and authentic in her play with the baby. He had never seen a girl unclothe herself so casually and freely. Unfamiliar sensations filled him, and he could feel his heart beating painfully against his chest.

Suddenly, the girl lifted her eyes upwards and noticed him. Judah blushed guiltily, but the girl merely smiled at him, as if she had known all along that he was spying on her, and waved at him.

"I am very glad that you came to visit me and that we had the chance to meet," said Maluma behind him. He rapidly spun towards her and walked away from the balcony corner, hoping Maluma did not notice what he had been gazing upon.

"How old are you, Judah?"

"Fourteen and a half," he answered automatically, thoughts running wild through his head.

"Good. I have a request for you."

He looked back at her inquiringly.

"Miriam is fifteen. She has no friends her own age in Jerusalem. She primarily speaks Greek, though she understands a little bit of Aramaic and Hebrew. Will you consent to escort her for a walk in the city? One of the slaves will drive you to the city and escort you. You can come with your sister, if you are shy…."

"I will come at noon tomorrow," he replied immediately, trying to appear indifferent, but his overly rapid response had revealed his true feelings.

"Come in the afternoon. Summer is nearly here, and noon is far too hot already."

The next day, Judah once again arrived at the home of the merchant. The maidservant that he had met the previous day opened the door to him and signaled that he should sit and wait at the foyer. Within a few minutes, Miriam and Maluma appeared from the second floor corridor and descended down the stairs. Miriam was wearing makeup much as she was the first time he had seen her, which gave her a feminine look older than her years. She wore a gown that was fastened at the waist and over her left shoulder, leaving her right shoulder bare. Judah recalled her fully bared figure from the day before. Had he seen another Jewish girl wear such a clearly Hellene style, he would have felt a certain repugnance, but at the sight of Miriam any such reservations immediately melted away. Her lustrous black hair poured down her shoulders. She descended the stairs lightly, greeting him with the sweetest smile he had ever seen. Judah stared at her, completely forgetting about Maluma's presence. In the many times he had rehearsed this moment in his imagination over the past day, he planned what he would say when he saw Miriam. Now, however, the words choked up in his throat.

A carriage driven by one of the house slaves waited facing the house, prepared to drive them to the walled city.

Unlike Judah, who was tense in her presence, Miriam was relaxed and uninhibited from the very first moment. She gently held his hand and pulled him with her towards the carriage, seemingly inadvertently brushing up against him as she did. The smell of her perfume and the sensation of her hand made him dizzy. He was familiar with the female friends of his sister, Hannah, and had often spoken to and laughed with them, but the sensation he felt sitting next to Miriam was completely different from anything he had ever known before.

During the carriage ride, Miriam led the conversation. She spoke in Greek, with the same foreign accent that he had first heard yesterday, and which became increasingly pleasant to his ears the more she spoke. Judah answered her in broken Greek, occasionally forced to use a word in Aramaic to fill in the gaps. Miriam expressed interest in his family and his origins, especially their priestly stature, and showered him with questions. She also asked about Jerusalem, the Temple, and his gentile friends, often hopping from one topic to another with a rapidity which dazzled him, so excited was she at finally having someone her own age to speak to. Occasionally, between his answer and another one of her questions, she revealed details about herself, her family, and life in Alexandria. She spoke in a constant stream, often laughing, with her eyes constantly glowing in happiness. Judah's linguistic difficulties and philological combinations amused her.

To Judah, she seemed the most beautiful girl he had ever met. Her liberated, uninhibited behavior and her carefree nature put him at ease. Gradually, he returned to himself and freed himself from his awkwardness.

The driver halted the carriage in the central street in the center of the city, at an intersection with another brood street. Jerusalem had no plazas or squares, and this was the only place wide enough to accommodate the carriage. Opposite the parked carriage was a tavern and an inn whose Cypriot owner was a former officer in the Jerusalem garrison. Judah only knew the place from the outside. The tavern was open every day save for the Sabbath, and at every hour, including at night, although the considerate Cypriot made sure to close the tavern's doors then, so as not to disturb his Jewish neighbors. During the daytime, however, the place was always loud with the sounds of raucous laughter, shouting, and music. The inn rooms on the ground floor, in back of the public room, served the prostitutes who worked in the premises. Above them, in the second floor of the building, were the true rooms used by overnight patrons and longer-term accommodations as well. Religiously observant Jews kept well away from the establishment, and its primary clientele were gentiles, soldiers of the Jerusalem Garrison, and merchants and other travelers visiting the city. The place was also a popular locale for the Hellenizers, particularly youths on the cusp of manhood. The driver winked at Judah and told them that he would await them inside the tavern, disappearing within its bowels almost instantly.

Judah led Miriam on a tour of the narrow alleyways in which the daily life of the city took place. Here, amongst the tiny and crowded houses, the traders and craftsmen labored. Miriam wrapped her arm in his, surprising him yet again. They talked as they walked through the streets, occasionally falling silent, growing used to the pleasure of each other's presence.

After strolling together for a considerable time, Miriam halted and stood before Judah, examining him with a long and thoughtful glance. He was embarrassed by her forthright gaze and glanced aside, but she turned his face back towards her with her index finger, forcing him to meet her eyes. He was nearly a head taller than she was. His chin, upper lip and cheeks were fuzzy with light thin hairs, the first growth of beard and moustache. Miriam knew that she would soon have to marry a Jewish husband in Alexandria. She toyed for a moment with the thought of her parents receiving word that she was marrying a priest's son in Jerusalem. From a religious point of view this would be considered a very good match. Businesswise, it probably would not be considered a good catch, however.

"What are you thinking about?"

She lightly blushed, concerned her facial expression had given her away.

"Nothing much, just what you said earlier," she evaded answering him directly. She drew closer, stood on the tips of her toes, and whispered into his ear, "Thank you for taking me for a tour of the city." Her lips lightly brushed against Judah's earlobe, tickling him lightly, triggering an almost electrical current which reached to the tips of his toes. She looked into his eyes smiling mysteriously. He, blushing fiercely, smiled back.

"Did you want to ask me something?" she asked provocatively.

"Me? No, what do you mean?" he replied innocently.

"I can see that you do," she persisted. "It is not good to keep things locked inside," she said, placing her hand on his chest.

He took a small step backwards, embarrassed at the contact of her hand on his body. "Yesterday, when you were bathing with the baby, did you know that I was watching you? Why did you not cover yourself?"

Miriam shrugged, her face radiant, "Why should I? I was bathing in the yard, and I knew I could be seen."

"This is not considered proper conduct amongst us. That is how the Hellenizers act... not us."

Miriam flinched backwards. The thought that her behavior was repugnant to him striking her like a blow.

"In Alexandria this is proper! There, we appreciate the image of the body and feel comfortable to display it. Does that bother you?"

He considered it for a moment, admitting to himself that he would disapprove if his sister Hannah behaved that way. "No, I do not mind. I even like it."

They continued walking, without saying a word. Miriam folded her arm in his again. She was relieved by his answer. For Judah, on the other hand, walking close to Miriam—and the occasional brush of thigh to thigh and arm to chest—was a new and almost overwhelming experience.

"The Jews of Alexandria think that it is a privilege to live in the Holy Land and especially in Jerusalem," said Miriam after a while.

"So why don't you return?"

"It is not so simple when one's entire family is there, and you have a home and a business… life in Egypt is very comfortable. Many Jews have done well and grown wealthy and have many servants and slaves. There are rich Jews here as well, such as my uncle, Simon, but there are more affluent Jews in Alexandria."

"Do you think there is a chance of another war between the Ptolemys and the Seleucids?"

"They say that there isn't. The queen of Egypt, Cleopatra, is the sister of King Seleucus…."

"Who would have believed that such a beautiful and cultured Hellene would associate with such an inferior hidebound traditionalist?!" A voice suddenly sounded behind them.

Judah's back stiffened. He identified the voice as soon as it spoke. Three stout youths wearing Hellen style tunics were standing a few steps behind them. Judah knew all three of them. It was Elianus and two of his closest cronies, Menachamus and Xenophon, all three scions of Hellenizer families. Elianus still craved vengeance, ever since the day he had been defeated and humiliated in the battle of their respective bands a year ago.

"Although according to what I hear maybe you aren't such a traditionalist after all," continued Elianus, "practicing in the pankration with highborn gentiles."

Judah was surprised. They only started practicing yesterday. Did everyone know already?

"I am prepared to face you, one on one," continued Elianus, trying to provoke Judah. "What do you say? Defeat me and I promise to let you have this Hellene."

The rustle of the city around them seemed to fall still. Elianus gave a superior smile, awaiting Judah's response.

Judah refused to take the bait. Elianus had grown strong in the past years. He was taller by half a head than Judah, broad of shoulder and muscular, the result of much weight-lifting and boxing. He was delighted to demonstrate his strength at every opportunity. Whenever a fight between youths broke out, Elianus turned out to be involved in one way or another. Whoever dared to face him soon found himself defeated and brutally beaten.

"You will win", said Judah after a long pause, feeling humiliated, the words costing him considerable effort.

Elianus beamed with satisfaction. This was not the revenge he sought, but he was prepared to make do with it.

Miriam took Judah's hand and moved to stand beside him. "Pay them no mind. If I wanted a Hellene I would have taken a real one, not a cheap knockoff," she spat out defiantly at the surprised Elianus. "Come on, let's go, the air has just turned rancid."

When they drew away and were about to turn into a side street, Elianus called after them, "Hellene, if you ever want a real man, I'll be waiting."

The sounds of laughter from Elianus and his friends echoed in Judah's head long after they had left the trio behind.

At dusk, Judah returned home and found Rebecca and

Hannah busy at work, preparing dinner.

"Judah, go find your brothers. Grandfather and father will soon return, and we will all have dinner together," his mother said.

Judah exited back to the street exactly as all four of his brothers arrived together: his two older brothers—Yohanan, the eldest, thoughtful and serious as always; and practical Simon—and his two younger brothers—bellicose Elazar, and mischievous Jonathan, the youngest.

"Look at the lover," said the grinning Simon. "The whole city is abuzz about you."

Judah frowned, uncertain whether Simon was referring to the incident with Elianus.

"Why are you troubled little brother?" Yohanan, the eldest, asked softly, putting his arm around Judah's shoulders. He led him aside, permitting the rest of the brothers to enter the house.

Yohanan's eyes were serene. He possessed some sort of inner calm, as if he possessed the life wisdom of an older man. His parents often joked that he had received the character and life experience of the grandfather for whom he was named.

"She is older than I am. It doesn't really matter," muttered Judah.

"Enjoy the moment and don't think too much. If you want to talk, I am here."

Judah smiled in embarrassment, wondering if he should tell his brother about the incident with Elianus.

Following dinner, Judah helped grandfather Yohanan to his home. Their grandfather lived alone in a small, one room apartment near their family home. The home in which Matityahu and his family lived belonged to Yohanan, but following the death of his wife, their grandfather preferred to rent a small room in a nearby house, and invited Matityahu and his family to move into his old home.

"What is troubling you, boy?"

"What do you mean?"

"You have been sitting all evening with a glum expression."

They arrived at the entrance to the apartment. Yohanan gave Judah a light shove from behind, urging him to enter. They sat down, the old man on his bed, the grandson on a bench before him.

Judah briefly described the events which took place with the Hellenizer youth.

"The priests from the countryside are not like the priests of Jerusalem," Yohanan said after reflecting on the matter. "We are men of the land, shepherds, hunters, laborers. We do not study boxing and wrestling in the villages, but we know how to protect what is ours."

"You mean I should have fought him?"

"Yes!"

Silence prevailed for a few moments. "I wanted to fight him, grandfather…"

"So why didn't you?!" demanded Yohanan.

"He trains, like many Hellenizers, in wrestling and boxing with one of the garrison soldiers. I saw him fight a few times. He enjoys it, and defeats anyone who stands against him. I thought I didn't stand a chance against him, and now I feel like a coward."

"It is well to know your strengths and weaknesses. Not many do," said Yohanan in a somewhat more approving tone. "You need to know how to fight, and we Jews have forgotten how to. We have remained a nation of shepherds, slingers, and archers, but that is not enough. Once, we were nation who knew how to fight. We held this land and protected it against all challengers with our own hands. The Greeks brag of battlefield tactics and formations as if they were the ones who invented them... when they were still living in mud huts we already had generals who won battles, conquered fortified cities, and drove off invading armies. You want to beat this Hellenizer ruffian? Be patient. I have made sure this Greek teacher of yours will teach you how to fight their way."

Yohanan stretched out a loving hand and stroked Judah's head. "Remember that you win with your heart, that is the most important thing. The way you describe this boy, he is a coward. Only brave with those too weak to fight back. As soon as you gain some training I am sure that you will defeat him."

***

When Judah's parents—Matityahu and Rebecca—met, she was the daughter of a long established Jerusalem family, whose entire life had been spent in the city where her relatives, both near and far, lived. Matityahu, on the other hand, was a village man. After they married, Rebecca moved to Modi'in, Matityahu's home village, where their children were born. But Rebecca dreamed of the day she would return to live in Jerusalem. The conquest of Coele Syria, and Judea with it, by Antiochus III, brought with it the opportunity to do so. Antiochus declared that those returning to repopulate Jerusalem would receive various tax deductions and benefits, in order to encourage the settlement of the city. Yohanan, the father of Matityahu, decided to take advantage of the opportunity. Rebecca and Matityahu and their children moved to Jerusalem with him. Matityahu was comforted by the fact that the family would descend to Modi'in every year, shortly after midsummer, to stay with his brother Joseph. At this time Jerusalem was relatively empty of visitors and even permanent residents, and business at the store was weak.

The family was preparing for their trip to Modi'in several weeks in advance this year as well. Matityahu hired two carriages and horses. Rebecca organized equipment and clothes, and, of course, gifts from their store for Joseph and his family. It was planned for the whole family to make the trip, with the exception of young Yohanan, who volunteered to remain behind to help look after grandfather Yohanan, who was too old to make such a trip.

The frequency of the meetings between Judah and Miriam grew over the passing weeks. Miriam would always greet him with a smile, her eyes stroking him, telling him all. Every time they met, even if it was after a brief interlude apart, she was overjoyed at meeting him as if they hadn't seen each other for a week. They talked about everything, improving in the meantime their proficiency in Aramaic and Greek, spending hours together both within and without the city.

Judah would have been happy to spend the entirety of every day with Miriam. It was enough for him to see her to feel his heart expand. When they were apart, she was on his mind every moment. During his pankration training he imagined she was sitting in the audience, watching him, and he strove to excel for her. From time to time he also fantasized about running into Elianus again, while accompanied by Miriam, so that he could defeat him with the maneuvers he had learned in his pankration practice. During his Torah studies in the mornings, and during Kratos' lessons as well, he sunk into daydreams more than once about the future. He even imagined himself as a young man arriving in Alexandria, presenting himself to Miriam's father and asking for his daughter's hand in marriage. Sometimes he would wake up from his daydreams in embarrassment to the sound of his friends' laughter. This was not the first time he felt love stir his heart, but this time he felt it with a strength he had never felt before. It burned within him, at times stimulating and exciting, filling him up like an overflowing river, and at times withdrawing, filling him up with doubts and uncertainty.

A few days before Judah's family trip to Modi'in, Judah and Miriam climbed to the top of the mountain overlooking the Temple from the East. The mountain was tall, the tallest in the environs of the city, and climbing up it made drawing breath, let alone carrying on a conversation, difficult. They reached a vantage point from which a breathtaking view revealed itself to them. Mountaintops all around, Jerusalem in the center and the Temple arising from it on the other side of the valley separating them from the city. The vista was so impressive that it distracted Judah from the thoughts which troubled him and his peace of mind. Miriam was supposed to return to Alexandria by the end of the summer, and this left them only a short time to spend together.

"You barely said anything today," said Miriam.

"I am thinking of our visit to Modi'in; I thought I might ask my parents to stay behind in Jerusalem."

"There is no point. I am returning home," said Miriam sadly.

"When?! You were only supposed to leave at the end of summer…"

"My uncle told me yesterday that he is leaving to Syria in a few days for a combined business trip and family vacation. We will all ride in carriages to Jaffe, and from there they will take a ship North to Antioch and I will sail with a handmaid back to

Alexandria."

A deep sadness was in her eyes. From the first she knew that their relationship had no future. She liked Judah from the moment she first laid eyes on him, but she thought that she would be able to control her emotions and have no more than a light summer fling before her return to Alexandria as a woman destined for a pre-arranged marriage.

Judah embraced her, pulling her to him. When they first met he was embarrassed at making physical contact with her. With time he grew addicted to it. His body was burning with desire, frustration, and rage.

Miriam surrendered to his embrace, wrapping her arms around him and placing her head lightly on his chest. After a time she pulled away and smiled a sad, loving and sweet smile that melted him up inside, as so often happened in her presence. She held his palms in her own hands and kneeled on the ground, pulling him down after her. Her two hands gently stroked his cheeks and then she leaned towards him and pressed her lips to his for a long, long, moment. Judah cooperated with her, overwhelmed with roiling waves of pleasure.

"We still have a few days," she whispered, "I want to make the most of them."

*Note to reader—you may now watch a movie relevant to the chapter you have just finished by either clicking the code or scanning it in an appropriate application. Alternatively, click on the following link: https://youtu.be/nKvmDZ8hGGY

177 BCE—Heliodorus

> Dramatis Personae
> **Bold** = main character
> * = historical figure

- **Kratos**—*A Greek tutor*
- **Eupolemus***—*A Jewish boy from a priestly family, son of Yohanan ben Hakotz*
- **Matityahu*** *and Rebecca*—*Parents of Judah*
- **Yohanan***, **Simon***, **Judah***, **Hannah***, **Eleazar*** *and* **Jonathan***—*The children of Matityahu, by age*
- **Phidias**—*Pankration trainer*
- **Tiamos** *and* **Glitarius**—*Seleucid and Roman classmates of Judah*
- **Heliodorus***—*Chief Minister of the Seleucid Kingdom*
- *Reuven—Cousin of Judah*
- *Korinthos—Commander of the Seleucid garrison in Jerusalem*
- *Ligatos—Commander of the garrison's Cavalry*
- *Solo—Commander of the garrison's infantry*

A bit over a year had passed since Miriam had left Jerusalem and returned to Alexandria. Judah no longer thought of her, though he could still not bear to think of other girls. The maidens of Jerusalem, however, found him to be of considerable interest. At sixteen he had matured and grown tall, achieving the towering height of his older brothers, Yohanan and Shimon. He was extremely muscular and possessed a handsome countenance which left few girls indifferent. He was of particular interest to the daughters of the Hellenizers, who sought to attract his attention, being well informed of his affair with the Alexandrian beauty.

Eupolemus barged into the room radiant and eyes sparkling. "Why hello to you all: the four wise men, the most beautiful daughter of Jerusalem—and who is this here?" he said, shaking his head in supposed amazement at Judah, "What is a donkey doing amongst such noble steeds?"

The brothers and Hannah smiled in delight. Eupolemus was impudent and uninhibited, and had become a close friend of Matityahu's family in spite of being a Hellenizer. His frequent and sudden incursions into their home had long ceased to surprise them. They enjoyed his sharp and witty tongue, which stung Judah mercilessly. Judah, who lay on a mattress at the edge of the room, rose slightly, leaned on his elbows, and looked over him calmly.

"Why is a Canaanite street dog troubling noble steeds such as ourselves?"

"Ohhhhh…" muttered the brothers, half laughingly, egging the friendly banter on.

"Look at that pack of old maids, trying to provoke such good friends as us into a fight," Eupolemus changed tack suddenly and directed his barbed tongue at Judah's brothers. "Come quickly. The Greek and the Roman are waiting for us."

Suddenly, the brothers grew serious and stifled their laughter. Eupolemus, whose sharp mind was even faster than his witty tongue, immediately understood who stood behind him.

"Priest Matityahu, how are you this fine evening?" he asked with his honeyed tongue, as he turned around.

"Don't you 'priest' me, you delinquent!" answered Matityahu with mock anger, his eyes sparkling with laughter. "Where do you think you are taking my son at this time of the day?"

"Oh, forgive me sir, the Greek teacher, Kratos, warned us never to dare to be late to the pankration training and we must hurry...."

"Why do you associate with such scoundrels?" Matityahu cut him off, addressing Judah, as his other children broke out in laughter. "He is lying to my face without any smidgen of shame. It's a good thing I trust **you**. Don't come back too late."

Eupolemus was actually speaking the truth this time. Phidias, their pankration trainer, was a veteran warrior and a pankration contestant in his own right as a youth. In the twilight of his military career he had been placed in the Jerusalem garrison, but as a soldier throughout most of his life, he was strict about maintaining schedule discipline—conduct which his youthful students found onerous.

Tiamos and Glitarius were already waiting for them on the main street of Jerusalem. Tiamos was impatient and signaled at them from afar to hurry. Together, they walked towards the garrison fortress where their trainer awaited them.

"In the pankration, we do more than learn how to fight," Phidias told the youths in a meaningful intonation. He had been training them almost every day for over a year and felt obligated to pound wisdom into their heads as well as drill fighting routines into their bodies. "We need to think, to fight with our minds. If you wish to train simple warriors, you will teach them boxing. If you wish to train generals, masters of strategic and tactical thinking, then pankration is what is needed! The secret to winning in pankration is thinking. If my opponent has an advantage in fighting at arm's length, then I will lead him to a close contact, face-to-face fight, or even a ground fight, where one can overcome the opponent with a choke or a submission hold[4]. In pankration, you must learn how to read your opponent, understand his strengths and weakness in regard to you, and determine the correct way of combating him accordingly. This is a battle of the minds, not merely a contest of strength. This is how a general should act in battle. Most of the victories of Alexander the Great came from outthinking his opponents."

"Our general could also use a bit of trade sense, negotiation skills, if you catch my drift," said Eupolemus with a sly smile, his fingers rubbing against each other in the universal gesture of counting money. "Soft words and a golden coin can gain you much more than bared blades and harsh deeds."

Phidias wrinkled his face in distaste. He liked the Hellenizer priest's son, but he was frequently annoyed by his cynical witticisms. "I only hope that when you grow up you will learn to use the negotiation skills you are learning at home for good," he chastised his errant student—but with a smile.

Glitarius seemed to be holding back from speaking out.

"You wanted to say something, Roman?"

"You can apply your mind to a boxing match, just as to pankration," said Glitarius hesitantly. "In fact, I would say this is true of any type of arena fight. The most famous warriors in Rome, the best gladiators, are famous for their cunning minds, not merely for their strength. That is how they win fights. The most beautiful battles are those in which a smaller combatant

---

4   A wrist lock which will break the opponent if he fails to surrender.

battles and defeats a larger opponent."

The three other youths exchanged amused glances, certain that Phidias would be angry at Glitarius, who dared compare his beloved pankration to other forms of combat. Phidias seemed for a moment to be on the verge of fulfilling their expectations, as his brow grew stormy and his eyebrows drew together as if he was about to admonish Glitarius.

He surprised them. "You are correct," he told Glitarius, shaking his head at the three other youths in silent reprimand. "Any combat style or form has room for tactics and intelligent fighting. However, in pankration this is particularly true, since all fighting techniques are permitted, so that greater room for maneuver exists. Furthermore, there is no chance of a single individual being the best warrior in all styles of combat—arm's length combat, close combat, and ground grappling. That is why a professional pankration fighter must take into account the possibility that one day he will meet an opponent who is his superior in one type of fighting, forcing him to lead the fight to a more advantageous context…"

After the training, Phidias and Judah walked from the fortress into the city.

"They are about to travel far away from here," said Phidias.

"Tiamos' father has already returned to Antioch. He hopes the king will promote him to a higher ranking position."

"The destiny of those children was written before they were even born," said Phidias as they walked. "This is the way it is in such families; the fathers pave the path ahead of their sons. Tiamos will be an officer in the army of the king, Glitarius will be a senator in Rome. Eupolemus will obviously be a merchant, a swindler and conman," Phidias said, shaking his head.

"Are you sure?" asked Judah, raising his eyebrow, driven to

protect his friend.

"No, not really. Eupolemus is young and cocky, but he has much potential. However, in order to realize that potential and achieve greatness, he needs a few hard knocks in the head from his trainer," laughed Phidias, thumping his chest, "as well as gentler lessons from tutors such as Kratos, and the influence of proper young gentlemen such as yourself," added the trainer, and affectionately smacked Judah on the back of his head.

"So what about me? What will I be?"

"Your family is made up of true priests. You will no doubt join your elder council, just like your grandfather."

"I am not sure of that. My grandfather is a member of the council, this is true, but that role does not suit my father."

"Will you want to continue training after they leave?"

"Of course! But I cannot pay…"

Phidias placed his hand on Judah's back. "You won't have to. I take money from the rich kids like Eupolemus because not filching their parents would be criminal—and as a garrison soldier, this is a supplement to my income that I cannot turn down. But I enjoy training you and you have already reached a level sufficient for us to train together."

"Why did you stop competing?" asked Judah, "Kratos says your talents are wasted."

Phidias sighed. "My dream was to be an Olympic champion. I had a pretty good chance; I was the champion of my city and was prepared to represent it in the games. However, I was young and arrogant, and I got into too many fights. Eventually I was exiled from the city."

They continued walking down the road to the walled city in silence. Judah was happy at the chance of continuing his training even after his friends left the city, but restrained his enthusiasm in Phidias' presence.

"How are things with you?" asked Phidias.

"As usual. Father dreams of moving back to Modi'in, mother is attached to the store and her family in Jerusalem and doesn't want to leave. So long as grandfather Yohanan is alive…."

"I meant your politics," Phidias cut him off.

"Oh, that," Judah blushed, "well, what do you want to know?"

"The king appointed Olympiodoros as the master supervisor of all temples in Coele Syria and Phoenicia. He is charged with **wisely** supervising their good conduct." Phidias sardonically stressed the word 'wisely.' "His real goal, of course, is to look after the economic interests of the king."

Judah's expression clearly indicated that he did not understand what Phidias was aiming at.

"He never bothered with you up to now; he couldn't find the time to reach a minor city which isn't even a Polis. He needed to unite the kingdom, spread the royal cult, ensure that everyone celebrates their holidays according to our calendar, and ensure that all temples pay their taxes. Judea, now… Judea is different. Your priests manage your calendar, and it is an inseparable part of your traditions. That is why he preferred to focus on the temples of other nations."

"So what has changed now?"

"I suppose that he wasn't able to squeeze enough funds out of the temple treasuries. The king sent his chief minister, Heliodorus, son of Iskilus, to tour the cities and the temples of this province in order to milk them for all they are worth. He will soon arrive in Jerusalem, perhaps together with Olympiodoros. Your people should get ready for trouble."

"But what will he want with us?" Judah still could not understand.

"The king requires a great deal of gold and silver to finance his army. A skilled warrior like myself costs coin, and quite a bit of it," replied Phidias with a smile.

"How much money could we have in the Temple?"

"How would I know? We are forbidden entrance, but rumor describes the Temple treasury as being vast."

The day of the departure of Tiamos' family arrived. In the early morning Judah walked slowly to the store. His mother had prepared a farewell present to Tiamos' mother, a colorful scarf with the words "Peace be upon you" embroidered onto it. Judah added his own necklace, with a Star of David pendant, a personal gift from him to Tiamos. Legend had it that King David, the great warrior king and general who had united all of the tribe of Israel into a single great kingdom, had that symbol painted on his shield.

Rebecca held her son's face between her two hands. "They don't have a homeland like we do. They are a nation of conquerors alien to the land they rule. Today they are here and tomorrow somewhere else. But the friendship which has grown between you is true and strong. It can outlast the miles between Jerusalem and Antioch and the passage of time. Hurry up, so that you won't be late to the meeting with him."

Hannah, his sister, instinctively understood how he must feel and offered to join him.

They left the store and walked silently towards the gate of the city. Judah was lost in his thoughts. When they reached the main street, near the Cypriot's tavern, they saw that many people had gathered there. All of them seemed excited, worried, and concerned, and all were looking up the main street towards the Temple.

Someone called his name from one of the adjoining alleys. Judah saw Reuven, one of his many cousins, arrive at a run.

"Judah, Hannah," panted Reuven. "A disaster is approaching. The Chief Minister of the king is coming to rob the Temple. A huge column of cavalry is on its way. The entire city is in chaos. Where do you think you are headed?"

Judah did not answer. He felt his stomach churning. Phidias had warned him of this a few days ago. He should have told his father and his grandfather. They could have warned the High Priest.

Reuven ran away from them, intent on warning others. More people crowded in around them. Men and women, elders and children. A large group clustered together and began marching up the street towards the Temple.

"Go home," Judah ordered his sister, "this could get dangerous."

"So where are **you** going?" Hannah enquired sharply.

"I have to bid farewell to Tiamos."

He ran the entire way. The gates of the city were flung open. He passed by them without halting. Continuing to run rapidly westwards, through the city quarters beyond the walls, ascending the hill on which the spacious homes of Jerusalem's wealthy elite and foreign dignitaries sprawled. As he caught a glimpse of Tiamos' family home from a distance, he saw the standard with their family crest being removed from the building. The gate was wide open and a loaded wagon stood in the yard. He passed the yard panting and entered the house. The entryway was packed with a high pile of closed chests, probably equipment which had yet to be loaded. He heard voices from the back yard and exited it. Two men he did not know were standing there and speaking amongst themselves. Judah returned to Tiamos' home without addressing them.

"Tiamos!" he cried out.

"I am here," called a cheerful voice from the second story of the building. A moment later Tiamos descended the stairs, his arms open to embrace Judah, his mother and Kratos trailing behind him.

"My brother," said Tiamos and warmly embraced Judah. "You seem flustered, what is it?!"

"They say the chief Minister is on his way to rob the Temple. Everyone is gathering in the city… can this be possible?" Judah asked Tiamos' mother and Kratos.

Kratos shrugged and shook his head, concern plastered on his face. He knew nothing about this. Tiamos' family's departure had lost him his primary pupil, as well as the diverse class he had established, but he had received a number of lucrative offers from the leading Hellenizer families of the city to remain and tutor their sons. That was how he had ended up primarily tutoring moderate Hellenizers who had adapted the Hellenist lifestyle outwardly, but in their inner hearts continued to believe in the one God and uphold the same Jewish customs and laws as the traditionalists. The thought that the Seleucid Temple Supervisor would ignore those traditions and force his way into the Temple of the One God, forbidden to all but the High Priest, troubled him.

"I know little of such matters," replied Tiamos' mother in reply to Judah's questioning gaze, "but Ligatos is here, and he will surely know."

Tiamos signaled for Judah to follow him to the yard.

"He is the commander of the cavalry of the garrison. He is handling the sale of our house and the shipment of the equipment, and knows everything that is happening in the province, better than anyone else."

Ligatos, however, had no calming words to share. "Your friend is right, Tiamos," he said with a severe expression, "The Chief Minister is supposed to arrive in the upcoming hours for a routine tour of the local temples, and given the particular sensitivity of this matter to the Jews, the garrison has been put on standby. That is why only a small cavalry detachment will be available to escort your departure from the city."

Tiamos noticed the strained expression on Judah's face. "You must want to return home now. Thank you for coming to say goodbye." He pulled Judah tightly to him. "I will never forget you. You were more than a brother to me." Judah locked his gaze with him solemnly and they stood there for a long moment, forehead to forehead, silence between them. Then Judah broke away and ran back home.

An hour later, Matityahu and his five sons left their home, headed towards the Temple. The sun was already high in the sky and its rays beat down strongly on their heads. The elders had gathered in the Hall of Hewn Stones, the innermost chambers of the Temple. Grandfather Yohanan was there as well. A great crowd had gathered in the Temple courtyard since the morning hours, standing in groups, trying to gather support from each other, some of them praying, some listening for any fragment of information. Rumors came and went, passing from one man to another, raising and lowering the threshold of anxiety from one side of the scale to the other depending on the rumor. At first, Heliodorus was said to be arriving at the head of a great army, together with the Temple supervisor, to transform the Temple into a Hellenist fane. A moment later this rumor was disputed by another, which decried it as groundless, claiming that Heliodorus was arriving on a mission of peace. The atmosphere was tense and drenched with fear, making Judah feel even guiltier for not immediately sharing the warning he had received from Phidias a few days ago.

As twilight fell, a whisper spread through the assembled multitudes. Heliodorus had arrived in Jerusalem, accompanied by no more than a squad of cavalry. They rode directly to the Jerusalem garrison fort. A sigh of relief rose from the crowd.

Shortly thereafter, Hunio left the Temple, headed towards the fort, accompanied by the chief elders. Judah saw them in the distance, as he stood within the tightly packed crowd. The potbellied Hunio moved with great effort, like a man unused to physical activity, for whom even a simple walk was a significant strain. A relative hush spread throughout the crowd, which tensed in anticipation of developments.

In the fortress, Hunio and his companions were received with the utmost respect. The soldiers lived amongst the Jews of Jerusalem and met with them on a daily basis. Jews were considered by them to be an autonomous nation rather than a conquered subject people. The High Priest and his men were responsible for collecting the royal taxes and maintaining public order, so the garrison was left with very little to actually do. Accordingly, only a small garrison was placed in Jerusalem, containing no more than a score of cavalry and twice as many infantry, as well as several officers, logistics personnel, servants, and so on—no more than a hundred people all told. Korinthos, the commander of the garrison, and his two officers—Ligatos, commander of the cavalry, and Solo the Cypriot, commander of the infantry—had lived a number of years in Jerusalem and were familiar figures in the city. While Korinthos maintained a certain distance from the commoners of the city, as befit his position as garrison commander, Ligatos and Solo would often walk the streets of the city and were known by many.

Hunio and the elders were led into the garrison's reception room. Two slaves swiftly arrived and served refreshments to the tense elders. After a few minutes, the three officers of the garrison—Korinthos, Ligatos, and Solo—entered the room. Korinthos directly approached Hunio, who stood slowly as the three entered the room, and held the soft hands of the potbellied priest warmly in his own two calloused hands. Heliodorus comes and he will leave, he thought, but I need to keep on living with them here.

"Hunio, my friend, what brings you and your honorable companions here? What are you concerned with? I hear that the entire male population of Jerusalem is assembled in the Temple. Why? What is the matter?" asked Korinthos.

Hunio shook his head, indicating that Korinthos was not fooling him.

"The elders of the Jewish people are with me here," he replied sternly, both honoring his companions and seeking to draw comfort from their presence, "as we see that the minister of the king has arrived in our Holy City. We will be delighted to host him with all due honor, but we have heard that his intention is to defile the Temple."

"Nonsense!" responded Korinthos heatedly, "Don't you know that we safeguard you?"

"Never has a gentile entered the Temple! We Jews pay the royal tax regularly, fully, and on time. Why then do you seek to injure the very heart of our faith? An injury to the Temple **is an injury to every Jew wherever he may be**...."

Hunio's final words were said loudly and with great agitation. They echoed throughout the chamber in a warning which left a strong impression on everyone in the room.

Korinthos pondered what to say. The internal politics of the

Jews of Jerusalem were well known to him. Hunio but barely maneuvered and maintained his position between the opposing factions. The Hellenizers, headed by the Tuvia Clan, were the most powerful single faction in the city, and consistently sought to undermine Hunio's rule. They had connections and plots that reached the very highest ranks of the court of Antioch. Korinthos was used to thinking of Hunio as a fat, tired, weak individual. It always seemed that his mind was troubled with the intrigues that surrounded him. And yet here he was, standing firmly, fire in his eyes, daring to hint that should Heliodorus dare enter the Temple it would lead all of the Jewish people to an uprising. Korinthos was familiar with the holidays in which Jews travelled to Jerusalem to celebrate, coming from all over the Seleucid kingdom and even foreign Hellenistic and non-Hellenistic kingdoms. Hunio's threat therefore seemed all too plausible to him. His impression was that the situation was far more severe than he had initially thought. Life in Judea, he was now convinced, would not go on as usual should Heliodorus enter the Temple.

"You are arriving at conclusions on the basis of false rumors," he told Hunio. "Heliodorus has just arrived. He is bathing the dust of the road off and will soon arrive to speak with you. Sit down in the meantime; relax, eat and drink. Things are not nearly as bad as they seem to you."

He gestured at the servants standing at the side of the room to treat the guests generously, and then left the room with the other two officers.

Some of Hunio's companions approached him and shook his hands or patted him on the back. Those who remained seated nodded their heads, making it clear that Hunio's brave words had impressed them as well. Hunio was satisfied. His words were meant to consolidate his own position amongst the elders just as much as they were meant to sway the Seleucid officers.

Korinthos walked rapidly down the corridors of the fortress on his way to his quarters, which he had cleared in honor of Heliodorus.

A brief washing was all that was required to make Heliodorus appear fresh and energetic, as if he had just woken up from a night's sleep. On the table an ornate helmet rested, decorated with two golden stripes and feathers. It was clearly a ceremonial helmet, rather than one intended for use on the field of battle.

"What's on your mind, Korinthos? You look a bit peaked," Heliodorus asked casually.

"Not at all, Minister. All is well," Korinthos answered mechanically, surprised that Heliodorus could read his expression.

"It is the same everywhere," Heliodorus told his servant who smiled in response. He turned back to Korinthos. "The officers in every city I visited—not to mention your Strategos, Apollonius son of Thresas[5]—behave as if I had come to take their own money. Or perhaps they think it is **their own money**…"

Korinthos was insulted at the injurious insinuation. "Your honor, in Judea, perhaps unlike other provinces, we have noth-

---

5   Apollonius was a common Hellene name at the time. The man mentioned here is the Strategos of all of Coele-Syria, rather than the contemporary Apollonius the Meridarch of Samaria, who is more familiar to those knowledgeable of the story of the Maccabees, and who will later make an appearance in this book. Similar name duplication also occurs for other characters both Hellene (Phillipus, Ptolemy, etc.) and Jewish (Yohanan, Jason, etc.). When such duplication occurs it will be identified through the use of titles, patronyms, appellations, or, when necessary, with footnotes.

ing to do with the collection of the taxes. From the days of the father of King Seleucus, Antiochus the Great, the chief of the Jews is their High Priest, and he is in charge of tax collection."

"Even better. Well then, what are you concerned about? I have come to see if there are any additional funds which should have been sent to Antioch. If all is well then all is well."

"Sir, anywhere else this might be a purely financial affair, but here, in Judea, this is a religious affair."

"What do you mean? I have no interest in their odd beliefs. The personal secretary of my father was a Jew. The majordomo of my family estate in Antioch is a Jew as well. I have no intention of harming them. That is why I didn't bring the Temple Supervisor with me. I only came to find funding sources for the royal treasury which, to remind you, pays your salary and that of your soldiers."

"Sir, their Temple is the most sacred site in the world to them. Their faith prohibits the entry of any non-Jew into the Temple. The Great King himself has forbidden us to tread there."

As he spoke, Korinthos handed two scrolls over to Heliodorus. "These are not the original documents, but I trust the Jews to have copied them correctly. They present these decrees to any new garrison commander who arrives in the city."

Heliodorus took the scrolls and examined the first. He recognized at once that this was a copy of an epistler prostagma, an official decree, but when he saw the seal and signature he was stunned. It was nothing less than a formal decree by Antiochus the Great himself, the father of the current king, to Ptolemy, the Strategos of the newly conquered province of Coele-Syria. The decree was dated to the days immediately following the conquest of Coele-Syria from Egypt. Heliodorus began to read the certificate carefully:

"Greetings from King Antiochus to Ptolemy.

Given that the Jews have shown their enthusiasm and support to us from the moment we set foot on their land, and given that they had set up a glorious introduction for us, and that their council of elders had approached us and submitted to us, offering plentiful supplies to the army and the elephant and fully cooperating with us in expelling the Egyptian soldiers from the fortress.

Accordingly we have seen fit to reward their actions and to restore their city, which had suffered so greatly in the events of the war, resettling it and encouraging its scattered exiles to return to it. To start we have decided, out of awe and respect to the heavens, to provide them, for the purpose of raising sacrifices a subsidy to the sum of..."

Heliodorus skipped two paragraphs in which the benefits to the Jews were enumerated and continued, skimming over the writing, focusing on only a few sentences:

"Let all of the people be governed by the laws of their ancestors. The elder council, the priests, the scribes of the Temple, and the holy singers will be exempted from the poll tax and from... so that the city might be resettled more quickly I hereby declare a tax exemption... those taken from the city by force of arms and who live in a state of slavery, we hereby set them free, they and their children, and order that their property be returned as well."

Heliodorus handed over the decree to his servant and more closely examined the second scroll:

"No gentiles may enter the precincts of the Temple, and the entry to the Temple shall be forbidden to the Jews as well, save for those permitted to enter following purification in accordance to the laws of their ancestors. Let no one bring into the city the flesh ... of the animals forbidden to the Jews..."

"Incredible...." muttered Heliodorus. "This is the first time I have heard of this. This does change the picture somewhat, doesn't it?"

"All of the residents of the city have gathered in the streets and in the Temple," said Korinthos, "As far as they are concerned the entry of your honor into the Temple is an unparalleled insult."

"What will they do?"

"The rumors of your lordship's coming have preceded you. The High Priest, Hunio, wishes to meet with you. He is their leader, and with him are a number of other honorable elders. I know him well. I have never seen him quite so upset. He told me explicitly that the entry of your lordship into the Temple will enflame the Jews throughout the kingdom and even beyond. This matter extends far beyond Judea."

Heliodorus spun on his heels and sat on his bed, deep at thought. Korinthos waited for a moment, permitting him to process what he told him and then added.

"One other thing, my lord. I do not like to mention it, and may my lord forgive me if my words sound cowardly, but my entire garrison here is barely fifty warriors. Together with the forces commanded by his lordship, we are barely a hundred warriors. If...."

"I understand you!" Heliodorus cut him off sharply. "Ha! I am not here to start a riot, but I am the **Chief Minister of the king**! My arrival in this pathetic shithole is the same as if the king himself had arrived here."

Heliodorus rose and picked up the ceremonial helmet. "Come and let us meet your High Priest!" he said as he stormed out of the room.

Korinthos entered first into the room containing Hunio and

his companions, his two officers at his heels. He drew himself erect by the door and declared, "The honored Chief Minister of the king, Heliodorus son of Iscilus. All rise!"

Heliodorus entered the hall and seated himself on a tall chair set in the middle of the room. The group of Jewish elders in front of him remained standing. In the royal palace matters were designed in such a way that the king's throne was placed on a tall platform, at the top of a deck of stairs, so that even when people faced their seated monarch, it was the king who held the higher position. Here, an opposite effect was in effect. When Heliodorus sat down he found himself looking from below at the people standing before him.

"Please sit down, gentlemen," he said.

"Your lordship," said Korinthos after Hunio and the others were seated, "this is High Priest Hunio, chief of the Jews."

Hunio stood up heavily, wishing to speak while standing, out of respect to Heliodorus. However, once he stood, he was once again taller than Heliodorus. Heliodorus could not suppress his smile.

"Shalom," he said in Hebrew, to the amazement of all present. "Peace be upon you, High Priest Hunio," he continued, this time in Greek. "Please, be seated. This is a friendly meeting." He was pleased with the nods and relaxed stance of Hunio and the elders—a single word in Hebrew had done a great deal to mollify them.

Hunio sat back down into the couch, his great weight sinking into its pillows. "Welcome to our Holy City, honored minister."

"My family has employed and still employs your people," said Heliodorus. "The man in which I put my greatest trust, the majordomo of my estate in Antioch, is a Jew. His name is Nikon, son of Alexandros. Perhaps you know him?"

Hunio shook his head in negation, as did the rest of the elders.

"In any event, you can be certain that I have the utmost admiration towards your people. I would be honored if you considered me to be your friend."

"I thank my lord for his offer of friendship and gladly welcome it," replied Hunio.

"I am told that you have heard a terrible rumor about the purpose of my visit."

"Honored Minister…" Hunio sought to reply, but Heliodorus signaled to him to wait.

"I was sent to every city in Coele-Syria and Phoenicia to collect funds that were meant to arrive at the royal treasury. In order to safely manage and safeguard the kingdom, coin is necessary. That is simply the way of the world. These funds are needed to safeguard public order and safety, and to pay the wages of the soldiers who **guard you**."

Heliodorus paused for a moment, passing his gaze over the members of the Jewish delegation.

"The king has been told that your Temple contains considerable treasure. These funds rightfully belong to the king and he is entitled to take them."

"Your lordship, the funds in the Temple treasury are funds deposited to safeguard the welfare of orphans and widows." Hunio protested, trying to speak as moderately as he could in spite of his outrage. "Who could close off his heart to their plight and to rob those poor souls who have deposited their property in the Temple of the god of Israel, the all-highest God?"

"The entire Temple treasury belongs to orphans and widows?! How exactly did they secure such funds if they are so poor?" Heliodorus raised his voice and glanced at Korinthos with a well-contrived expression of wonder.

"A considerable portion of the money belongs to the noble Hyrcanus of the house of Tuvia, a righteous and innocent man, loyal to the king, who guards the eastern marches of his kingdom from marauding Arab tribes, keeping them from pillaging the king's lands. Whatever villains may have whispered in the ears of the king, they were speaking lies intended to injure me, no more. Nor is the treasure as great as your words might imply. The entire Temple treasury contains no more than four hundred talents of silver and two hundred talents of gold."

Heliodorus was surprised at Hunio's willingness to reveal the extent of the Temple treasury, as well as with its contents—which were indeed considerably lower than he had expected. "Very well, orphans and widows," he grumbled, "what about the funds of this Hyrcanus?"

"My lord, removing them from this man is equivalent to robbing him. He is an honorable individual whose lands stretch over much of the Transjordan. This is a man who maintains extensive trade relations with Egypt—and a close personal friendship with the queen of Egypt, Cleopatra."

Matters are becoming more and more entangled, thought Heliodorus. This is all I need—driving these Jews to rebellion, and also offending a friend of Cleopatra, the sister of the king and queen[6]. But I cannot back down now. "I am prohibited from failing to fulfill the order of the king, and he ordered me to bring him the funds in the Temple treasury. His order cannot be transgressed. Tomorrow morning I will enter to inspect the treasury."

---

6   The Seleucids, like the Ptolemys and other Eastern dynasties, practiced the custom of marrying brother and sister, for both religious/ritual purposes and to keep power within the family.

"Your lord, your entry into the Temple of our god will violate the sanctity of the place!" Hunio rose in protest, his face an open book of turbulent emotions.

Heliodorus rose as well, determined to have the final word and end the audience. "If you speak truth then I will consider my course of action and it may be that your contribution to the royal treasury will be light." He turned and rapidly left the room, before the high priest sought to respond.

In the Temple courtyard, spirits had settled down in the meantime. The expedition of Hunio and the elders had yet to return, but the tense atmosphere had somewhat relaxed given the news of the limited forces which had accompanied Heliodorus. Judah, who had been sunk deep in thoughts about the events of the day for some time, was startled out of his reverie by a friendly pat on his back. It was his brother Simon, who was standing beside him, and it snapped him back to reality at once.

"This is no time for daydreaming, kid," Simon said with mock seriousness. Yohanan, who stood nearby observed them with a glum smile and then turned his gaze aside. At the age of nineteen he was already taller than most men. Now he used his height to look over the heads of the assembled multitudes, looking for any sign of developments in the situation. He was the most serious of the five brothers, and felt a greater duty, being the eldest son. Judah reddened, embarrassed. "Simon, if we weren't in the Temple...."

Simon grinned, but signaled for Judah to lower his voice, nodding at their father as he did. "You can't, and you know it," he whispered so that only Judah and his younger brothers could hear. "Even with all of your training with your gentile friends, you know I could swat you like a fly."

"Hey, I'm with Judah," said Elazar, joining in with a childlike delight.

Simon glanced at Jonathan mock-gravely. "Well, who are you with, little brother? With **the winner** or with the losers?"

"With you, of course."

"It's a deal! Wrestling match at home when this is all over," Simon pronounced.

Later, Heliodorus and Korinthos met alone at the top of the garrison-fortress' watch tower.

"Korinthos, I have a feeling that Strategos Apollonius has deliberately stirred up trouble. The king does not care who leads the Jews so long as they pay their taxes, keep quiet, and show loyalty. Our kingdom is made up of many nations and tribes and they need to be handled with caution. The connection between Apollonius and the local opposition, who approached him directly rather than going through you; the fact that he left the sensitivity of the Jews in regard to their Temple out of his reports, even though he must have been well aware of it; the treasury, which is not nearly as extensive as we have been told; all this adds up to an indication that he intended to provoke unrest, which would lead to a change in the local leadership. I wouldn't be surprised if the local opposition provided him with a hefty bribe."

Korinthos listened silently. Heliodorus was considered to be one of the most powerful men in the kingdom. The manner in which he spoke to him and revealed his innermost thoughts was an unambiguous expression of trust. Such a connection with the second most important man in the kingdom was a once-in-a-lifetime opportunity for the commander of a minor garrison.

"In the palace we are used to intrigues," continued Heliodorus.

"I suppose that you too must have your spies. Is there anyone you can trust to transmit this high priest a confidential message from me, meant solely for his own ears?"

Korinthos considered the matter. Once Heliodorus raised the possibility of spies, he understood that he really didn't know who of his own men he could fully trust. "I can rely only on myself, sir. I will personally transmit the message. I don't think that will be considered unusual considering what is happening."

"Very well. Speak to him in privacy. Tell him that I am on his side. I will not enter their Temple tomorrow, but I cannot return to the king empty handed. He must prepare fifty gold talents and a hundred silver talents by tomorrow morning. That is a quarter of what they have, according to his own words. I trust him to manage that much if he wishes to keep his position. Tell him to report directly to me any unusual moves his opponents seem to be plotting with Apollonius. He must send word of such plots directly to Nikon, my Jewish financial manager in Antioch."

Korinthos only nodded, stunned with these developments.

"One more thing, my friend. Until I handle the Strategos, you should be careful as well. My reach is powerful and long, but I am far away. Do not share this information with anyone, and report to me about anything that happens here."

176 BCE—Hunio III

Dramatis Personae
Bold = main character
* = historical figure

- **Hunio III***—*High Priest, head of the house of Zadok*
- **Jason** *(Yeshu[7])**—*Hunio's brother*
- Hunio IV*—*Son of High Priest Hunio III*
- **Yohanan***, **Simon***, **Judah***, **Eleazar*** *and* **Jonathan***—*The five sons of Matityahu by age*
- Grandfather Yohanan*—*The father of Matityahu*
- The Belgas*—*A Hellenizer priestly family, rivals of the House of Zadok*

Hunio gazed at Jason indulgently, trying to display generosity of spirit towards his younger brother. He placed both of his hands on his potbelly, "the hill of repose and serenity," as he affectionately called it.

"Hunio, try to listen to me this time with an open mind, free of prejudice," Jason said, trying to smile and speak pleasantly

---

7   The Hebrew name of Jason, as identified by Josephus Flavius two centuries after the events of this story, was identical to the given name of Jesus.

in spite of his disgust with his brother. "Believe me, I wish to ensure the well-being of our people just as much as you do. But times have changed. Only the citizens of cities that have received the status of a Polis have rights or recognized status in the kingdom. Trade between all lands within and without the kingdom is flourishing, but we are not reaping the fruits of that commerce. Competitions in which athletes from all over the world participate are taking place—but we are left on the outside. A citizen of Antioch, should he wish to travel and see the kingdom, will not even bother setting foot in a city that is not a Polis—such a city would be of no consequence to him."

Hunio sighed and shook his head. "What do we have to do with all that? Jerusalem is the Holy City, the center of life for the Jews of the world. It is them that we want to come, not the idolaters who will profane our Holy City."

"Hunio, when a rich visitor arrives with his family to Jerusalem, he will stay in an inn, eat in the taverns, and purchase gifts and mementos of his visit. Don't underestimate the value of that tourism. Some cities in the world have grown rich entirely on account of it. I have been in Athens and I have seen the massive flow of visitors who arrive in it from the four corners of the world. You know what is happening in Alexandria, and you must understand how much the visitors contribute to the local economy."

"Yeshu," said Hunio, deliberately using his brother's Hebrew name. He made a habit of ostentatiously ignoring the name Jason, which his brother had adopted upon reaching manhood. "Jerusalem enjoys the pilgrimage of Jews from all over the world. It is bursting to the rafters three times every year[8]. I do not mind the idolaters coming to visit here. Perhaps even some good will come of it, and they will get some sense knocked into their heads. But I am not prepared to attract them at the cost of us becoming no different from them."

Hunio leaned down towards the table and picked up a handful of grapes. These grapes are sweeter than honey, he thought. Why must he bother me at my home? I could be enjoying a nice afternoon nap right now, maybe having the boy play me a nice melody. I should see how I can be rid of him.

"Help yourself Yeshu. Do you see how ripe the grapes are? The difference between us, you see, is that I will be happy to see you eating well, enjoying life and putting on a little weight like I have...."

A little?! Thought Jason in disgust. His brother was as fat as a cow.

"You now, on the other hand, would like to take the food out of my mouth," Hunio smiled, delighted with his ambiguous insinuation. It was not his food, of course, that his brother wanted to take from him, but the title of the High Priest. "You want me to be thin and built like one of those Greek athletes you so adore."

Jason replied with a forced smile, his eyes cold, as his brother continued speaking.

"Yeshu, the leaders of the Jewish community in Alexandria sent me a message that they would be delighted to see a large religious center established in Egypt. Queen Cleopatra

---

8   Jewish tradition defined three holidays (Passover, Shavuot/ Feast of Weeks, and Sukkot/Feast of Tabernacles) in which Jews were commanded to make a pilgrimage to the Temple in Jerusalem.

promised a generous subsidy to promote its establishment. She highly values and honors her Jewish subjects. As far as the Jews of Alexandria are concerned it would be a singular honor of this religious center, which will be a center of learning and Jewish scholarship, were to be headed by a priest from the house of Zadok—a scion of the line of High Priests."

You think you can be rid of me so easily, you obese slug, thought Jason, his thoughts nearly bursting out of his tightly controlled mask. You go to Egypt. You are such a Ptolemy lapdog that this will suit you. The expression of false friendship which was on his face only a moment ago made way for a severe expression which was more reflective of his true feelings.

Hunio, who was not particularly sensitive to the feelings of others, didn't pick up on his brother's hostility. "My son, Hunio the Fourth, is in Egypt, discussing the matter with the Ptolemy king. You, of course, are the natural candidate to fill this role, should you but wish it."

Jason adopted a friendly expression once again. "Hunio, I am not seeking a position for myself. I wholeheartedly believe that our world is undergoing a change and that we must change along with it. We must integrate with Hellene culture, and do more than integrate—we must lead, take the initiative and determine how we make the transition into this brave new world. That is the only way we can advance and evolve, but still preserve what is truly important in the ways of our people. I can greatly contribute to this process of reform, and I would love to do so under your leadership. Know that if you support this process, you will enter the history of our people as one of our greatest leaders, together with Moses, Joshua, King David..."

"Enough! You have gone too far this time Yeshu!" Hunio leaned forward sharply. "These ideas of yours are borderline sacrilegious. How can support of Hellenization be considered a reform?! Don't forget who we are. Our people are still paying for the sins of our kings. It is not for nothing that God has placed us at the mercy of the gentiles. The Torah is a trust given into the safekeeping of our family. We, more than anyone else, are obligated to preserve it unchanged until the kingdom of God is renewed on earth."

What a fiery speech; how unfortunate that the only thing behind it is fear of change, mused Jason. Then he tried again: "Hunio, hear me out…."

"No, you listen to me!" Hunio cut him off. "If we had changed our ways every time our imperial rulers changed then we would have had to first become Egyptians, then Assyrians, then Babylonians, then Persians, then Hellenes—and at some point, nothing would be left of us. Nothing at all. There is no shortage of such nations who have been assimilated and been completely absorbed by the empires which conquered them. Where are they now? And who are these Greeks anyway? What culture do they have anyway? Who are they to call the nations of the East barbarians?! They are idolaters, no more. I do not say there is nothing we can learn from them, but to treat them as if they were the enlightened, cultured ones whereas we have no culture worth preserving—that is nothing more than pathetic toadying."

Hunio leaned backwards, panting heavily. Before Jason could answer, he leaned forward again, whispering, as if he were sharing a dread secret. "I will tell you something else. You admire these Seleucids too much. Their current king is a weakling. He is not his father, who nearly reconquered the empire of Alexander the Great and Darius. Egypt, on the other hand, is stronger than ever. Their army is ready, and its commanders are clamoring for the queen to act. It may well be that within a short time the tables will turn, and this land will return to Egyptian rule—together with us. The Egyptians have respect for us. Many Jews hold key positions in their court and army. We are not required to Hellenize to be treated as equals!"

Hunio rose, indicating to his brother that their meeting was over. Blood flooded his face and he imagined himself flushed, upright, and enraged. The thought that this is how he must appear to his disrespectful younger brother brought him satisfaction. "You weary me. It seems I will not get my rest today; I must go to the Temple. Farewell, brother."

He spun away, leaving the room without waiting for a reply.

Jason was left alone in the room. Absentmindedly he picked up a bunch of grapes. They are indeed ripe, he thought. The land justifies its repute as a land of milk and honey and more. Grapes, pomegranates, dates, figs and all sorts of sweet fruit grow here. He leaned back and placed his legs on the table. You leave me no choice brother. I will have to do it without you.

***

Judah was lying down on his stomach atop a carpet back in the family home, dozing lightly, when Simon sat on him with his full weight.

"Ahhh… fatty, get off me."

"I'm not fat, I'm muscular."

"Well, whatever you call it, just get off me! I'm up."

Simon rolled off him, laughing out loud.

"Well, you need to replace me and escort grandfather back. Wash up and get dressed in white, because he is in the Temple."

"What is happening there?"

"I accompanied grandfather to the Chamber of Hewn Stones

for the elders' meeting. I was kept waiting for an eternity, listening to their endless debates for and against a Polis in Jerusalem. For and against a gymnasium and an ephebia[9]. Hunio's brother, Jason he calls himself, is trying to sway them to his way of thinking. He says that Jerusalem should be made into a Polis and opened up to the West. He doesn't understand that he doesn't have a chance. Most of the elders are in Hunio's pocket."

"They aren't in Hunio's pocket. Grandfather says that half of them are the men of Belga and the Tuvia clan, which is in favor of reform."

"Trust in Hunio; he is the High Priest."

"That doesn't mean much to the Hellenizers. Last year there was very nearly fighting in the streets against them. The garrison was reinforced with soldiers and only thanks to them was order kept."

"You are beginning to sound like father... in any event, grandfather understood that I was dying to get away and released me. He asked that you come to escort him back."

Judah slowly ascended the stairs to the Temple. The Temple is not to be approached at a run, grandfather Yohanan had repeatedly told his sons and grandsons. On holidays, when the entire Hashmonaim family was assembled, their grandfather would stop at the bottom of the Temple stairs and speak to the entire extended family. As the firstborn of his family, Yohanan was the head of the extended family. He always stressed that a nation which had almost lost its homeland and the Temple once, and had received a second chance, must never take things for granted or grow complacent. He was especially concerned

9   An institution devoted to training young Hellene citizens for
     military service to their Polis.

about how the new generation of Hellenizers, amongst them many of the youth of Jerusalem, showed a distinct lack of interest in preserving the traditions of their ancestors.

Judah halted and gazed in awe at the Temple. In spite of the familiarity of the sight, the education he had received at home had sunk in deep into his bones. As he entered into the outer compound, a strange feeling filled him, a mixture of awe and pride in the achievements of his people and their covenant with God, with humbleness in the face of this symbol of the will of the divine on earth. He crossed the outer courtyard, the singing of the Levites surrounding him on his way. He recalled the laughter of Miriam when he told her of his sensations when he visited the Temple. She confessed to him that though Alexandria had immense buildings, some of which dwarfed the Temple, she too was awed by the Temple in Jerusalem. In spite of the long time which had passed since he last laid eyes on her, he still felt a prickle of yearning when his mind dwelled on Miriam.

At the entrance to the Chamber of Hewn Stone stood grandfather Yohanan. He seemed tired, and leaned on his cane. He noticed Judah upon his entry into the hall. Beside him was Jason, haranguing him with a tireless stream of words, refusing to pass up the opportunity to explain his position and sway an elder councilmember with such a righteous reputation.

"Yeshu, do you know my grandson, Judah?" Yohanan tried to change the subject of conversation and nodded towards the approaching Judah.

Jason, however, could not be so easily distracted. "It is precisely in order to secure his future, and that of the other youths of this great city, that I am laboring," he answered without even glancing in Judah's direction. "If you don't want him to remain an inferior subject in this kingdom, he must become a citizen of the Polis of Jerusalem. If we do not lead the process, it will eventually be forced upon us by others."

Judah reached them and stood beside his grandfather. Yohanan drew himself erect, pushing his cane against the flagstones. His expression softened once he saw his grandson.

"Yeshu, your father was a great leader. My father and all of our family supported him loyally, just like many of the elders. We did this because we knew that his spirit was loyal and concerned with the welfare of his people."

Yohanan spoke slowly, pronouncing each syllable slowly. That was his manner of speech lately. Age burdened him, and one of its marks was that his speech had become slow and heavy, as if he had a hard time finding the words that would express his thoughts.

"Your father, with his sharp instincts," continued Yohanan, "understood that Antiochus III was going to defeat Ptolemy. He knew that kingdoms come and go, but that we must cleave to our faith and to the Torah. To remain Jews, a single unified people uniquely defined by our faith in a single God, worshipped in his one and only Temple, in a single Holy Land. It may be that you are right. Perhaps we do need to open up to the Hellenistic World; but we must do so without losing our legacy. Woe to slack hands, and to the sinner who walks a double path!" he concluded, quoting the wise priest ben Sira.

Jason lowered his gaze to the flagstones and moved his weight from leg to leg. The way in which Yohanan brought up his father made him uncomfortable. He knew that had his father been alive he would have opposed his actions.

Yohanan put his hand to Jason's chin and gently pushed it upwards, forcing him to meet his eyes. "If you undermine your brother, you will bring a great evil upon us. You will be no better than the Belgas, who try to seem like Greeks to such an extent that they renounce their legacy as priests. Be wise, not right. Act patiently and try not to harm he whose honor must be safeguarded."

Jason stepped backwards, bitter and disappointed. "I am the son of the High Priest, just like my brother. The good of our people is all I am concerned with—even if I think it lies elsewhere than he does. Peace be upon you." He turned away and began walking away rapidly, crossing the hall on his way outside.

Yohanan leaned on Judah's arm and gestured at him to begin walking. "There is nothing good about this old age," he moaned. "My legs can barely carry me, my back aches when I sit, when I lie down—in fact, in whatever position I am in. My eyesight is bad, I can't read, and I can't hear very well. Sometimes I can't choose the right words. It's hard to speak. Soon, someone else from the family will have to take my place at the council of elders."

Judah embraced him warmly with one arm. "Grandfather, it's all right. We are here for you."

***

Grandfather Yohanan's decline was very swift. His body failed time and time again and recovered only after they called the physician. After every such failure his condition deteriorated further. He almost completely lost his speech. His family members respected him and told him of their affairs and current events, and an outside viewer might assume he was attentively listening, but in practice his body had ceased to serve him, and his thought had lost its clarity. Every action and every movement became impossible without close assistance. The head of the Hashmonaim family descended into a twilight world of hallucinations and delusions, lost every physical ability and became completely dependent on his family members, one or more of whom had to be by him at any given moment. The physician would arrive almost every day, and often found grandfather Yohanan in a state of apathy on the verge of unconsciousness, from which he could barely rouse him with his medications.

Matityahu was ill at ease regarding the extension of his father's life by the physician. One day, he instructed his sons not to permit the physician to enter their home before he himself arrived.

A few days later this happened again. Jonathan, who was there at the time, went out onto the street and yelled at the passersby to call for his father to come. That was exactly when the physician arrived and sought to enter. To his amazement, the sons of Matityahu blocked his way and would not let him pass. The physician argued with them, shouted, and even tried to break into their home, before Matityahu arrived, his expression carefully blank. Matityahu placed a heavy hand on the physician's shoulder and asked him to wait outside. He entered his home and after a moment which seemed to the physician to last forever, reemerged. In the meantime, a crowd had gathered before the house. Neighbors, people who knew the family, and just curious idlers. Matityahu addressed the physician, "After the previous time in which you saved my father's life, our ancestor, the angel Metatron, the chancellor of heaven[10], appeared before me. I asked him in my dream why God was being so cruel to my father, who was a righteous and loyal man all his

10 According to the predominant priestly belief of the time, Chanoch ben Yarad, a seventh generation descendant of Adam, was the founder of the priesthood. Chanoch learned writing, knowledge, and wisdom from the angels, wrote them in books he transmitted to his son, and then ascended the heavens, where he underwent apotheosis into the Archangel Metatron.

life, and would not let him die with dignity. Metatron shook his head and replied by directing the question right back at me. He asked **me** why **we** were being cruel to my father...."

"What are you talking about?" the doctor cried out and tried to push past Matityahu, "Let me in to treat your father!"

Matityahu blocked his path. "It took me time to understand the words of the angel. My father was never meant to suffer."

"Who are you?!" cried the doctor, "Who are you to determine when your father should pass way? That is not for us to decide!"

"And who are you?! Who are **you** to prevent my father from moving on when his time has come?!"

The physician glanced from side to side, seeking support amongst the crowd. "I will call Hunio—it is forbidden...."

"Hunio was already here yesterday. He respects my decision."

"It is my duty... to save any man, under any condition, from death," whispered the doctor, his shoulders bowed. "Who is to decide who is to be saved and who is not?"

"You must save those who can live. If you are merely extending the life of a man whose life is already indistinguishable from death, you are not saving his life but merely extending his death—and his suffering. Let the man himself choose his time of death so long as he is of sound mind. At this time, I command my sons that when my time comes they will permit me to die in peace and not interfere with God's plan. And if a man has not spoken on the matter when he was capable of it, let his sons decide for him, as I am doing now."

Judah heard his father's words, and his heart went out for him. It was clear that Matityahu had agonized over his decision.

A few hours later the suffering of grandfather Yohanan ended.

All of the elders and dignitaries of Jerusalem and the neighboring villages arrived to accompany the righteous priest to his final rest.

Judah, who was highly attached to his grandfather, found saying goodbye particularly difficult. "Never doubt yourself, and place no limits on yourself," Yohanan used to tell him. "It is man who builds himself walls and fences—and he too is the one who can break them down."

175 BCE — Jason

> Dramatis Personae
> **Bold** = main character
> * = historical figure

- **Hunio**—*High Priest, head of the house of Zadok*
- **Jason** *(Yeshu)* *—The brother of Hunio*
- *Seleucus IV*—*King of the Seleucid Kingdom between 187-175 BCE. Son of Antiochus III, husband of his sister, Laodice IV*
- *Laodice IV*—*Queen of the Seleucid Kingdom, sister and wife of Seleucus IV*
- *Heliodorus*—*Chief Minister under Seleucus IV*
- *Tuvia Clan*—*A Hellenizer family of Jerusalem (other than the traditionalist, Hyrcanus ben Tuvia)*
- *Jeremiah*—*One of Hunio's aids*
- *Mithridates (Antiochus IV)*—*The brother of King Seleucus IV and Queen Laodice IV. Titled Antiochus IV after ascending to the throne*
- *Azilus*—*A Seleucid officer*
- *Hyrcanus ben Tuvia*—*An affluent Jew ruling an estate in the Transjordan; a Hunio loyalist*

Loud voices in conversation emerging from Hunio's home announced the arrival of Jason. Unlike his long established custom of receiving his guests with plentiful refreshments—refreshments which Hunio himself usually devoured—this time the table held only a single pitcher of water and two cups. His weakening position, the ongoing rivalry with the Tuvia clan and the Belga priests who led the Hellenizer factions, the ongoing pressure of the Hellenizers to enact reforms and adapt the traditions of the Jews to accommodate Hellenism, and above all Jason's undermining of him in the name of transforming Jerusalem into a Hellenist Polis—all these had left their mark on Hunio. Over the past few months he had lost much of his appetite, and even some of his weight.

"Greetings, Hunio," he heard Jason say in a flat and emotionless tone. Jason stood at the entrance to the room, his body language clearly displaying his hostility to his brother. Hunio rose and approached him with open arms, a smile across his face. Jason remained cool and expressionless. He knew that his brother was distressed, and had responded to his invitation but had no compassion towards him.

"Jason, thank you for coming." For the first time in his life, Hunio addressed his brother with the Hellene name he had chosen. "I am leaving for Antioch. Heliodorus will ensure that I receive an audience before the king. The situation simply cannot go on as it is."

Jason shrugged. "According to what I've heard, King Seleucus and the Queen Laodice are not exactly fond of us. Why do you think they will help you?"

"Why not?! We pay our taxes every year, on time and in full. In these troubled times, with the Parthians rebelling in the East, the Armenians harassing the northern borders, and the Nabateans the southern borders, we are quiet and dutiful subjects not causing them any grief."

"Once that would have been enough. But times have changed. They are trying to forge a unified Hellenistic kingdom which runs according to the law and customs of the Greeks."

"All we insist on is the freedom to worship our God according to our own usages and laws, as we have done for centuries. The Persians weren't bothered by this, nor was Alexander the Great himself and all of his heirs, including their own father."

"We do not perform the royal rituals, which every other city in the kingdom performs. The king wishes the kingdom to follow a single unified lunar calendar. We are alone amongst his subjects in insisting on following a different calendar. We need not abolish the laws of our ancestors in order to adapt to the new way of things—just interpret them a bit differently. We must adapt ourselves to the Greek culture which is common throughout the world today."

Jason recited the words almost indifferently. They were part of the speech he had preached to anyone willing to listen to him over the past few months. "But what is the point of this conversation?! You know what I think. Now, when you feel the ground beneath your feet is unsteady, you remember to call me?!"

"This is different, Jason. This is not a religious or cultural struggle between us and the Hellenizers. This is a political and business struggle between families. Our family is struggling to maintain its position versus the Belga priests, who want to assume preeminence, and the magnates of the Tuvia clan, who are prepared to sacrifice their people in order to advance their narrow interests...."

"They want to live in a Hellenist Polis as citizens with rights! They have no problem with our family," Jason cut off his brother impatiently.

Hunio stared at Jason, trying to find any hint of empathy towards him on his face. He decided to take a somewhat different line of argument. "Look, Heliodorus and I have a good relationship. Regardless of whether the king and queen are fond of us or not, they want the kingdom to be peaceful and they fear Egypt. I have good grounds to assume that, with Heliodorus' support, I can win them over. I have called you here so that we might reconcile, for our family's sake, in the name of our departed father. If we unite we will be stronger against any domestic enemy. Help me and I will help you. We will overcome this challenge and then, together, we will see what other steps we can take to move forward, as you put it."

You're too late, thought Jason. Had you sought my friendship earlier, perhaps the Tuvias would not have gotten to me and we really could have won together. But he had no intention of revealing his thoughts, and so simply shrugged and said in a conciliatory tone, "I am glad to hear that that is what you think."

"I am leaving tomorrow at dawn. I must return by the beginning of the seventh month[11] in order to fulfill my role in the Temple on the Day of Atonement[12]."

---

11 In this period, the Jews maintained a sacred 364 day solar calendar, which divided the year into 12 months and 52 seven-day weeks. The Sabbath was defined as a holy day of rest. The first month of the year was in the spring, corresponding to the modern April.

12 The Day of Atonement was held on the seventh month of the ancient calendar, and was considered to be the holiest day in Judaism. This is a day of fasting and repentance, and was the only day in the year in which the High Priest entered the inner sanctum of the Temple.

"I will await your return," said Jason, not meaning a word he said. It was now his turn to make a display of fraternal solidarity. He smiled, spread his arms, and advanced to embrace his brother. "Travel safely and return soon."

Hunio did not know how to respond to the surprising gesture, but he did not give much weight to the matter. In his mind's eye he already saw himself standing before the king and queen in the palace in Antioch.

Hunio's journey from Jerusalem to Antioch was planned to last three weeks. He left in a caravan, accompanied by clerks, priests, servants and armed guards. At night the travelers rested in towns and villages inhabited by Jewish communities. Everywhere they traveled, Hunio was received by the local Jews with great ceremony and enthusiasm, as befitted the holiest man of the Jewish people. The Jews would crowd around him, kiss his clothes and his hands, and ask for his blessing. Hunio took pleasure in their adulation. The Jews of Jerusalem saw him on a daily basis and therefore saw no reason to view or treat him with such awe. For the first time in a long, long while, Hunio felt relief from the heavy stress which had burdened him over the past few months.

On the fifth day of the journey, his caravan was intended to reach the city of Tyre, where a large, well-established Jewish community existed. As in every previous day of the journey, two horsemen rode ahead of the main body of the caravan to inform the members of the Jewish communities in the towns and villages along their way that the High Priest Hunio was about to pass through. One of the horsemen was Jeremiah, one of Hunio's aides, and the other an armed bodyguard.

That morning, about an hour after the caravan embarked on its way, three horsemen dressed in the formal livery of the king galloped past them on their way from Antioch. Hunio was resting at the time in the carriage of his wagon, and the caravan did not tarry, but over the following hour more of the king's messengers rode across the path of the caravan a number of times, or else could be glimpsed in the distance, riding down various side paths. It was clear to everyone in the caravan that something of profound importance had taken place.

A short time later the outriders returned, well ahead of schedule. Hunio, who had been updated regarding the unusual activity of the road, had moved to a bench on the front of his wagon and anxiously awaited Jeremiah's report.

"What do you have to report?" called out Hunio to his aide, "Why have you returned?!"

"My lord, I carry ill tidings," responded Jeremiah as he approached, "King Seleucus is dead."

Hunio gasped, as the air rushed out of his lungs. "What did you say?! But he is still a young man! How did this happen?"

"I found out about this as I passed through a village on the way to Tyre, but waited until I arrived at the city before I returned to get more information. I met with the heads of the Jewish community there. They don't know much beyond the fact of Seleucus' death, primarily rumors. They could tell me that the king was ill for a long, long time, and that the people who have managed the kingdom in practice have been Queen Laodice and the Chief Minister Heliodorus."

Hunio felt relieved when he heard the name of his putative ally. He reconsidered the situation anew in his mind.

"What shall we do, eminence? Shall we return to Jerusalem?" asked Jeremiah.

"We will continue to Tyre and make our decision there," replied Hunio, who wanted to consider matters further.

Even before they arrived in Tyre, Hunio decided that it would be wise to continue on the journey, and to ensure that they would be amongst the first to console the bereaved queen. This might be a good opportunity to ingratiate himself with the queen, the sons of the deceased king, and the members of the court.

Three days later, the caravan arrived in Antioch, but Hunio was disappointed at his reception. Though the formal reason for his arrival was to offer consolation to the bereaved, he could not secure an audience at the palace. The nobles and ministers of the kingdom, the envoys of neighboring kingdoms, even the leaders of the Jewish community in Antioch were all able to secure access to the palace with no particular difficulties. Hunio, the High Priest of the Jews, on the other hand, was forbidden entry. He recalled Jason's words to him in their previous conversation, before he had embarked on his journey. 'They are not fond of us… we do not perform the royal cult rituals, which every other city in the kingdom does.' Queen Laodice was the High Priestess of many of the royal cult rituals, and Hunio wondered if that was the reason for his cold reception. He hoped to at least secure an audience with Heliodorus, the Chief Minister, whom he considered to be a friend and ally, but he too sent word that their meeting would have to be postponed to an uncertain date in the future.

Hunio found a certain comfort in the welcome of the Jews of Antioch who showered him with honor and affection. Knowledgeable individuals in the community reassured him that matters were working out for the best. Heliodorus had been appointed the regent of the kingdom and was even rumored to be the lover of the queen. Hunio's mood improved for a time. He hoped that, as de facto ruler, Heliodorus would be able to support him more openly, and fully, than in the past. In the meantime, a message came from the palace, reassuring him of the intention of both the queen and Heliodorus to meet with him soon. Encouraged, Hunio decided to extend his stay in Antioch.

But then the wheel turned yet again. Word spread throughout Antioch that Mithridates, the brother of the dead king, was returning from exile in Rome.

A delegation from the dignitaries of the Jewish community arrived at the home that had been provided for Hunio by those dignitaries.

The head of the community summarized developments in a self-important tone. "The nobles of the kingdom do not look with favor upon Heliodorus' attempt to hold on to power. They will support the brother of the king, even though he has been held hostage in Rome for many years. It is said that he also enjoys the support of Eumenes II, king of neighboring Pergamon in Asia Minor. Rumor has it that the army of Pergamon is escorting him here in order to ensure his ascension to the throne. It is precisely your good, and now inconvenient, relations with Chief Minister Heliodorus that make it necessary for you to remain until the situation stabilizes and you can establish a relationship with the new king."

Hunio was filled with fright at the thought that his relationship with Heliodorus might now be an obstacle in his path. He was terribly concerned with the possible results of his long absence from Jerusalem. On the other hand, he found himself in agreement with the head of the Jewish community in Antioch. If he returned to Jerusalem now, his rivals would be able to plot against him with the new king, who would be predisposed against him given his preexisting relationship with Heliodorus. Furthermore, Hunio did not want to end his journey empty-handed, especially given his long wait. With a heavy heart,

Hunio sent a message to Jason in Jerusalem asking him to fill in for him in his capacity as High Priest during the upcoming rituals at the Day of Atonement. In his missive, Hunio stressed to his brother their common interest: protecting the house of Zadok against their common domestic enemies, in the spirit of reconciliation and cooperation he thought they had achieved in their previous meeting.

And so it was that, for the first time in Hunio's life, and perhaps the first time since the Second Temple was constructed, the High Priest was about to observe the Day of Atonement and Sukkot outside of the Holy City.

The Jews of Antioch were actually delighted with him remaining in their city on these important holidays. Their joy was so great that many Syrian Jews made a special pilgrimage to Antioch that year, and saw themselves as absolved from performing the traditional pilgrimage to the Temple in Jerusalem.

***

As the leaders of the Jewish community correctly predicted, Mithridates, the prince who returned from exile, rapidly became the de-facto ruler of the kingdom. Officially, he and his nephew—the young son of Queen Laodice and their deceased brother, King Seleucus—ruled in common, but it was clear to all who truly ruled. Queen Laodice soon took her younger brother as a husband and maintained her grip on the crown, while Mithridates adopted his father's name as his own royal name—Antiochus IV.

Hunio sought, time and again, to gain an audience with the new king, but had no success. One morning an older officer who described himself as the emissary of the king came to visit him. Hunio received him, accompanied by several of his staff, but the officer, Azilus by name, sought to speak with him privately.

"The king was happy to hear that the Jews of Antioch were hosting you with the full dignity appropriate for the High Priest of the Jews," Azilus told him. "You are hereby formally invited by the king to permanently remain in Antioch."

Hunio was astounded at the man's presumption. "I thank the king for his generosity," he said without making any attempt to conceal his anger, "but my people need me in Jerusalem, and that is where I intend to return just as soon as your king sees fit to find some time to meet with me."

Azilus fixed his gaze on the High Priest for a long moment, not bothering to reply.

Hunio, frightened by the response and by the realization of the inappropriateness of his speech, began to feel a light, uncontrollable tremor in his feet. After a moment that seemed for Hunio to stretch on forever, Azilus said, "Your friend Heliodorus is under investigation for participating in the plot which brought about the death of the previous king, Seleucus. I **suggest** that you don't leave the city before the king **permits** you to do so."

Jeremiah stormed into the room, "Eminence, soldiers are surrounding the house!"

"What is this?" Hunio asked Azilus in a faint tone. The tremor in his legs had returned.

"They are intended to safeguard the house and accompany you wherever you might go. For your own safety, of course. The king looks after his guests," said Azilus indifferently, and left the room without bidding Hunio farewell.

Hunio understood perfectly. The soldiers were there to keep him from escaping. He wrote two separate missives. The first to Jason, his brother, and the second to his eldest son, young Hunio. He wrote both in a secret ancient Hebrew script, which was only known to a small circle of priests from the House of Zadok.

Two weeks passed before he received the first reply, from Jason. Jason wrote him shortly, in Greek, that he was coming to Antioch. Hunio felt his heart fill with gratitude at the thought that his long estranged brother was coming to help him in his hour of need. He even imagined that Jason intended to offer to take his place in Antioch as a hostage. However, another missive arrived three days later from his eldest son, young Hunio IV. It was a long missive, written in the secret priestly script, and it clarified to Hunio III that he had been wrong every step of the way, both in the trust he put in Jason and in leaving Jerusalem. Young Hunio wrote that Jason and the Tuvia clan had joined forces. The Tuvias, who so far had supported the Belga priesthood, had transferred their support to Jason, who used his position as officiator of the High Priest's role at the public rituals on the Day of Atonement and Sukkot[13] to solidify his status in the city. He spread rumors that the position of the High Priest has passed on to him permanently, and lately was heard openly saying that Hunio would never return to Jerusalem. Hyrcanus, the only one of the Tuvia clan to always support Hunio, removed all of his money from the Temple and cloistered himself in his estate in the southern Gilead. Jason had indeed left for Antioch—not in order to assist Hunio, but in order to promote his own personal agenda.

---

13   The Sukkot (Feast of Tabernacles) was held four days after the Day of Atonement and was considered one of the three holidays on which Jews were commanded to make a pilgrimage to the Temple in Jerusalem. The customs of the Sukkot holiday include sleeping and eating in straw Sukkah (temporary huts) for seven days in commemoration of the journey of the Children of Israel during their exodus from Egypt to the Land of Israel.

Hunio felt his world collapse around him. He now understood, far too late, that he had cleared the way for his brother to assume his position.

A few days later, early in the morning, Hunio received word that Jason had arrived in Antioch the previous evening and was immediately admitted for an audience with the king. His brother had not even bothered to pay him a courtesy visit prior to meeting the king.

Later that same morning a messenger came to Hunio and informed him that the new High Priest of the Jews would come visit him later during the day, prior to his return to Jerusalem. It was in that way, by the wording of the messenger, that Hunio first understood that he had been officially stripped of the High Priesthood. All he had left to do was to await the arrival of the brother who had betrayed him, in a house that had been transformed into a prison.

At noon he heard the neighing of horses in the street. Through the window he saw Jason enter the courtyard of the house. A detachment of cavalry had escorted him and was awaiting him outside. Hunio turned from the window and stood in the center of the room, facing the door.

Jason entered at a brisk pace and stood before him, his expression firm. For a long moment the two brothers faced each other, saying nothing. Hunio was the first to break the silence. "Why?"

Jason replied, his tone unapologetic, "I always thought you were not suited for heading the priesthood. It is unjust that you inherited the title merely because you were firstborn. I hated you for your arrogance, for your decadent pleasure-seeking ways, for being so sure of being right that you would never listen to me. But know this: I never would have taken this step if I hadn't known **that unless I did, then someone else, someone**

not of our family, would have done exactly as I did."

Hunio's shoulders drooped. He was prepared for a confrontation with his brother, was prepared to denounce him as a faithless traitor, but Jason's direct and brutal words took all of the wind out of his sails. "So that's the way things are? You made a deal with the king?" he asked quietly.

"He confirmed my appointment as High Priest. You will remain in Antioch but be treated as an exiled king. Jerusalem will become a Hellenistic Polis with a gymnasium and an ephebeia, where the youth will be trained in preparation for receiving citizenship in the Polis."

"A gymnasium and an ephebeia?! In the Holy City?! You will need Greek trainers and tutors. Who will pay them? More taxes on our people?"

"Whoever wishes to become a full citizen in the Polis, with all of the rights and duties that entails, will pay those fees out of his own pocket. There are plenty of people for whom this will be important and worthwhile. This investment will enable them to become equal citizens of the kingdom, just like the citizens of the other Polis throughout the world. You simply do not understand how much this can contribute to Jerusalem, economically as well as culturally. Of course, we will have to adapt ourselves to their lunar calendar. The king is adamant on putting the entire kingdom on a single unified calendar."

"You have agreed to change the calendar marking our holy days?!" cried out Hunio, "We received it directly from Heaven. The marking of the holy days, the years, the months and the days, from creation to the present day?! We can state with complete precision on what day of the week every month and every holiday will begin a thousand years in advance. Our count of the days and months is holy and not to be discarded!"

"It is a beautiful tradition, that is true, but not something which is worth setting ourselves against the explicit will of the king."

"You have sold the High Priesthood to a foreign king. You do not understand what manner of disaster you have brought upon us," whispered Hunio in horror. "Our people believe that the High Priest is from a holy seed, who hears the voices of the angels and passes on the word of God. Now what will they say? If the king determines the identity of the High Priest, then does that mean that God speaks to him?!"

"Times have changed. Father also gave in to the demands of the day and established the council of elders. This intervention by the king is a one-time event—and it leaves the position of the High Priest in the family."

Hunio slowly turned around and faced the window, turning his face away from his brother before Jason could see his expression of despair and loss.

"What about my family?" he asked despondently.

"They are my family as well. I am responsible for them. Whoever wishes to join you here can do so. Should young Hunio wish to remain in Jerusalem he is more than welcome, but it goes without saying that he is **not** my heir."

Hunio shrugged helplessly. Staring outside he noted a horse with a sumptuous and ornate saddle standing between the cavalry, riderless. "You ride a horse? Not a carriage?" This was a meaningless issue, but there was nothing significant and worthwhile left to say in any event.

"Yes, the Hellenes like to see their leaders ride a horse like one of their warriors," replied Jason, smiling thinly. A moment later he added, "If you need anything, write to me. Farewell, Hunio."

Through the window, Hunio saw Jason leave his new and permanent home in Antioch, mount his horse, and lead the cavalry far away, towards Jerusalem, the city which was once his.

174 BCE—The Hellenizer Regime

Dramatis Personae
Bold = main character
* = historical figure

- **Matityahu***—*Father of Judah and his brothers*
- **Jason***—*High Priest, the younger brother of the previous High Priest, Hunio, whom he deposed*
- **Rebecca**—*Wife of Matityahu*
- **Yohanan***, **Simon***, **Judah***, **Hannah***, **Eleazar*** and **Jonathan***—*The children of Matityahu and Rebecca by age*
- **Phidias**—*Pankration trainer*
- **Eupolemus***—*Friend of Judah, son of Yohanan ben Hakotz*
- *Elianus and his father—Extreme Hellenizers*
- *Joseph—Brother of Matityahu*
- *Apollonius*—Meridarch (govoner) of Samaria*

Jason and the Hellenizers announced a new constitution for Jerusalem, that of a Hellenist Polis, whose laws would dominate over the traditional laws and traditions of the Jews. Accordingly, new governing institutions and municipal administrations were established, including a courtroom whose judges were appointed solely from the citizens of the Polis. The body of citizens in the new Polis amounted to no more than three thousand heads of households. These were men who wished to be accepted as citizens, accepted Greek law, and were confirmed by an admissions committee which was made up of Jason and representatives of the leading Hellenizer families.

Jason's initial steps were cautious as he tried to form the impression that the transformation of Jerusalem into a Polis would only affect the Hellenizers, not the traditionalists. It took a few weeks before the first traditionalists realized they were being transformed into second-class citizens, and another few months before this realization percolated amongst the general public. Just as the political and economic status of the traditionalists was degraded, so was the position of the elder council. Jason established a Citizen's Council, and all important decisions were made by it. The elder council, headed by Yose ben Yohanan and Yose ben Yoezer, became a secondary religious institution, with little influence on non-religious spheres.

For Matityahu and many other traditional Jews like him, Jason's revolution was the straw that broke the camel's back. Matityahu had dreamt of returning to Modi'in for many years. Once Jerusalem was transformed into a Hellene Polis, he saw no reason to remain in the city. Matityahu gathered his family together to announce the news. The somber atmosphere and serious expression on their father's face made clear to his children that a serious matter was about to be discussed. "Jason and his supporters are trying to present developments as a mere change in outer appearances, but I believe that these are evil times for believing Jews such as ourselves. I refuse to live in a Hellene Polis. I have decided to return to Modi'in."

The children looked at Rebecca, their mother. Her face was drawn in sorrow, but she nodded her head in agreement.

"Yohanan and Simon, you are now of age. I want you to

return with us… but I leave the choice to you," Matityahu added in a measured tone, concealing his emotional storm as much as he could. "Should you choose to remain, either together or only one of you, the store and the home will be left for you to look after. Just remember that as faithful Jews you will never be considered citizens of the Polis, and the tax burden you face will likely rise."

Yohanan had always been drawn to the spiritual. He had dreamed of one day being counted amongst the regular staff of priests and Levites at the Temple. Accordingly, he was torn. His heart implored him to remain near the Temple. On the other hand, the business of running the store and managing it held no attraction for him. "I'm returning with you, father," he said, swiftly reaching a decision.

Matityahu's eyes widened in joy. He glanced to Simon.

"I am prepared to move to Modi'in tomorrow," Simon answered decisively.

"Father, I wish to remain in Jerusalem," spoke out Judah, surprisingly, whom Matityahu had no intention of offering such a choice to.

"Jason is doing everything to attract trainers and set up a gymnasium and an ephebeia. He has hired Phidias as a pankration trainer, and Phidias has offered me and Eupolemus work with him as assistants. The fees Jason will pay us as trainer's assistants are extremely high, and I can help my family more in this way than if I join you in Modi'in."

Matityahu's face grew dark. He had not even considered leaving Judah behind. "You…."

"You can stay," Rebecca inserted herself into the exchange, cutting her husband off.

Matityahu looked upon her in astonishment. There was a

spark of liveliness in her eyes, the first he had seen after weeks in which she seemed depressed and despondent.

"We still have family here. Some of them are even citizens of this Polis. We trust you will be all right," Rebecca raised her eyes to her husband in a silent plea. She felt, somehow, that by Judah remaining in the city some part of her would remain there as well.

Matityahu muttered something that could be interpreted as assent, his expression making clear he was far from satisfied with this development.

Judah, who was blind to the interplay between his parents, rushed to his mother and embraced her in gratitude.

***

Jason would occasionally arrive in the gymnasium to watch the training, either by himself or escorted by others. The prestigious institute was his personal creation. He would encourage the trainers and the trainees and promise them rewards and much honor if and when they should represent Jerusalem in the competitions.

One day, as he was watching the pankration and boxing matches, Elianus' father burst into the gymnasium, dragging his son after him. The trainers and the trainees heard him shouting at Jason in anger, demanding that his son be appointed assistant boxing trainer. Phidias ordered his pupils to remain in place and began moving in the direction of the shouting. Judah followed at his heels. He had a longstanding rivalry with Elianus, ever since the battle on the hill between their respective gangs in their youth. Eupolemus followed them as well.

The boxing trainer stood by Jason's side and waited for an

opportunity to interject a few words, but Elianus' father would not cease yelling at Jason.

Ever since the gymnasium had been established, Elianus had ceased practicing boxing. From the moment the training had become more serious and professional, more directed at arena contests, the trainees were required to maintain greater training discipline—and this did not suit Elianus, who preferred to carouse at nights. He and Judah had met several times in the years that had passed, but they no longer entered into conflicts. The body which Judah had laboriously built up over the years indicated his great strength, and everyone in the city knew that he took his pankration training with the greatest possible seriousness.

Phidias, who knew all of the boxing trainees very well as a result of common training he occasionally held with the trainer of this field of sports, intervened in the conversation between Elianus's father and Jason.

"Your son isn't good enough to be an assistant instructor here," he said bluntly.

"Who in Hades are you to interfere in this conversation? I am a citizen of this Polis and my business is with the boxing trainer and with Jason, not with you," Elianus' father thundered at Phidias.

"I am the senior trainer for arena sports in the gymnasium, and I decide who the trainers are," Phidias replied evenly.

Elianus tugged at his father's arm, "Father, let it be, let's go," but the father angrily shook his arm free. "Jason, I demand you intervene."

"You know what?" said Phidias, "I have a proposition for you. Let your son prove just how good he is in the field of boxing, in which you think he is so much of an expert that he can train others."

Silence fell across the training field.

Judah's senses tensed. He was the best fighter in the gymnasium and he knew that Phidias intended to assign him the task of beating Elianus down.

Eupolemus, however, was the first to respond. "Senior trainer, I will fight him."

Phidias shook his head in negation. "No, Judah will," he declared. Phidias thought Eupolemus could defeat Elianus—but he wanted to play it safe and unsettle Elianus and his father as an added bonus. "I know you can defeat him, and easily," he told Eupolemus, deliberately loud, "but I need someone with a gentle touch. You might injure the lout."

Judah stepped into the center and gestured at Elianus, inviting him to do battle.

Elianus paled. His head turned rapidly from Judah to his father and then back to Judah. He examined Judah's muscular arms, and his sculpted chest and stomach muscles. Then his eyes met those of Judah, and what he saw there evidently swayed him. "Come father, I have no interest in teaching the milksops here how to box," he lied, trying to salvage the final shreds of his dignity, "I'm going."

A few days later, Jason arrived at the pankration training ring once more. This time, he was clearly excited as he assembled all of the trainers. He informed them that Apollonius, Meridarch of Samaria, the neighboring Meridarchy, was about to hold competitions in the Polis of Samaria. The games would include participants from Polis' throughout Coele-Syria. This was an excellent chance to test the abilities of the athletes of the Polis of Jerusalem in a true contest.

The trainers of the various fighting styles unanimously opposed this. They believed that their trainees were not yet ready for a contest. However, Jason was insistent. "Make them ready," he ordered, adding that the contestants from the other Polis were hardly professional athletes, merely citizens of the city who happened to train in the gymnasium.

Following the conversation, Jason called Phidias, Judah, and Eupolemus aside.

"I expect these two to compete and represent us," Jason told Phidias, gesturing with his head at Judah and Eupolemus. Phidias shrugged and turned to Judah. He opposed the very idea, but so long as he was charged with carrying it out, Judah was clearly the right man for the job.

"I will be delighted, but I will need the blessing of my father to participate, for a nude contest is not considered appropriate for a son of a traditionalist priest," replied Judah.

"You need not compete in full nudity. In Greece it was customary to compete in this manner, but not in Syria. You can wear a small loincloth to cover your private parts," said Phidias.

"Excellent! It is decided, then," ruled Jason "I had thought that you would be happy to represent your city and your people. I will join our team at Samaria—and I expect to see you win. I will pay you an additional monthly salary for the competition, and if you should win I will raise your wages. Besides, aren't you still a bachelor? Just think about what your appearance in the contest will do for your reputation with the women of Jerusalem. You can easily have the most beautiful girls of the city if you win."

"Ah, now we are talking, sir. For women he will compete for free," said Phidias, a smile spread across his face.

Judah blushed momentarily. His tanned and muscular appearance, status as an assistant trainer in the gymnasium, and being a priest accepted by both traditionalists and Hellenizers made him into an extremely popular bachelor in the city as it was, and he enjoyed the attention.

"I ride for Modi'in on Friday. I will speak to my father about this. Should he have no objections then I will compete."

Jason immediately turned to Eupolemus.

"Err... I am thinking about traveling to Antioch soon, to enlist in the king's army," Eupolemus said hesitantly, to the amazement of all present, who were hearing about this plan for the first time.

"What are you talking about, boy..." Phidias began to say, but Jason cut him off sharply. "Forget about it! You have a contract with me; you are obligated to your job as a trainer until the end of the year. I refuse to permit you to travel anywhere!"

Eupolemus now understood that he erred in revealing his intentions before they had consolidated into a final decision.

"I am not planning on travelling immediately. Nor am I sure I ever will. I was just talking about the distant future."

Jason frowned, "You belong to the gymnasium and must represent it. Think about how proud you will make us if we win!"

Eupolemus nodded submissively. "Very well, I too will speak to my father and ask for his permission."

Jason was far from satisfied at this unenthusiastic response, but left well enough alone. He walked away from them abruptly, casually waving farewell, and shouted over his shoulder to Judah, "How many days will you spend in the country?"

"Four days. I will be back on Monday."

"Very well. Speak to me when you return."

On Friday evening an expensive meal was laid out in Matityahu's home in Modi'in in honor of Judah's arrival. Joseph, Matityahu's brother, and his entire household joined the meal. At the end of the meal, when the men exited to the yard to enjoy the evening breeze, Judah raised the two issues which occupied his mind. The first were the games in Samaria. The second was the idea, newly seeded in his mind, to join Eupolemus on his journey to Antioch and to enlist in the king's army.

As if the walls had ears, the women of the household all chose that moment to leave the house. His mother was grumbling, his uncle Joseph was incredulous, and his brothers and cousins made merry at his expense. Only his sister Hannah was silent in concern. She knew her brother well—well enough to know that whatever he had planned would quite likely come to pass.

"No Jew, and certainly not a priest, should leave the Holy Land in order to fight as a mercenary for a gentile king," Joseph claimed.

"Joseph, the Holy City is the habitation of both gentiles and Hellenizers. Most of our people live scattered far beyond the bounds of the Holy Land, and many of them, priests included, serve in the ranks of the Hellenist kings. Eupolemus is also a priest, and he intends to travel as well," Judah refuted his uncle.

Matityahu listened to the exchange in silence, and then pronounced his ruling. "I do not oppose your participation in the contest provided you do not do so naked. As for the other thing, leave it be for now."

The next day, the men rose at dawn and went out to pray in the synagogue. It was a large hall which was erected as the sole public building in the village and was used to perform various events and ceremonies, as well as being a gathering place to read from the Torah on the Sabbath and on holidays.

As the eldest son of the deceased Yohanan, Matityahu had assumed the role of village priest upon his return from Jerusalem to Modi'in, as his brother Joseph stepped aside in his favor. As a village priest, he did not receive any tithes or service from his flock, but managed his own fields and herds by the sweat of his own brow so that the role had no economic advantage—only responsibilities.

On the Sabbath morning he would usually speak after the reading of the Torah scrolls. He was not much of a public speaker by nature, and took pride in being a man of action; a man of many deeds, few words, and laconic[14] speech. However, on the Sabbath he spoke at greater length, this being his duty as the village priest, and he fulfilled this duty with a willing heart.

"It is told in the book of Samuel that David, at the time that he fled from King Saul, travelled with his men to Acish the Philistine, King of Gat. Some say the Philistines themselves come from the environs of Hellas originally. What did the future King of Israel do at the court of this gentile king? He and his men served as mercenaries. That was how he acquired military experience and learned the ways of the deadly enemies of the Tribes of Israel. Centuries earlier, the daughter of Pharaoh raised our teacher Moses as a son. This shows us that Moses was raised as a gentile in the royal Egyptian palace. And of course, who was it who received the sons of Jacob in Egypt to begin with, centuries before that? None other than Joseph, minister to the Pharaoh. God directed the three greatest leaders of our people to study and serve under the gentiles... God chose us to be a shining example and testimony to the other nations, but at the same time he directed our steps to study from the gentiles. We are a

---

14   In Lacedaemon, homeland of the Spartans, brief speech was valued over rhetoric, hence the term laconic.

peaceful nation, but we must grow familiar with the ways of the gentiles and how they fight."

Confused mutterings rose all around. The men of the village did not understand Matityahu's meaning.

"How, then, are the Hellenizers any different from what you preach? Did not they too learn the ways of the gentiles and adopt them to their bosom?" asked a voice from the crowd.

"It is not to them I refer, my friends. Rest your mind," Matityahu calmed them, and looked at Judah with love. "Yes, the Hellenizers studied the ways of the gentiles, but they do not sift out the good from the evil but adopt their customs wholesale and abandon the traditions which make us who we are." Matityahu paused and met the eyes of the men in the crowd, "Judah, my son, has asked for my blessing to join Eupolemus, son of Yohanan ben Hakotz, in enlisting in the army of the king."

The congregation exchanged glances in astonishment.

"So now, at this time of the sacred Sabbath, amongst observant and faithful Jews, friends and family, I bless you, my son, and provide my consent to your request. May the God of Israel keep you and return you to us hale and whole."

Matityahu spread out his arms, and Judah hurried to embrace him as the congregation gathered around them, surrounding them both with their loving approval.

***

The audience in the stadium of Samaria jeered out at the Jewish competitors. Eupolemus fought well, but inexperience and over-enthusiasm got the better of him, and he was defeated in his very first battle.

Eupolemus was frustrated with his defeat, but focused on

helping Judah learn from his experience. "I could have beaten my opponent, but I started off too quickly and ran out of breath," he told Judah when he left the ring. "Give yourself time to get used to the environment, start from afar. We are far better than they are."

Jason suddenly appeared behind Phidias and whispered in his ear, "The boy has to win at least one match; otherwise we will be a laughing-stock."

Phidias turned towards him and held back his temper. It would not do to give the High Priest a piece of his mind. Instead, he chose milder words. "This is their first contest, and everyone fights to win, as you know. The most important thing is that they leave the contest in one piece."

Jason was not pleased with the answer, but the stern visage of Phidias made clear to him that he had best hold his peace. He grumbled something under his breath and walked away.

However, by the time Judah's very first battle was over, the crowd had turned its coat. Unlike the other competitors, who displayed inferior technical skills and tried to overwhelm their opponents through brute force and without any thought behind their actions, Judah, who took Eupolemus' advice to heart, fought cunningly, constantly catching his opponents flat-footed and off guard. He struck at his opponent from a distance while advancing rapidly, snapping a blow or two and then leaping back before his opponent could strike back or grapple with him. His opponent seemed helpless, even pathetic, and soon lost his self-confidence completely. Judah, in contrast, soon freed himself from his pre-fight tension and doubts and began to enjoy himself, while being careful not to become complacent. After Phidias shouted at him to stop playing and finish the fight, Judah launched a flurry of deadly blows at the face of his opponent, this time without withdrawing. Within a few seconds, the stunned opponent kneeled and raised his finger in surrender.

In Judah's second fight, his opponent was a veritable giant of a man who had easily overpowered his own opponent in his first fight. The crowd cheered exuberantly for the giant. Phidias, standing at Judah's side before he entered the ring, asked him if he had any last request before he died. Then he roared out in laughter and slapped Judah's shoulder affectionately, leaning in to offer some final instructions before the fight began.

The giant charged immediately at Judah, seeking to grapple him. Judah gave the giant no chance to place his massive arms on him. He dodged aside agilely and skipped around the giant lightly, launching rapid punches and kicks at the giant, constantly dodging or withdrawing before his opponent could close on him. The human mountain attempted to charge Judah again and again but ended up hugging the air. Every such attempt exposed the giant to another precise and powerful strike, gradually wearing him down. That was when Judah charged forward and struck at his opponent relentlessly and precisely, offering him no respite, until he collapsed.

The rapturous cheers of the crowd surrounded him for many minutes. This was the point the crowd adopted Judah as its favorite contestant and honored him with constant cheers.

In the third fight, Judah won within a few seconds. He struck first, surprising his opponent with a direct punch straight to the face, which penetrated his opponents' half lifted hands, crushing his nose and slamming his head back. Giving his opponent no chance to recover, Judah gripped the stunned man from the back, knocked him to the ground, and began choking him, applying pressure to his carotid artery, halting the flow of blood to his brain. His opponent was of Macedonian origin, a citizen of the city and a scion to a family of military colonists. He refused to surrender before his family and fellow citizens, and collapsed into unconsciousness, from which he only recovered a few moments after Judah was declared the victor.

The contestant in Judah's fourth and final fight was a tough brawler from Gaza, a man with extensive experience and many fights behind him. The many scars which decorated his face and body, and his smashed nose, indicated that fighting was a way of life to him. As this was the final fight of the contest, the Gazan had already fought and defeated three other opponents, testifying to his skill.

Judah and the Gazan both fought with determination and ferocity, exchanging blows from a standing position, grappling on the ground, and then breaking free and standing up once again. Neither of them could overcome his opponent nor achieve a significant advantage, but nor was either of them prepared to quit. And then, at some point, after the fight had dragged on for far longer than was common in a pankration match, the Gazan suddenly gave up. The crowd did not realize what had happened, for the Gazan still stood and fought, but Judah saw that the Gazan's eyes were no longer focused on him, but were darting from side to side, giving away his desire to escape the fight.

The experienced Phidias noticed this as well and yelled at Judah to ratchet up the pressure. Judah did so, constantly striking at his opponent, trying to exploit the sudden opportunity to break the stalemate.

The Gazan began to withdraw. Judah knocked him to the ground and sat on him, pinning him to the ground with the weight of his body and pounding him with blow after blow. After a few moments the Gazan ceased fighting back. He still hadn't surrendered, but his eyes were those of a defeated man.

As soon as Judah noticed this, he immediately stood over him. His opponent remained on the ground, his breath heaving, his hands gripping his face.

Judah raised his hand up in victory and spun before the crowd. The entire crowd rose in applause, even in the dignitary box. Even Apollonius, the governor of Samaria, clapped in appreciation.

Judah bent down and offered his hand to his opponent, helping him to his feet. The gesture was received with surprise by the Gazan and won Judah ever more enthusiastic applause from the crowd. After the Gazan found his feet, Judah warmly embraced him, and raised his opponents hand upwards, signaling to the crowd to honor his opponent as well. The crowd went wild. The applause and cheers continued long afterwards and were heard far beyond the walls of the stadium.

As was customary in such contests, the victor approached the governor to receive his congratulations and the victory laurel. Judah, who was unfamiliar with this custom, innocently left the ring and headed back to Phidias, bemused at the roaring laughter of the crowd. Phidias led him to the governor's seat, Eupolemus accompanying them from the rear. Jason was already waiting for them there, glowing with delight.

"Jason, your lads just proved that Jerusalem is a worthy Polis," Apollonius told Jason, and then turned to Judah. "Well done, lad, you fought well. Just don't get carried away with the feeling of victory. Remember that this was a ring, and that you did not face true warriors. Had you fought a real soldier, someone like me for example, with swords rather than fists, you wouldn't have stood a chance."

The governor's words were met with outbursts of laughter from his entourage. Judah, insulted, tensed and barely held back a cheeky retort. Phidias, sensing the mood of his charge, rapidly pulled him away.

"What were you thinking?!" he reprimanded Judah after they had distanced themselves from Apollonius. "I saw that you were about to reply to the governor. You are still a lad, while he is an experienced warrior—and he was right. There is a huge difference between fighting in the arena and a real battle with weapons. You have no idea what being slashed and hacked at is like, of how it is to feel a terrible pain overcome you. Only in a true battle do the real warriors reveal themselves. Only when the blades ring are those who piss themselves in fear separated from those who are more aroused by the clash of arms than by the soft arms of a beautiful woman. Only then does one see who falls to the ground and screams in pain at the first scratch from those who continue to fight even after they are cut repeatedly by the enemy blades."

"All right, all right," grumbled Judah. "Then teach us to fight with weapons. We will grow experienced, and that stuck-up windbag…"

Eupolemus burst out in laughter, "Phidias, admit that Judah is right. He really is a windbag. What's with the lectures? Let us enjoy Judah's victory."

Phidias did his best to maintain a stern demeanor but failed. "Well, that governor really is irritating. The truth is, you really are inexperienced in battle, but if I had to choose who to go to war with, you or him, I would not hesitate for even one moment—I would take you."

173 BCE—Eupolemus

> Dramatis Personae
> **Bold** = main character
> * = historical figure

- **Eupolemus***—*A friend of Judah, son of Yohanan ben Hakotz*
- **Tiamos**—*Hellene friend of Judah and Eupolemus, who studied with them under Kratos*
- *Glitarius*—*Roman friend of Judah and Eupolemus*
- *Kratos*—*Greek tutor under whom Judah, Eupolemus, Glitarius, and Tiamos studied*
- **Yohanan***, **Simon***, **Judah***, **Hannah***, **Eleazar***, and **Jonathan***— *The children of Matityahu and Rebecca by age*
- *Democritos*—*Former officer in the Royal Guard, old friend of Kratos*
- *Jason***—*High Priest, the younger brother of the previous High Priest, Hunio, whom he deposed*
- *Hunio***—*Deposed High Priest and brother of Jason*
- **Phidias**—*Pankration trainer*
- *Poseidanus*—*Trading vessel captain who carries cargo and passengers across the Mediterranean*
- *Papalagos*—*Manager of the household of Glitarius' family in Rome*
- **Cassandra**—*Sister of Glitarius*
- *Marcius Porcius Cato***—*Roman patrician who filled many senior positions in the Roman Republic*

Eupolemus was the only member of Kratos' old class with whom Judah was able to maintain a strong connection. Eupolemus had begun to play a role in the trading business of his family a few months ago and had, as a trader, begun to travel the world with his father. However, he had not given up on his dream of enlisting in the royal Seleucid army. Every few weeks Eupolemus would return to Jerusalem and the two would meet and reminiscence.

Prior to one such meeting, Judah received, much to his surprise, a letter from Glitarius, their common Roman classmate. As Jerusalem and Judea were not part of the Roman Empire, the letter had passed through many lands before it miraculously reached its destination. Glitarius wrote to Judah and Eupolemus little of himself and much about Rome. He praised the glory of the city and its military power, and invited his two old classmates to come visit him.

Eupolemus was very pleased to receive the letter, but could not conceive of ever actually reaching Rome. He still intended to enlist in the Seleucid army together with Judah. Their plan was based on the hope that they would be able to be accepted into a unit of Macedonian-Greek settlers as the sons of notable men.

The Seleucid army, as a rule, kept those who were not descended from the Greco-Macedonian conquering armies of Alexander the Great and his heirs in small auxiliary units, such as the cavalry recruited from the distant Persian and Median provinces. The Seleucid regime was extremely reluctant to arm and train native Coele-Syrians, both Gentile and Jew, for it distrusted their loyalty and feared that they might one day revolt against Seleucid rule, or side with the Ptolemys in Egypt. In order to overcome this obstacle, Judah and Eupolemus equipped themselves with letters of recommendation from the commander of the Jerusalem Seleucid garrison, Jason, Kratos, and Phidias. These letters presented them as pankration fighters, citizens of the Jerusalem Polis—even though only Eupolemus was a citizen—and as young men who had been brought up in the manner of well-born Hellenes.

The second part of their plan was to locate Tiamos, their old classmate, and his father in Antioch, hoping that they would aid them in entering the select ranks of the Seleucid Royal Army. Kratos had also referred them to his friend Democritos, whom he knew from his time in Antioch. Democritos had previously been an officer in the royal guard and even served as a trainer and an instructor. Kratos was convinced that Democritus' connections and service record would facilitate their acceptance into the ranks of the Seleucid Royal Army.

Jason, who was in good humor and who had favored the two friends since Judah's achievement in the competition in Samaria, surprised Judah when he lent him a thoroughbred horse for the journey. "If you are accepted into the army as a cavalryman you may keep the horse as a gift. If not, you must bring the horse to my brother Hunio in Antioch. Tell him it is a gift from me to him," Jason told him magnanimously.

A few days later they hit the road. Phidias rode beside them out of the gates of the city. The tough warrior was moved by his emotions and did not wish others to see him in such a state when he bid his young charges farewell. When time came to say goodbye, the three dismounted and Phidias removed a large package from his horse. Opening it up, he displayed a variety of weapons and other equipment: two swords and matching daggers, a leather medicine pouch, and more.

"You can probably make better use of this equipment than

I can," he told them, "and with your thoroughbred horses, you had better wear your weapons openly, just to keep bandits from developing false hopes."

"Thank you… for everything," said Judah.

Phidias grasped them by their shoulders, locking gazes with them gravely, and said,

"Listen up, you two, and keep my words in mind, because you won't have a trainer at your side where you are going.

Eupolemus, you are a good thinker, and skilled in persuasion and negotiation. But as a common ranker you will be expected to act without thought or backtalk. You will not be able to argue with your commanders or impress them with your ideas. Once you gain experience and prove yourself this might change, but you will always be subject to superior officers, and the army is a tough place, based on rank, orders, and honor. Still, don't lose your distinctive qualities. An army's Achilles heel is frequently its logistics and supplies. A warrior who is familiar with trade can often be more valuable than a skilled swordsman. If you learn to act wisely and earn the trust of your commander, they will appreciate you and rely on you in turn.

Judah, what I told Eupolemus is partially true for you as well. You are also clever and swift of thought. However, you have been gifted with superlative strength, speed, and combat skills, which will make you stand out in training immediately. But beyond this, even if you are not really aware of it, something about you makes men want to stand beside you and follow you. On the other hand, you carry yourself like a trustworthy and loyal man, and I am certain that your commander will also come to rely on you. See this as an opportunity.

I love both of you as if you were my own sons. I do not know if I will still be here when you return, but if I am not I will leave your families a letter describing my plans. Write to me when you return safely."

They embraced firmly, saying no more.

Judah and Eupolemus first turned to Modi'in. During his employment in the gymnasium, Judah had been able to save a considerable sum of money. When he reached his parent's house, he divided his funds into two portions. He hid away the lesser part in a small leather pouch which he carried on his travels. He wished to give the larger portion to his father, as a gift, but Matityahu refused to accept it. He told Judah jocularly that if a father gives his son money, they are both satisfied, but if the son gives money to his father than they both have cause to sorrow. He then added, more seriously, that he would keep the money in trust and would await Judah's return.

When Judah and Eupolemus left Modi'in, the entire village turned out to bid Judah farewell. Saying goodbye to Judah's mother and sister was particularly difficult. They both wept, and Judah also had a hard time controlling his emotions. Matityahu embraced him for a long moment, pressing Judah close to him without saying a word. His four brothers walked with him to the edge of the village, a flock of cheering and shrieking children at their heels. The brothers maintained a tough countenance, but all five brothers knew that this was a mask for great brotherly love and turbulent emotions. Judah and Eupolemus mounted their horses and rode out. Judah's brothers remained standing for a long time, watching them as they disappeared over the hills on their way to the coast.

Judah and Eupolemus intended to ride North on the sea highway, passing through the ancient Phoenician cities of Ptolemais[15], Tyre, and Sidon and continuing northwards to Antioch, capital of the Seleucid kingdom. They reached Ptolemais after three days of sedate riding, rented a room at an inn, and went out to explore the city.

This was Judah's first visit to a port city, and at first he was excited at its vibrant pace of life. Ships entered and left, goods were loaded and unloaded, and the markets and stores were filled with thronging customers. However, after his initial impression passed, Judah discovered that the city was not welcoming to strangers, particularly not Jewish strangers. The streets were filled with all sorts of suspicious types, layabouts, peddlers, and beggars, who saw strangers such as themselves as easy marks. At some point their tour of the city became unpleasant and a sense of wariness in the face of danger filled them. Ptolemais turned out to be disappointing from a Jewish perspective as well. Its Jewish community was small and its members preferred to conceal their Jewishness as much as they could, fearing gentile harassment.

They left the city with a sense of relief the very next day. Their experience in Ptolemais suppressed their desire to halt at Tyre and Sidon, although they knew that both had well established Jewish communities, and they decided to proceed directly to Antioch without further stops on their way. Unlike Ptolemais, Antioch was a pleasant surprise. The Jewish community of the city was vibrant. Its members walked the streets proudly, secure in their stature and wealth. Some were businessmen and property holders, while others held senior positions in the administration of the kingdom and the Polis. They had their own communal institutions, including a number of synagogues.

---

15   Modern Acre.

They were proud of the fact that Hunio, the former High Priest, was now one of them.

The fact that Judah and Eupolemus were the sons of priests from Jerusalem won them a particularly warm welcome. They were invited every evening to dinners with Jewish families at which they were asked to speak of events in Jerusalem and Judea. Their hosts were used to Polis life and saw with approval the transformation of Jerusalem into a Polis and the establishment of the gymnasium. The youth and children were excited at their status as pankration fighters, and they repeatedly asked Judah to speak of his experiences in the Samaria contests. The older members of the community were more interested in the social and economic conditions in Jerusalem. To their mutual disappointment, none of their hosts seemed to take their plan of enlisting in the royal army seriously.

Judah and Eupolemus noticed that every house they were hosted at boasted at least one maiden of marriageable age. Their hosts were not shy about imploring them to remain in Antioch, attempting to convince them of the superior lifestyle the Jews of Antioch enjoyed over those of Judea. They even received quite a few offers of employment and blunt hints that they might win extensive economic benefits should they select a bride from amongst the daughters of their hosts.

A few days after their arrival in Antioch they were able to locate Democritos, Kratos' friend, who agreed to help them. There was word of tension in the East and the North of the kingdom against the breakaway provinces of Parthia and Armenia, as well as rumors of war against Egypt, particularly given the death of Queen Cleopatra, sister of the Seleucid king and queen. However, Democritos told them that there was no recruitment drive for the royal army and there was no indication of when such a recruitment drive might take place.

Democritos advised them to gird themselves with patience and await developments in Antioch. In the meantime, impressed with their muscular and tall stature, he offered to arrange lucrative employment for them as mercenaries and body guards.

The search for Tiamos was another source of disappointment. They had no success and could not find any individual who was familiar with the family.

After a stay of about four weeks in Antioch, Eupolemus arrived at the conclusion that the longer they remained, the less likely they would be to realize their ambitions of a military career. He found himself dwelling upon Glitarius' letter. Given that Rome was increasingly the capital of the world and the rising power of the present age, he thought, perhaps they should have set their course to it to begin with.

Judah completely rejected this idea. "Joining the royal army, from which the governors who rule our people and homeland come, is one thing. Sailing to the end of the world to become a mercenary or even a legionnaire in Rome is something completely different—better to travel to Egypt, where many of our people serve in the Ptolemy army."

Democritos, on the other hand, was supportive. "The Seleucid kingdom has been a power in decline ever since Antiochus the Great was defeated by the Romans. The Parthians and the Armenians were doing as they pleased and the Egyptians were constantly plotting to restore Coele-Syria to their rule. King Antiochus is frightened of the Romans and will take no military action without receiving Roman consent. Joining the Roman Army might therefore be a very good idea, at least if you seek an active military experience."

Eupolemus deliberated, and finally decided to continue on to

Rome. In spite of his love for Judah, it was the knowledge that Judah would not be travelling with him that swayed him. Somewhere in his heart he realized that this was his chance to move out of Judah's shadow and prove his worth. The two friends visited deposed High Priest Hunio, and found him bitter and frustrated, angry at the Seleucid regime, his brother who had betrayed him, and the priesthood at large for putting up with the situation. Still, Hunio willingly accepted the thoroughbred horse his brother had gifted him. Judah doubted if the heavyset man ever intended to ride the noble steed, but that was none of his business. Jason's horse was loaned to him and was not his to keep, and in any event Eupolemus intended to let him have his own horse, which would be useless on the long sea voyage to Rome.

Three days later, in a port city near Antioch the two friends bid each other farewell. Judah headed back to Modi'in and Eupolemus sailed on the ship Kalirma on the way to Rome. The Kalirma was a typical trading vessel which had also been adapted to the transport of passengers. The captain was a veteran seaman called Poseidanus. Rumor had it that in his youth he was the commander of a warship in Rhodes, but there were also opposing rumors which adamantly insisted he was once a pirate. Either way, he was now an independent trader and rented his ship out to transport merchandise and travelers on the trade routes connecting the port cities of Syria, Rhodes, Greece, and Italy. Eupolemus paid Poseidanus for a ticket to Rhodes, the current destination of the Kalirma, where he hoped to find another ship which would bring him to Ostia, the port city of Rome.

This was not the first time in his life he had sailed on a ship, but knowing that he was about to embark on an adventure whose end was unknown made this trip feel different and unique. He enjoyed standing on the deck, watching the line of the horizon, feeling the salt and the air and the winds stroke his face. The mariners told their passengers that dolphins frequently joined the ships and escorted them on their journey, leaping out of the water as they swam, and all of the passengers watched from the deck, hoping to catch sight of the noble sea beasts.

Due to the winter there was concern with stormy weather; however, they were fortunate enough to enjoy a calm sea and a steady breeze, and the ship advanced rapidly across the waves. Over the next few days, the ship approached the coast and the sea changed its color from blue to turquoise. Over the beach rose the Taurus Mountains, steep and heavily forested. The coastline was twisting, revealing between its folds small bays which where brilliant in their beauty, seaside villages sprawled over some of them whereas others were pristine and free of human habitation.

On the fourth day of their voyage, as the Kalirma coasted along the coastline, the passengers saw three long galleys leave one of the bays and advance rapidly towards the ship. The passengers were struck with fear, realizing they were pirates. Eupolemus took position at the stern of the ship, his personal equipment bag with the weapons by his side. The money within it was all of his property. Without it, he could not continue his journey or return.

Poseidanus emerged on deck and looked at the approaching galleys. The men seated by the oars were well armed with swords, axes, and daggers, and were dressed in a motley variety of clothing, no doubt loot they had captured from the passengers of ships that they had captured. Poseidanus kept his cool. He ordered the crew of his ship to belay any efforts at flight, well aware that this was impossible in any event. The wind was too weak to give his sailing vessel the speed needed to evade the oar propelled pirate galleys. To the terror of his passengers, when the galleys caught up with the Kalirma, its crew fully cooperated with the boarders, one of the crew even tossing down a rope ladder to the boarders.

Three of the pirates climbed up the rope ladder to the Kalirma's decks, their greedy glances at the passengers of the ship revealing their intentions. Poseidanus led the three into the bowels of the ship and conferred with them for a time in his cabin. The loud laughter that rose from the cabin slightly allayed the concerns of the passengers. Shortly thereafter, Poseidanus and the three pirates returned to the deck, one of the pirates now bearing a small cloth bag. They shook hands with Poseidanus, giving another greedy stare at the passengers before disembarking from the ship.

Then the Kalirma continued its journey. Poseidanus was uncharacteristically silent for a long, long time afterwards. When he was asked how he had gotten the pirates to release them without robbing them he merely said gruffly, "Who said they didn't rob us?" and descended from the decks to cloister himself in his cabin.

After another ten days of sailing, with short stops in the ports of Asia Minor on their way, the Kalirma reached the island of Rhodes. As the ship approached the harbor, the astonished passengers, Eupolemus among them, gazed upon the Colossus, the enormous statue of Helios, the god of the sun. The statue had collapsed to the ground about fifty years ago following an earthquake, but even laying down was still considered to be one of great wonders of the world.

Poseidanus suggested that Eupolemus wait nearby, just in

case, while he sought cargo to deliver. He was fortunate enough to sign a contract that very evening to transport wine from Rhodes to Ostia, which meant Eupolemus could remain aboard the Kalirma rather than taking passage on another ship.

And so, after a few weeks at sea, the Kalirma arrived in Ostia during the noon hours of the Kalends, the day of the new moon, the first day of the month of April, on the 580th year since the founding of Rome. The port was almost inconceivably crowded. Thousands of ships and boats were anchored at the docks, making their way to and from the port and loading and unloading merchandise. Numberless people were occupied with moving goods and equipment from the port warehouses to the ships and from the ships to the warehouses. In spite of the tightly packed streets and the crowded docks, Eupolemus was impressed with the orderliness with which the port conducted its business. It seemed every man knew his role and his task. By the time they managed to dock, the sun was near to setting, and Poseidanus decided to unload his cargo the next morning. He gave his crew shore leave but admonished them to return the next day at sunrise.

Poseidanus liked Eupolemus so much that he decided to help him find his Roman friend. "Rome is unimaginably vast," he said, "As large and vibrant as Ostia is, the greatest port we docked in during our voyage, it is no more than a small suburb of Rome. I suggest you do not make your way to Rome alone. Join me on shore; we will send a messenger to your friend to announce your arrival. Let him come and pick you up from the port."

Poseidanus went to a large warehouse at which the shipment of wine was supposed to arrive. Over the next few days, he would circulate amongst the merchants of the city and attempt to secure shipment orders that would fit in with his planned return to the ports of Greece and Syria. The owner of the warehouse was absent from his office, so they met the warehouse manager instead.

"You have arrived on the Kalends, named after the word Calendarium, which means account book," explained the man. "On this day harbingers walk throughout the city and remind the citizens that they must pay their debts. My master has ridden to Rome to his patron in order to settle his debts with him."

Poseidanus was disappointed; had they arrived a day earlier, they might have made use of the assistance of the warehouse owner to transmit a message to Eupolemus' friend during his travel to Rome.

"Who did you come to visit in Rome?" the manager asked Eupolemus.

"A childhood friend by the name of Glitarius Marcius."

"Marcius? I do not know this family. Do you know what his full name is? The middle name is the father's clan, and that is what matters."

"I think he wrote the name…." said Eupolemus, and withdrew the letter which Glitarius had sent to him and Judah from his equipment satchel, "Here it is: Glitarius Fabius Marcius."

The warehouse manager leaned back in awe.

"Fabius?! The house of Fabius is one of the most renowned and glorious in Rome! My friend, why did you not mention this earlier? My master will be delighted to aid any friend of this house. Wait here!"

The warehouse manager left his office and returned after a few moments, accompanied by another man. "It has all been taken care of, my friend. I will send one of our men to my master in Rome. He will make sure your friend is found and made aware of your arrival."

As they left, Eupolemus said softly, "I think this may be a misunderstanding. As far as I know, my friend's family, though patricians, are low of rank and make their living by trade."

"We will live and see," responded Poseidanus. "The Roman house is a wide circle of men, almost a tribe. It may be that the immediate family of your friend is not wealthy, but it still belongs to this honorable house. Besides, why should you care, so long as you benefit? Come, we will sleep in the inn tonight. We deserve it after so many days at sea."

The next day a slave of the Marcius family arrived at the inn with an open two seat chariot to pick Eupolemus up. Glitarius and his family were on vacation outside of the city of Rome, but their majordomo had decided, on his own judgment, to make arrangements to transport Glitarius' friend who had arrived from a distant land. Eupolemus bid farewell to Poseidanus, though not before the latter informed him, with much delight, of the bitter disappointment of the warehouse owner. It turned out that he had returned to Ostia in fury after having invested many hours in locating the home of Glitarius' family. He then discovered that it belonged to such a distant and minor branch of the house of Fabius that he would derive no conceivable gain from the efforts he had expended in aiding them.

The travel from Ostia to Rome in an open chariot was a pleasant experience. The entire path was paved, a fact which Eupolemus found nothing short of amazing. Not even the larger cities of the Eastern Mediterranean he had visited had paved streets. The more the chariot drew close to Rome, the more his amazement grew. The size of the city was incredible. Over the six centuries of its existence the sons of the city had established a sprawling Empire and made their capital the center of the entire world. Eupolemus felt a pinch of envy in his heart. The

Children of Israel had lived in their nation for centuries and had established a great kingdom by the time Rome had been founded... God, had you not told us that we were the Chosen People?! Eupolemus asked the silent heavens.

When they arrived at the Marcius household, the majordomo who had secured his passage from Ostia greeted him.

"Welcome. I am Papalagos. The family has travelled on a vacation and is likely to return in a few days. Only a few slaves, and myself, a freedman, are left to look after the household," the man said self-importantly.

Eupolemus thanked him, carefully selecting the correct words in Latin. "I would be pleased to tour Rome until they return and improve my skill in your language."

"Rome can be very dangerous, particularly at night and especially for strangers," Papalagos responded in trepidation, clearly terrified at the very thought of his guest touring the city. "I ask that you do not leave the household after dark, and in any event only travel with the escorts which I will provide you with."

Rome left Eupolemus with conflicting impressions. On the one hand, it had great temples and public buildings, as well as sumptuous villas in the residential quarters of the wealthy patricians. On the other hand, the city was also enveloped by a sprawl of slums packed with insula, apartment buildings which rose over ten stories high, which seemed like mouse tunnels rising into the air. The streets flowed with sewage, and they were packed with all types of filth—even animal and human corpses. Many parts of the city were crowded, choked with soot, the smells of frying food, stink and raucous noise. The roads and alleys were choked with traffic jams, a phenomena he had never seen in the cities of the Eastern Mediterranean: wagons, chariots, and masses of pedestrians blocked each other in complete indifference.

On the fifth day following his arrival in Rome, the Marcius family returned home. Eupolemus exited to the courtyard to greet his friend and found that Papalagos had already updated them regarding his arrival.

Glitarius was the first to leap out of the carriage. He ran to him and embraced him in a display of emotion which was very un-Roman in its lack of restraint. When they had last seen each other they were boys, and now they were young men at the height of their power.

Cassandra, Glitarius' sister, descended from the carriage after him. Eupolemus looked at her in amazement. She was younger than Glitarius by two years. When they lived in Jerusalem he had a chance to see her every once in a while, but he had seen her as a child, and had little to do with her. The young woman who descended from the carriage now was so attractive that no man could remain indifferent in her presence.

Eupolemus was never shy with women. He drew himself erect, his eyes widening slightly, and then narrowing in a mixture of playfulness and casual arrogance, his mouth quirking in a restrained smile, as he met her eyes with presumptuous self-confidence.

Cassandra was used to men playing the peacock with her. She met his eyes and smiled, but her expression made it clear she was not interested.

Glitarius, who picked up on the byplay, whispered in his ear, "Forget her, my friend. She is courted by the highest ranking patricians. And as for you, you will meet many other beautiful women in Rome."

In the meantime, the parents of Glitarius descended from the carriage, and Eupolemus, embarrassed at the impact of Cassandra upon him, and even more by his casual rejection, forced himself to look away. Glitarius' parents received him warmly and invited him to join them for dinner. Glitarius and Eupolemus then entered the inner courtyard of the home, as the rest of the family members ascended the stairs to their quarters. Attentive slaves leapt from the background to unload the wagon's equipment.

"Please, tell me about what has happened over the years since we last saw each other. Where did you get these muscles? Did you continue with the pankration? How is Judah?" Glitarius rained questions down on him.

Eupolemus shared his experiences during his journey with Glitarius, including his plan to enlist in the Seleucid army, Judah and his participation in the pankration contest, the voyage to Antioch, and the trip to Rome.

"It is a shame Judah did not come with you. You should have arrived a month ago. March is a never-ending festival of celebrations in Rome. You could have come with me to the Circus Maximus or seen a gladiator contest. These are sights you will never see in Jerusalem."

"How about my idea of enlisting in a Roman legion instead of the Seleucid army?"

"I am not sure. It may be a good idea. I personally am not experienced in military affairs, but Rome has a constant demand for soldiers. We will consult with my father regarding this matter when we dine with him tonight. Tomorrow I am invited to dine at the home of Marcus Porcius Cato, who was once a Censor, one of the most prestigious positions in Rome, whose job is to safeguard the morals of the city. His son and I are friends. Cato's recommendation would open up every door in Rome, and would certainly help you enlist in the Legions. I will see if I can secure an invitation for you as well."

Marcus Porcius Cato would occasionally host young men in his villa rustica outside Rome. Some of them were friends of his son, whereas others were promising young men he wished to promote or whose company he enjoyed. Glitarius sent a messenger to Cato's farm with a letter requesting Cato's permission to bring Eupolemus with him. Obviously he exaggerated somewhat, introducing him as a scion of the most prestigious priestly family in Judea. A positive reply came the next morning. A few hours later, the two were already making their way outside the city towards Cato's villa.

"So, you are the priest Glitarius told us about?" enquired Cato upon receiving them in his home's reception hall, "To what nation exactly do you belong, and how did you come to join us here?"

"My nation, and the territory where we now dwell, are named after one of our tribes, the Tribe of Judah. Originally, we were called the Children of Israel, and our land was all of Canaan."

"I have heard of you. An ancient and odd people. You believe in a single god, read sacred scrolls, and have no statues to represent the divine. You also only work six days of seven and release your slaves on the seventh year. You are not fond of work? And what is your fascination with the number seven?"

Eupolemus was surprised at the pace of the questioning. Cato spoke seriously and softly, and seemed genuinely interested in his answers.

"We believe, as you said, in the existence of a single supreme God, sir. Our belief is that God has ordered man to rest on the seventh day, which is the Sabbath. On that day we pray and read the sacred books we call Torah. I have heard that my lord is a great expert in agriculture. We let the land rest every seven years as well, which is how it renews its strength and gives better crops over time. We believe that man, even if he is a slave, also renews his strength if he rests every seven days."

A number of young men had gathered around them, listening to Cato question the foreigner. Some of them chuckled at the words of Eupolemus.

"We Romans honor the tradition of our ancestors. The ancestral laws of another ancient people are something that every true Roman will honor, even if they are different from our own," Cato said, raising his voice and glaring in reprimand at the chuckling young men, who quickly fell silent.

Eupolemus felt uneasy at being the cause for their reprimand, and quickly changed the subject of conversation. "My lord's name has spread far and wide as a pursuer of justice and a lover of the law. Our sacred scrolls say: You shall not pervert justice; you shall not show partiality, nor take a bribe, for a bribe blinds the eyes of the wise and twists the words of the righteous[16]."

Cato seemed pleased at his words. "Well said. That is why I hold these meetings here: to educate the younger generation in the spirit of morality and the laws of our forefathers. I am favorably impressed with you, young man."

Cato addressed Eupolemus again later in the evening. "Your homeland is ruled by young Antiochus. Did you know that his father dared to challenge Rome?"

Eupolemus nodded in confirmation. He had earlier decided not to mention his father's connection with Antiochus III or the fact that he had managed to secure benefits for the Jews from him.

"I was the one who led to his father's defeat eighteen years

---

16   Deuteronomy 16:19.

ago," Cato raised his voice so that all those in the room would hear. The conversation in the hall fell silent as all turned to listen to their host.

"I was forty-three at the time. Antiochus III was titled 'the Great' after he subdued the barbarians in the East, defeated the Ptolemys, and conquered your homeland from them," said Cato, directing his words at Eupolemus. "Were that not enough, he sheltered Hannibal of Carthage in his court, who had often defeated the armies of Rome on the battlefield, keeping him as an adviser. Antiochus invaded Greece and defied Rome's demand he withdraw. Rome was in a state of crisis. It was clear that if Antiochus were not stopped in Greece, Italy would be next!"

Cato fell silent dramatically, and then rose from his couch and continued to speak standing, as if he were addressing the Senate. "The citizens of Rome feared that they were now faced with an enemy greater than they had ever known. Given the needs of the hour, I did not hesitate to offer my services to Rome and do battle. Although I had previously been Consul, I saw no dishonor in serving under the current Consul. Antiochus had positioned his army in the Hot Gates, Thermopylae, where the Lacedaemonians nearly halted the Persian army in its tracks three centuries previously, and fortified the site far better than the Spartans ever had, waiting for the Roman army to come. The Barbarians never managed to breech the Spartan defenses of the pass even though they faced only a handful of warriors, albeit Spartiates. Who knows how the barbarians were able to nonetheless overcome the Spartans?"

"A traitor revealed a hidden pass through the mountains and they struck the Spartans from the rear," said Glitarius.

"Indeed, so it was," replied Cato. "I decided to learn from the barbarians. Sometimes a single man can shape the destiny of his people and write history in his own hands. I led several hundred warriors through the mountains until we reached the rear of Antiochus's camp. We attacked at dawn, with the main Roman army launching a frontal assault at the same time. The Seleucids understood that they were surrounded. Antiochus 'the Great,'" mocked Cato, "fled like a coward and his troops followed. Thousands of them were slain by us."

The audience in the hall was delighted and applauded as one. Cato's eyes sparkled with pride; this battle had been the peak of his military career. When the excitement died down, Cato sat down by Eupolemus. "So what brings you to us? You hardly look like a priest," he added with a smile.

"I wish to enlist in a Roman Legion, sir."

"I see no problem with that. Rome will be delighted to have you join its ranks," answered Cato. He rose, slapped Eupolemus on the shoulder in approval and moved on to mingle with his other guests.

Glitarius approached his friend. "It seems that the old man is fond of you. What did he say?"

"That I should have no problem joining a legion."

"Excellent. But you had better secure a written recommendation from him. I will ask his son to take care of it."

172 BCE, Northern Iberia— The Legion[17]

Dramatis Personae
Bold = main character
* = historical figure

- *Clemanus—Squad (8-10 soldiers) commander in Fifth Legion*
- *Marcus—Decurion, commander of cavalry squad in the Fifth Legion*
- *Gato—Century commander in the Fifth Legion*
- *Tiberius—Cohort in the Fifth Legion*
- *Quintus Marcellus—Commander of the Fifth Legion*
- **Eupolemus***—*Childhood friend of Judah, son of Yohanan ben Hakotz*
- **Flavius** *and Albus—Infantry soldiers of the fifth legion*

Clemanus, the squad commander, informed his soldiers that they would be leaving the following morning on a scouting patrol. This was their first operational mission

---

17 A Roman legion at the time was apparently composed of ten cohorts of 480 warriors; each cohort was composed of six centuries, and each century of ten squads. The exact structure and size of the units was finalized during the reforms attributed to Gaius Marius in 107 BCE.

as soldiers of the Fifth Legion. It was true that this was merely a scouting mission, rather than going to battle, but at least they were leaving the camp ground, fully armed and prepared for confrontation. The patrol was made up of their infantry squad and a squadron of cavalry to accompany them.

The warriors gathered themselves in the assembly point at the entrance to the camp. Clemanus' infantrymen were flanked by a line of ten mounted cavalrymen. Gato, the commander of their Century, waited for them to finish assembling.

"Centurion, the seventh squad is ready," Clemanus declared, and straightened before his commander.

The leftmost cavalryman smirked in scorn and said derisively, "Rather late being ready. I hope you aren't late when my horsemen I and need you in battle."

"That's enough, Decurion," Gato mildly reprimanded him, well aware of the limitations of his power versus the cavalrymen, many of whom were members of the noble patrician class. Indeed, the cavalry of the legion answered directly to its commander and were not usually under his command. "Outside the walls of the camp you will all have to stand by one another…."

Gato reviewed his soldiers lingering over each one. They are young, inexperienced, but filled with enthusiasm, he thought.

"Listen up, soldiers! As soon as you step out of this camp, you are no longer ordinary human beings. You are soldiers of the fifth Roman Legion," Gato emphasized each word in the sentence. "You are the representatives of the Roman Republic, the mightiest power in the world."

Gato paused, glaring at the troops, before he continued, "The walls of this camp are the boundary between civilization and barbarism. Beyond it live barbarians, independent tribes who see Rome and all those who represent it as an enemy. It is our duty to safeguard this border, and to protect our world from theirs."

Eupolemus was not particularly happy about the Romans viewing the local tribes as Barbarians. However he might feel about the matter, Gato continued his speech. "The purpose of this patrol is merely to demonstrate our presence. The cavalry squadron will ride first, followed by the infantry squad. This is not a joint patrol. The cavalry will advance independently and will not wait for you, but both squads will follow the same trail to the river and alongside it. The other bank hosts a hostile Barbarian village, and we have already had conflicts with its inhabitant. Be vigilant!"

These young men smile too much, thought Gato as he reviewed his troops one last time. It is a good thing that Clemanus is a veteran trooper. Still, the Legion Commander is right to send them out on patrols. They will learn the terrain and get some idea of what it is like to be in contact with the enemy.

The infantry squad marched out of the camp at a rapid pace. At first, they maintained tight marching discipline, with the impact of Gato's words still upon them. Their gravity and seriousness evaporated as they left the camp behind, however. After long months of rigorous military hierarchy and training, marching and being barracked in the crowded camp, the soldiers were excited at the sense of independence and the wide open space. They marched in a column of four pairs on the sandy trail, following Clemanus, who led them from the front. Endless green fields of waist-high grass stretched on both sides of the path. The gentle breeze stirred the carpets of grass as if they were the waves of a turquoise sea.

The farther they marched from the camp, the looser their discipline became. The soldiers talked, laughed, and lost their vigilance and preparedness. From time to time Clemanus sent an admonishing glare backwards, trying to restrain them and restore order, but they all thought he was being pointlessly uptight. They were soldiers of the Roman Legion. Dressed in impressive combat paraphernalia, wearing gleaming weapons and their heads adorned with stiff-maned helmets, they felt themselves to be invincible.

After a march of about an hour they reached the river and began to march alongside it. They could see local Gauls on the other side occasionally who stared at them in hostility. Some even dared to shout and curse at them. These proud, fearless and free Gauls, who had pushed South into the Iberian peninsula over the past generations, felt nothing but contempt for the Roman soldiers fortified up in their camps. When they passed by the village the second bank of the river was already thick with a mob of hundreds of furious locals, shouting and waving their hands at them. A group of armed young men stood by the riverbank near boats floating in the water, arguing with an elderly individual who seemed to be the village chieftain. It seemed they were trying to convince him to allow them cross the river and attack the Romans.

Clemanus tried to keep calm, but increased the pace of their march. His soldiers stopped horsing around. The sense of danger was imminent and stretched their readiness to the edge. It was clear to all of them that they had no chance of peacefully emerging from any conflict which might take place. They breathed in relief when they withdrew from the village without the Gauls crossing the river.

After some additional time walking by the river, Clemanus turned them towards a path crossing the fields, back towards the camp. The soldiers marched in silence, shocked by their experience and deep in thought about the likely consequences of the Gauls in the village choosing to attack the badly outnumbered Romans. And then, out of nowhere, a long javelin pierced the air with a shriek. Clemanus noticed the javelin from the corner of his eye. His warrior instincts pulled him downwards, but another instinct, that of the commander responsible for his charges, overcame it. He turned back, shouting at his soldiers to duck. Before he could say anything else, the javelin pierced his back with enormous force, flinging him at his stunned soldiers. He was dead before his body hit the ground. Eight stunned soldiers stared, dumbfounded, unable to digest what had just happened and oblivious to the danger that the javelin attack from ambush would be followed up by an enemy charge.

Eupolemus was the first to gather his wits. He shouted "Battle formation!" and leapt forward, passing Clemanus' body and kneeling, his sword drawn and his shield positioned to cover most of his body. The other soldiers stirred into action and fell into formation behind him in two V shaped lines, the body of Clemanus among them.

A few moments passed, but the attack was not renewed. Eupolemus turned around and inspected Clemanus' supine body. He was dead by every appearance, but Eupolemus felt duty-bound to ensure it.

"Dead," he informed his friends softly. "Quickly, advance at the bushes from where we were attacked. Maintain formation."

Eupolemus spoke in a peremptory, low, authoritative tone. No one doubted his words. They felt greater confidence at him assuming command and telling them what to do.

Eupolemus began to advance, the soldiers following him. They left the path and entered the tall grass, their upper bodies protruding from the sea of grass. On top of a small hillock, no more than thirty paces away, they found a location where the grass was flattened. This was the ambush spot of the man who had flung his javelin at them. They understood that he had fled the location immediately thereafter, leaving behind a long trail of tracks in the grass.

They went back to where Clemanus' body lay on the ground. Saying nothing, Flavius and Albus bent and lifted Clemanus. Another soldier picked up his staff. All of them looked at Eupolemus, silently acknowledging him as their leader. Eupolemus nodded slightly as he accepted responsibility, and began to walk back towards the camp, his comrades falling in behind him.

None of them said anything all the way back to the camp. They walked huddled, deep in shame at the loss of their commander. Such thoughts are like a slippery slope, and the more you sink within them, the more they grow and overtake your entire perception with darker colors. Under such a mood, the soldiers were certain that as soon as they arrived in camp they would be dishonorably discharged from the legion. When the camp and its earthen rampart, topped with wooden fence posts and punctuated by guard towers, came into sight they slowed their march, as if trying to postpone the moment of their return.

Eupolemus noted the glum mood of his fellows. He too was agitated, his senses sharpened by the command position he had assumed with his comrades' consent. He felt responsible for their fate, at least until their return to camp. Halting, he turned towards them. They approached him slowly, standing before him and awaiting his words. Flavius and Albus, who carried Clemanus, gently lowered his body to the ground, inwardly relieved at the chance to catch their breath.

"About a month ago, another patrol just like ours was also ambushed," said Eupolemus.

They all grew attentive at once, eager to hear the rest.

"They hushed it up. The results of the incident were very bad, you see. The commanders didn't want word to spread. It all began similarly to what happened to us. A javelin from the ambush. The patrol commander killed. The soldiers, fresh recruits just like us, were shocked. One of them fled. Two others ran after him. Another one called them back and then ordered all the others to charge to the attack after him. But someone else shouted at him that he was not their commander and that they must take their commander's body with them and withdraw. The soldiers began to argue amongst themselves."

He examined his comrades. Suddenly lightning glinted in their eyes. The story about an ambushed patrol so similar to theirs, who conducted themselves much worse than they had, made them feel better by comparison.

All of the soldiers roused themselves and began to speak, breaking into each other's words.

"What happened to them?"

"Did they all die?"

"Did the three who fled survive?"

"How do you know about this story?"

"Compared to them we did much better," muttered Albus.

"What did you say?" Eupolemus asked Albus sharply.

"I said that compared to them we acted just right," answered Albus confidently.

"Exactly!" replied Eupolemus, raising his voice, "We acted just right. We were confused and shocked for an instant; that is only natural, but we immediately recovered, gathered into battle formation, protected Clemanus, and attacked the enemy just as Roman Legionnaires should. We must judge ourselves only by how we acted."

He looked over his comrades slowly. They all stood erect now.

"We have nothing to be ashamed of. If we view ourselves and what happened without shame, then that is how the commanders and the entire legion will treat us."

By their expressions, they all agreed with him.

"Now, about that story I just told you...." his friends looked at him with suspicion-tinged speculation, "I could have made things easier for you by permitting you to believe it...."

The fire in their eyes dimmed at once. "But you would have found out the truth sooner or later. And in any event, it does not matter since the story could have been true. I wanted to illustrate to you that everything is relative and that it is your choice how to relate to the ambush. Before you heard the story, you were mired in self-doubt, you were ashamed of yourselves, as if you had failed..."

He fell silent for a moment and then continued: "After you heard my story, even though it changed nothing of what actually happened to us, you were all filled with pride, and your eyes blazed with courage. So I tell you once again, we should be proud of ourselves. We have acted exactly as Roman warriors should!"

Later, in the tent, despondency spread once more. Everyone drew inwards, wrapped in his own thoughts. The image of Clemanus hurled to the ground by the javelin was too vivid and could not be wished away.

Activity was heard outside the tent, people's voices. Albus, who lay on the mattress by Eupolemus, sat up, trepidation in his eyes. The others felt it as well.

Gato entered the tent briskly. Following him, to their surprise, entered the Decurion of the cavalry squadron. The eight soldiers rose swiftly, tense and cautious.

"At ease, soldiers," said Gato. "No one here is blaming you. In a few moments we will be summoned to the Legion Commander. It is important for all of us to understand and analyze what happened. From the cavalry squadron, only Marcus," Gato nodded at the Decurion, "will participate. However, all of you, who were present at the site, will attend."

Gato turned his gaze to Albus. "You will present everything that happened. Speak clearly, briefly and shortly. Stick to the facts only. All the rest is not relevant," Gato emphasized. He had commanded raw recruits for many years. He could well imagine how these green troops must be feeling after losing their commander.

Albus hesitated. He knew that his comrades expected him to speak out.

"Commander, perhaps it will be better for Eupolemus to be the one to speak...," he said hesitantly.

"Accepting the command of whoever seemed most suitable at the ambush is one thing," Gato cut him off peremptorily, "but only a Roman born will speak out before the full command of the Legion!"

Eupolemus signaled Albus not to argue. The officers left the tent, and the soldiers prepared silently for the inquiry.

The tent of the Legion Commander was the largest in the camp, capable of containing over a hundred men. At its rear was a curtain which concealed the sleeping quarters. The area the soldiers entered was well lit by torches surrounding its circumference and at its center. The floor of the tent was well padded with carpets. Quintus Marcellus, the commander of the legion, was seated on a tall, ornate chair. To his left was a pole festooned with the flag of an angry bull, the sign of the Legion, painted on it. To his right a pole topped by a golden eagle, the symbol of Rome. Before him, the commanders of all the cohorts and a number of other officers were seated in a circle on simple wooden chairs.

At Quintus' signal, Gato and Marcus stepped into the circle and stood side by side with each other before the commanders of the Legion. The soldiers of the squad remained standing in a row at the entrance of the tent.

"Decurion Marcus Sartorius," Quintus initiated the proceedings, "report."

Gato's rank was higher than that of Marcus, but Marcus was a cavalryman, a Patrician noble.

"The truth is, sir, that I don't have much to say. I led my cavalry squadron on a separate patrol than that of the infantry. We passed through the same spot where they fell victim to ambush, but the barbarians did not dare attack **us**, and we saw nothing."

Quintus nodded and said nothing. He turned to Gato expectantly.

Gato turned around and gestured at Albus to come forward.

"Soldier, state your full name and tell us, in full detail, what happened," Quintus told Albus when he stepped into the circle and stood near Gato.

Eupolemus was happy for Albus for the chance to receive the attention of the commander of the legion. Quintus asked him several questions regarding their path from the camp and Albus answered him briefly. Eupolemus, who had heard and experienced and repeatedly reviewed in his own mind every moment of the disastrous expedition allowed his attention to wander.

Suddenly, he realized that the tent had fallen silent and everyone was staring at him. He straightened to attention, flushing, and felt a shiver crawl down his spine.

The perceptive Gato immediately intervened, "Eupolemus, Albus just told us how you took command of the patrol after Clemanus was slain. What happened from that point onwards?"

"First, introduce yourself. Who are you and where do you come from?" asked Quintus, seeming to realize that Eupolemus was not Roman born.

"My name is Eupolemus son of Yohanan. I come from a distant land in the East—Judea."

"I have never even heard of this land," replied Quintus in bafflement. "How did someone like you end up serving as a soldier in the Roman Legion?"

"I came to Rome to visit my childhood friend, Glitarius Fabius Marcius, with whom I had been educated and trained in the arts of war when he resided with his family in my country. Marcus Porcius Cato, his benefactor, offered his recommendation on my behalf, enabling me to enlist in the Legion."

A murmur of amazement passed through the tent at his words. None of the commanders had ever heard of the Marcius family, but their association with the house of Fabius made them high ranking in the eyes of all. Most of all, the personal recommendation from Cato the Censor made Eupolemus into an individual everyone should have been familiar with.

Quintus signaled the others to fall silent. He did not like the fact that someone in his legion, even if only a simple ranker, was so highly connected in Rome without him being aware of it. "You have mentioned some of Rome's most esteemed personalities. Your association with them requires you to meet high expectations. Describe to us your conduct after the ambush and we will judge whether you have met those expectations."

Eupolemus described shortly what had occurred, noting only the facts, without referring to the low morale of the soldiers or the pep talk he gave them prior to their return to the camp. When he finished speaking silence fell across the tent.

"And what are your conclusions from what happened? How do you think Clemanus' death could have been prevented?" Quintus asked him.

Eupolemus noted the surprise on Gato's face. It was unexpected, to say the least, for a Legion Commander to ask a common ranker such a question. He considered his words carefully. Everyone in the tent awaited his reply expectantly.

"There is no way to prevent an ambush or a surprise attack," he said evenly, "However, what determines the final outcome of the encounter is the manner in which the ambushed respond. The first moments are critical. In order to respond quickly, without even thinking about it, such situations must be repeatedly practiced. Only in this manner will we reach a state of immediate and optimal response to such situations. This is just like an arena fight. Many of the actions performed by the combatants are routines which are so deeply embedded in them that they do not even think about them when performing them—they seem to happen on their own. In this case, Clemanus was the only one who understood what was happening when the ambush took place, but instead of protecting himself, he turned to warn us. If we had been trained in protecting ourselves from an ambush this would not have been necessary." He hesitated for a moment, then added, "What we need is a unit of our own which will specialize in ambush and will simulate such attacks on other units, much like the training opponent of an arena contestant."

The officers in the tent looked to the Legion Commander, awaiting his words. Eupolemus spoke good sense, but his words could also be construed as criticism of the conduct of the Legion and the manner in which soldiers were trained.

Quintus nodded, considering Eupolemus' suggestion. He turned to a man seated in the circle of the commanders. Eupolemus recognized Tiberius, the commander of their cohort.

"Our first mistake was sending the units on patrol when they are completely separated from each other. What is the point of sending two patrols when they cannot offer any support to each other?!"

"The idea was to train as many junior commanders as possible. If we unite the two patrols, we will get a single patrol with one responsible commander," replied Tiberius.

"Not necessarily. I do not mean to unite them but to maintain communications and support between them. Each unit should have its own commander with his own mission, but the two forces must also remain in eye contact with one another and come to each other's support if necessary. This too is proper training for every soldier and commander prior to a real combat situation. Does anyone think differently?" Quintus turned his question to the other Cohort commanders.

"Very well, it is decided!" said Quintus, and gestured with his hand to his secretary. "Write it down as a new procedure, unless we choose to cancel all patrols for fear of the Barbarians eliminating all of our junior commanders."

Some of the commanders smiled. Quintus smiled for a moment as well, but then grew serious and turned to Gato. "We lost a brave soldier today, one of your valued junior commanders, and you are not pleased with our laughter, are you?"

Gato lowered his head silently, careful not to openly criticize the Legion Commander.

"Let it be clear that the death of a Roman warrior is not something we take lightly," said Quintus loudly. "His memory is honored, and we will yet settle accounts for his death. However, what is done is done. As warriors and as commanders we cannot take his death too badly. This is our fate, and may each and every one of us manage to die as Clemanus did, on his feet and weapon in hand."

The Cohort commanders nodded in agreement.

Eupolemus listened to Quintus's words with great interest. At that moment he felt that the entire long journey from Judea to Iberia was worthwhile, if only to hear Quintus's words.

"We will continue to investigate this incident, and when we conclude the inquiry we will determine how to punish he who dared attack Rome. We have the strength to do as we see fit, but we should do so with forethought."

Quintus gestured at his secretary and added, "In addition, we will establish a unit specializing in ambush and stealthy reconnaissance, just as this young warrior from Judea suggested. This unit will be used to train all of our patrols in responding to ambuscades, but might also be of use to us in special operations in the enemy rear."

Many of those in the tent stared in appreciation at Eupolemus. While his proposal had been elaborated upon and better defined by the Legion Commander, the original idea was his.

Quintus looked at him as well, a considering look in his eye, and then turned to Tiberius, "I place the responsibility for setting up and training that unit on you. It will later be directly under my command. It would be best that those amongst these soldiers who experienced an ambush in the flesh be included in this unit. Those most suitable amongst them, of course. Select twenty of the best soldiers in the Legion, two squads and a Centurion as a commander. I would consider making this fellow a commander of one of the two squads," added Quintus, nodding in Eupolemus' direction.

171 BCE—
The Fall of the House of Zadok

Dramatis Personae
Bold = main character
* = historical figure

- *Matityahu**—*Father of Judah and his brothers, village priest of Modi'in.*
- *Simha—An elderly Jew who moved from Jerusalem to Modi'in*
- *Joseph—Matityahu's brother*
- *Jason**—*High Priest since 175 BCE, brother of* **Hunio**
- *Rebecca—Matityahu's wife*
- *Laodice IV**—*Queen of the Seleucid Kingdom. Sister of Seleucus IV and his wife*
- *Mithridates (Antiochus IV)**—*King of the Seleucid Kingdom from 175 BCE onwards, brother to Seleucus IV and Laodice IV; also known as Antiochus Epiphanes—Antiochus the divine*
- *Perseus**—*King of Macedon*
- *Menelaus**—*Non Zadokite Jewish priest*
- *Yose ben Yoezer**—*Jewish elder and sage, president of the elder council*
- *Yose ben Yohanan**—*Jewish elder and leader, president of the court*
- *Yismachel (God will be joyful)—A Jewish priest*
- *Antigonus of Sokho**—*The first non-Zadokite president of the elder council; was appointed by the High Priest Simon the Righteous, father*

of Hunio and Jason
- *More-Tzedek*—A Zadokite priest.*
- *Yohanan*, Simon*, Judah*, Hannah*, Eleazar* and Jonathan*—the children of Matityahu* and Rebecca by age*

Matityahu sat on a chair at the entrance to his home, gazing westward at the horizon, his thoughts following the setting sun. Passover was over, and spring had come. A new year had begun. The hills were green with blooming vegetation. The fields were filled with flowers, and trees were covered with leaves.

Matityahu and his sons had not gone to Jerusalem at the two previous pilgrimage festivals, Sukkot and Passover. The stories and rumors about developments there amongst those who visited the city and the Temple made many traditional Jews keep away from the Holy City. As fewer traditional pilgrims arrived in the city and more traditional residents moved elsewhere, the Hellenizers' dominance of the city became increasingly brazen, to the point that those returning from Jerusalem described it as having changed its appearance and character completely. The council of the elders met but rarely. The High Priest, Jason, barely bothered to show up in the Temple. He was too busy with politics and Polis affairs. Pilgrims who had visited Jerusalem during the previous Passover told how, when Jason bothered arriving in the Temple, he did not even don the traditional clothing of the High Priest. The atmosphere of Jerusalem, even during the holidays, was that of a Hellene city which had no respect for Jewish tradition. It was said that during training in the gymnasium, the Temple priests would leave their watch and go watch the training athletes, and that many of the new Temple priests appointed by Jason only fulfilled their religious functions as if they were conducting a distasteful and meaningless duty, in a type of patronizing indulgence towards of their elders rather than a true expression of faith.

Joseph—Matityahu's brother—and Simha—an elder who had recently relocated to Modi'in from Jerusalem—approached him. Matityahu rose from his chair and handed it to the elder, who gratefully dropped into it.

"Matityahu, we must make the pilgrimage to Jerusalem in the upcoming Shavuot festival. At the rate that the city is being Hellenized, in a few years there will be nowhere to make a pilgrimage to," said Joseph with a sigh.

Matityahu did not reply. The mere thought of embarking on such a journey felt suffocating. "This Jason..." he finally replied in despair, "I do not understand how things run according to the new calendar. In the villages we continue to worship in accordance with the sacred Hebrew calendar. In Jerusalem it is the kingdom's calendar which determines the proper time...."

"In this, at least, Jason is following the proper path of tradition," Simha replied in a trembling and cracked voice. "It is important to him that the pilgrimage of the Jews of the Diaspora continue. It brings much money into the treasury of the Temple and the coffers of the merchants. He has circulated letters to all communities in the Diaspora, informing them of the time and date of the holidays. He personally still honors the holidays and the commandments. The radical Hellenizers think that he is too moderate, too gentle. They are already undermining him...."

"Rebecca also wants to come with us," added Matityahu. "I tried to persuade her that she should pass on this visit to Jerusalem, but when she wants something, nothing will sway her aside... Very well, on the upcoming Friday I will notify everyone. We will notify the neighboring villages as well—who ever will come is welcome. Jason will receive at least one large mission of proud Jews."

***

Antiochus III had managed, in his lifetime, to transform his kingdom into an Empire. His achievements were only marred by his stinging defeats by Rome. The surrender treaty had forced him to evacuate his army South and East of the Taurus Mountains and leave his son Mithridates in the hands of the leaders of the Roman Republic as a hostage. Following the death of the father, when *Seleucus,* Mithridate's brother, ascended to the throne, the Romans demanded that he send them his eldest son Demetrius as a hostage in place of Mithridates. Seleucus, however, tarried in responding to the Roman demand and left Mithridates in Roman captivity for many years. Only after Rome, increasingly insistent, backed him into a corner, did he send them his firstborn son Demetrius as a hostage.

Mithridates, embittered at his brother who had left him captive for so many years in Roman hands, moved to Athens for several years following his release, intending to sever any connection with his homeland. But then his brother suddenly died, and he returned to ascend to the throne of his kingdom only to find it weaker than ever: the Seleucid army had deteriorated badly from its proud empire-building days, the Parthians had risen in the East, the Armenians in the North, and the Egyptians threatened the South.

Mithridates had every intention of returning his kingdom to the glory days of his father. He adopted his father's name as his own, naming himself Antiochus IV, trying to send his subjects a clear message as to his intentions. For good measure he added to himself the title "Epiphanes", the divine. He had very serious intentions regarding Egypt and he made meticulous preparations for war with it. Over the past years he had been careful to quietly strengthen the army and build it up anew, a clear violation of the terms of his father's surrender treaty with Rome.

Recently, Mithridates' mood had improved following the arrival of news regarding the growing conflict between Macedon and Rome. The Romans accused the king of Macedon, Perseus, of violating his obligations towards them. It seemed that Macedon's military and economic growth had drawn the ire of Rome, which was intolerant of powerful states on its borders, particularly when such states had already fought them in the past. There were quite a few Roman senators who sought to provoke a war that would put Macedon in its place. Mithridates was equally avid to see warfare between the two states break out, thinking that this would provide him with the freedom of action he required to fulfill his ambitions regarding Egypt. And thinking of Egypt, on that morning a priest from Judea was waiting to meet him.

The Jewish priest Menelaus awaited his interview with the king outside the royal reception hall, pale and tense. This was his first-ever time in the palace. There is no sin in stealing from a thief, he told himself. Jason stole his position from his brother and now I will repay him in kind, measure for measure. The time of the house of Zadok in Israel has ended. Long live the new priestly dynasty....

The doors of the royal hall opened sharply. A royal clerk ushered him in.

Menelaus approached the stairs leading to the royal throne, following the steps of the clerk. At the base of the throne he lowered his body in a brief bow. The outraged clerk reprimanded him and ordered him to kneel before the king. Menelaus briefly hesitated and then swiftly knelt.

"Your majesty, it is a great honor for me to arrive at Antioch, to deliver to you the love of the Jewish people and their sincere concern for your wellbeing."

"I had thought your people did not kneel before anyone but your God?" a feminine voice snapped at him from behind the throne of the king as Queen Laodice entered the hall.

Menelaus flushed, tongue-tied, as his eyes met those of the queen.

"My queen, could you not resist the temptation of needling this poor priest?" asked Mithridates with a smile, as he extended his hand to his sister and wife.

Laodice smiled back at him. "They do not honor the royal cult of our queen mother. I am glad to see that he is at least paying you your proper respect."

"As far as I understand, the Jews of Syria and Antioch do respect our rituals. It is only those of the Meridarchy of Judea who do not do them proper honor. Come, my queen, sit beside me. Let us listen to what this honored priest wishes to **propose to us**," answered Mithridates, hinting at Menelaus that he well knew the reason for him seeking an audience. The king and queen locked their gazes on Menelaus, who felt like he had entered a tiger's cage.

***

The men made the journey from Modi'in to Jerusalem on foot. The womenfolk, who had joined them under Rebecca's influence, and with them the small children, crowded into two wagons. The journey was planned to be carried out at a sedate pace during the hours of the first day, with the pilgrims making their camp in one of the villages on the way to Jerusalem and completing their journey the following morning. On their way additional pilgrims joined them, swelling the group to a large crowd of men, women, and children.

True to his duty as the leader of his community, Matityahu preached the laws and customs of the holiday to the group following him. He told them about the sacrifice of the two loaves, which was performed in the Temple on Shavuot Holiday, and was unique in that it was composed of bread, unlike most sacrifices, which were forbidden to be baked with rising dough. The sacrifice was meant to symbolize the gratitude of the people to God for the bountiful harvests. Matityahu asked the children in the group various questions regarding the origin of the commandment. The crowd around answered with cheers whenever one of the children replied correctly, and with mocking jeers whenever a child replied incorrectly. This display helped distract the grownups from thoughts about what was awaiting them in Jerusalem. The quiz expanded to questions regarding types of sacrifices made at the Temple, the roles of the High Priest, and more, and the circle of respondents gradually expanded to include grownups as well.

Their good spirits lasted the next day as well, at least until the pilgrims arrived in the outskirts of Jerusalem. There, they gradually fell silent as they walked with heavy hearts towards the city until they entered its gates.

Matityahu took the lead, his mind having a hard time taking in what his eyes saw. Jerusalem had been made into a Hellene city for all intents and purposes. The atmosphere of the streets was festive, street performers crowded into every corner, bare-chested and tattooed men danced and sang, and peddlers circled their stalls, offering all types of souvenirs and refreshments. But many of the refreshments were not kosher, and the souvenirs included figurines which were forbidden by the laws of Judaism. Many of the visitors who crowded the city streets were Hellene in dress and custom, and it was impossible to determine whether they were Jews or not. No one greeted the pilgrims from Modi'in, and as they crossed the city they felt as if they were strangers in a foreign land. Some of the Hellenizers even stared at them in contempt. Occasionally they were subject to derisive catcalls as if, merely by arriving in the city, they were disturbing the Hellenizers' carnival atmosphere.

Matityahu recollected, his heart aching, his days living in Jerusalem, in which the pilgrimages were the occasions on which ties to the Jews of the Diaspora were reestablished. Those were days of spiritual exhilaration, in which every Jew felt he was part of something greater than himself, connected to the great extended family of the Jewish people. The streets of Jerusalem were filled at that time with a feeling of sacredness, packed with tens of thousands of people, all dressed in white, who walked back and forth to the Temple smiling and greeting each other as they walked. People who had not met each other in months, sometimes years, embraced, reminisced, and asked after those who could not arrive.

They went on through the city until they reached the Temple. There, in stark contrast to the indifferent, even hostile, attitude towards them in the streets of Jerusalem, they were received with great joy. The courtyard of the Temple was filled with a few thousand traditionalists. These were not the crowds of previous years—only a few of the Diaspora had arrived this year to carry out the pilgrimage. The spirit in the Temple courtyard was despondent rather than celebratory, and the people who gathered there felt as if they were under siege. The Temple had become a refuge from the streets in which they were catcalled, and sometimes even physically harassed, by gangs of Hellenizer teenagers.

The concerned Jews who clustered in the courtyard were reassured by the appearance of the large delegation from Modi'in. As they passed through the crowd many approached them, shook their hands and slapped their shoulders in greeting. The sons of Matityahu scattered rapidly, each seeking their friends from the days when they had lived in the city. The women were also drawn to their friends and relatives, greeting them with kisses and warm embraces.

Judah took advantage of the opportunity to leave the Temple, hoping to visit Phidias in the gymnasium and Kratos in the ephebeia. He hoped that one of them might have heard word of Eupolemus. He also intended to visit the house of Hakotz, the abode of Eupolemus' family, and try to find out there what had happened to his friend. He was surprised at the intensity of the hostility of the Hellenizers to traditional Jews, and the way the city had changed since the first year of Jason's High Priesthood, during which he had lived in Jerusalem alone.

Matityahu, Joseph, and a number of other elderly dignitaries in the group were invited to enter the Temple to attend a council of elders, heads of the leading families of the Jerusalem, and senior priests.

Matityahu and his men entered the hall and stopped at the entrance. An elderly man whom Matityahu did not know was standing and speaking to those present, who were seated on benches before him. In the first row were seated, side by side, Yose ben Yoezer, the President of the Council, and the priest

Yose ben Yohanan, the President of the Court. Near them, also in the first row, sat several high-ranking priests, their faces grave. In fact, it seemed that everyone in the hall was serious and concerned. The speaker halted his speech, welcomed those who had arrived, and invited them to seat themselves on the benches amongst the multitudes who were gathered there. Many of those seated in the hall welcomed the newcomers. At this difficult time, every patriarch who honored the hall with his presence was a much-welcomed reinforcement.

"As I said earlier," continued the elder once they were seated, "rumor has it that Menelaus is headed back to Jerusalem, escorted by the soldiers of the king. No one can find Jason. It seems he too has had word of the situation. Given these developments, he probably will not arrive to fill the role of the High Priest and perform the sacrifice of the two loaves…."

At that moment the echoing cries announcing the arrival of the High Priest arose from without. The entry of Jason to the Temple courtyard immediately raised the spirits of the thousands of faithful. In addition to being the High Priest, Jason was the Polis leader, so his arrival in the Temple was received by the faithful as a show of support, as well as a message to the Hellenizers that Jason extended his protection to the Temple and required that the sanctity of the site be honored. Even though Jason himself was responsible for the transformation of the city into a Polis and the empowerment of the Hellenizers, he remained a scion of the house of Zadok, the rightful High Priest, the preserver of the direct connection between the God of Israel and its people.

Within the hall, the elders of the nation waited silently. Tension was high. Everyone eagerly awaited Jason's response to the rumor of Menelaus' appointment to take his place.

Jason entered the hall at a brisk pace, standing at its center, patronizingly and impatiently signaling at the elder standing there to vacate the location and seat himself among everyone else. The expression of the elder made clear that his pride was injured, but despite the clear insult he honored the office of the High Priest and slowly moved aside.

Jason's face glistened with beads of sweat. He seemed tense but in control, seeking to conceal the rage he was filled with. He looked around him, sternly meeting the eyes of the elders surrounding him. He had no intention of flattering them. He knew that many among them were not displeased with his misfortune. Some of those seated in the priest's row were his own relatives, who had never forgiven his betrayal of Hunio, and some of them even maintained contact with his brother. Nonetheless, he knew that they, too, would support him if they thought it would benefit them.

Joseph, who sat near Matityahu, leaned towards him and asked him in a whisper who the elder who had been dismissed by Jason was. Matityahu shook his head to signal his ignorance. Someone in the row before them turned towards them and whispered, "That was the priest Yismachel, a leader of the congregation in Jericho. He was a Zadok loyalist until Jason overthrew Hunio."

"As were we all," responded Matityahu, but gestured at him to fall silent so that he could hear Jason, who had just started to speak.

"I'll get straight to the point. The priest Menelaus, whom I sent to the king with the annual taxes from Judea, promised the king double the taxes if he is appointed High Priest in my place. If this happens, then a terrible calamity will fall on all of Israel! For centuries, the divine commandment of keeping the

High Priesthood in the house of Zadok has been maintained. Many may have opposed my replacement of my brother Hunio, but this was an internal issue of the house of Zadok. The appointment of Menelaus is an affront to all of Israel…."

"When your Hellenizer friends toss you out you come to us!" someone from the crowd cut him off.

Jason turned, eyes blazing with fury at the speaker. No more was necessary to restrain him. Matityahu knew the shouter. He was a usually soft-spoken and pleasant man called Hillel ben Gera, who lived in Jerusalem with his family. He had a small workshop for pots and domestic tools, as well as a small plot outside the walls of Jerusalem on which his family nurtured an olive tree orchard. It was apparent that he hated Jason, but that he feared him even more. He sank down in his seat, as if seeking to disappear, shocked at his own temerity and terrified at Jason's anger.

"What's with him?" murmured Matityahu quietly, shocked at the man's lack of confidence.

"Poor ben Gera," whispered someone at his side. "He could not keep up with the taxes and fell into debt. He has become a serf of a Hellenizer who is a citizen of the Polis. Only thanks to Jason's intervention were his children not carried off into slavery to pay his debts. Many of the traditional Jews in Jerusalem and its environs have fallen into the same trap. The Hellenizers are making a killing on our debts. The more taxes are raised, the wealthier they grow."

Jason continued his speech. His audience, having watched him make an object lesson of ben Gera, did not dare interrupt him again. "Some of you may have a hard time understanding this, but what I did was aimed at preventing precisely the disaster we now face. It was clear to me that if we failed to make a change and open ourselves to the Hellene culture which dominates the world, we would risk war with it—a war which we would have no chance of winning. That is why I opened up a channel of mutual respect and communication between the advanced Hellene culture and our own ancient and illustrious legacy. Thanks to the changes I had made, we, both traditionalists and worldly Jews who have adopted Western Hellene culture, have remained a single united people. Yes, it is true that friction and difficulties between us exist, but had I not acted as I did, we would have found ourselves standing on the brink of an abyss. However, there are elements among us who seek more. These extremist elements, filled with greed and the lust for power, will do anything to promote their personal ambitions. These are the elements who are behind Menelaus' grasp for power. They seek total Hellenization, and to achieve their aims they require a priest whose authority does not derive from his lineage, and who will therefore totally be dependent on them."

Jason looked at his audience, trying to decipher their mood.

"Menelaus is arriving at the head of a column of the king's soldiers," said someone, "what does it matter what we say? The king has made up his mind."

Many nodded in agreement.

"The king does not care who leads us. All that he cares about is collecting as much tax as possible," answered Jason. "The commander of the local garrison is higher-ranked than the officer commanding the column accompanying Menelaus, and he and I have excellent relations. Moreover, he and the other local officers can scent the coming war with Egypt, and it is by no means clear who will be the victor. Under these conditions, they prefer me over Menelaus, due to my excellent relations with the Egyptians. They will give us a day or two to settle matters amongst ourselves, as was their custom until this time, and only then will they intervene to enforce order. Many of the citizens of the Polis support me. All those who wish to achieve progress without tearing our people apart, all those who wish us to stay united as the Children of Israel, traditionalist and worldly alike, will support me. If the people unite behind the House of Zadok, Menelaus and his supporters will back down."

Yismachel stood in place. He clenched his jaw and stared at Jason. It was clear that Jason's words did not penetrate his heart.

Silence fell across the hall as all eyes turned to Yismachel.

"The United Kingdom of Israel survived just three kings before being torn asunder by the high taxes forced on the people by a young king, who had isolated himself from the concerns of the people and their difficulties.[18] It is you who first volunteered to raise the tax burden on your people, without a moment's hesitation, all in the name of advancing your personal ambitions. Now Menelaus has done the same. None of you are worthy to lead our people...."

"If you support me, I will work to reduce the tax burden," Jason interjected, well aware of the incredulity with which his assurances were received.

Yismachel ignored him and carried on. "Some say we have no more need for a High Priesthood which is inherited across generations. Prophecy has ended, as has the transmission of

18　In the early days of the reign of King *Rehoboam,* son of Solomon, the representatives of the people asked that he ease the tax burden. Rehoboam decided to raise it instead and replied with the sentence "My father tormented you with whips, I will torment you with scorpions." Subsequently, a rebellion broke out which split the land into the kingdoms of Judea and Israel. Kings 1, Chapter 12.

the word of God to the people via the High Priest." Yismachel nodded towards Yose ben Yoezer and Yose ben Yohanan. "The sages claim that they are capable of interpreting the Mitzvot and leading the people. Such opinions were also heard during the time of your righteous father," Yismachel turned back to Jason. "He was attentive to the will of the people and concluded that the sages must be made part of the leadership. Accordingly, he appointed Antigonus of Sokho to be president of the elder council beneath him. Nonetheless, we all honored your father and remained loyal to him. You, by your flattery of the Hellenes and the Hellenizers, by turning your back on the traditions of our forefathers, by selling out your people, have, by your own actions, brought about the fall of your father's house!"

Jason paled at the harsh words flung at him. No one had ever dared address him in such a manner in public. He glared furiously at Yismachel, but was too stunned to respond. Yose ben Yoezer and Yose ben Yohanan shifted uncomfortably in their chairs. Others nodded in agreement and support of the words of Yismachel.

"However, in spite of my words," added Yismachel, "I think we have to support Jason. Not for his sake, and not out of misplaced loyalty to his family, but for the good of the people. If we permit the existence of power struggles for the High Priesthood we will be playing into the hands of the king, and eventually we will have a Hellen governor placed over us, just as every nation in the kingdom has, and we will lose the autonomy we have hitherto enjoyed in our internal matters as well. That is why I am approaching you, my friends, the elders of the nation and its sages, and claim we must support the house of Zadok, and notify the king that the tradition of our forefathers requires the high priest to come solely from the house of Zadok."

Jason took a deep breath in relief, holding on to the hope that the elders would accept the recommendation of Yismachel. He looked at the line of priests, hoping for their support. Amongst them sat a forty-year-old priest, a distant relative called More-Tzedek[19]. His father was amongst the leaders of the Jewish community in Damascus, and he had become one of the close associates of Hunio ever since he had become an exile in Antioch. More-Tzedek stared at him accusingly. It was clear that he held Jason responsible for the entire situation.

The elders consulted in whispers amongst themselves. Finally, Yose ben Yoezer rose and spoke. "Our minds are with Yismachel on this matter. But what guarantee do we have that the soldiers will close their eyes and permit us to work things out on our own?"

"Trust me on this," said Jason with great confidence. "The Hellenist authorities have the greatest respect to the elder councils of the Polis. They are considered to be representative of the will of the people...."

"That is inaccurate, Jason," Yose ben Yohanan replied firmly from where he was seated. "You yourself established the Polis Council, and made this Elder Council irrelevant! If the Polis Council is opposed to you, our support will have no effect. Moreover, we would be considered as acting against the will of the king, and it will be claimed against us that we are interfering in the affairs of the Polis."

Jason waited for a few minutes and then stated, as moderately as he was able, "The Polis council is split between support of me and support of Menelaus, and cannot therefore present a single united position. It is true that our people are now represented

---

19   Hebrew for "teacher of justice".

by two councils, one of the citizens of the Polis and one of the elders of the people. But the king is aware of this split—this is not unprecedented. Such a split has also occurred in other places where Polis were established but local leaders and traditions remained outside of it. When the king appointed me to establish the Polis in Jerusalem, the king's counselors themselves, in the presence of the king, cautioned me that I must respect the existing leadership institutions, at least for a transitional period of a few years...."

Cries of outrage rose from the crowd. Yose ben Yoezer stepped forward, facing Jason. "You just revealed to us that you intended to eventually abolish this council! How dare you imagine that we would support you now?!"

Jason placed his right hand over his heart and stretched his left hand forward to Yose ben Yoezer in supplication. "It is the exact opposite. This is the way of the Seleucid regime, but this is also the proof that I was right in my approach of cooperating with them but maintaining the ability to influence and adapt developments to our special character. I give you my word in the name of my Zadokite ancestors that I had no intention of abolishing this council. I say this to you clearly: the king will not wish to act in opposition to the will of the elders of the people presented by you. Do as you wish. I strongly advise you to support me for your own sake."

Jason had no intention of getting dragged down into further debates. He made do with his declaration and left the hall. The real war against Menelaus would be carried out by his armed loyalists, and he had little time to get ready.

Judah returned after a few hours to the Temple. He found his parents troubled and agitated. His father filled him in briefly on events.

"Did you meet your friend's father?" asked Matityahu, "It is precisely people like him that are important to us right now; people who straddle both sides of the dividing line, Hellenizers who are simultaneously loyal to the laws of our forefathers."

"They left, father. The Hakotz family moved to an estate outside Jerusalem. I visited Phidias and Kratos, but they too had heard nothing from Eupolemus."

The holiday continued with a tense environment and without the presence of the High Priest at the rituals. At the conclusion of the holidays, the pilgrims began to leave Jerusalem and return to their homes. Matityahu and the men of Modi'in left with heavy hearts, concerned for the future.

A few days after the Shavuot, Menelaus returned to the city accompanied by his military escort. Jerusalem was plunged into savage conflict. His supporters from the house of Tuvia deliberately inflamed the conflict using foreign mercenaries. Riots broke out between Jason's supporters and those of Menelaus. The garrison commander feared loss of control and intervened sooner than Jason had expected. He unleashed his soldiers against Jason's men, treating them as rebels against the king and his authorized representative, Menelaus. Jason lost control of his own men. Soon the streets of the city ran crimson with blood and were choked with the wounded and the slain. Jason, acknowledging defeat, fled the city.

During these dramatic events, the senior priests of the house of Zadok, once they realized that Jason had no hope of victory, launched a secret contingency plan. As Jews were being slain in the streets of Jerusalem at the hands of their brothers and Seleucid soldiers, and the High Priesthood of the House of Zadok faced an end, a group of priests led by More-Tzedek rushed to the Temple, feeling that the task of rescuing the entirety of Jewish heritage was on them. They secretly entered the Temple library and began to rapidly sort and pack the ancient and sacred vellum scrolls. Some of them, the Torah books and books of prophecy, were smuggled away to the mountains East of Jerusalem, and from there were carried to hiding places in the caves of the wilderness of Judah, in the cliffs facing the Dead Sea. A select few were chosen to live near the caves and preserve and guard the scrolls.

170 BCE—Riots in Jerusalem

Dramatis Personae
Bold = main character
* = historical figure

- **Kratos**—*Greek tutor of Judah and Eupolemus*
- **Matityahu***—*Father of Judah and his brothers, village priest of Modi'in*
- **Eupolemus***—*Friend of Judah, son of Yohanan ben Hakotz*
- **Menelaus***—*Non-Zadokite High Priest in Jerusalem from 171 BCE onwards. Appointed by Antiochus IV in place of the Zadokite Jason*
- **Phidias**—*Pankration trainer*
- Lysimachus*—*Brother of High Priest Menelaus*
- Andronicus*—*Representative of King Antiochus IV*
- **Hunio III***—*Zadokite High Priest until 175 BCE, when he was replaced by Antiochus IV with his brother Jason*
- Strategos Ptolemy*—*The current ruler of Coele Syria, oversees all of the Meridarchies in the province, including Judea and Samaria*

A wagon hitched to two horses slowly approached the village. A single man was seated on the coachman's seat, holding the reins lightly. A group of children playing in the field noticed the wagons first. Often, tax collectors reached the village with their armed guards. In those cases, the children were trained to run into the fields and call the men. But a single wagon did not seem to the children to be dangerous, and they gave in to their natural curiosity and approached the chariot. The wagon coach was covered so they could not see who was in it. The children halted shortly before the wagon. The coachman smiled at them. "Have no fear, children."

The curtain of the wagon carriage was brushed aside, and an older man got out, sitting on the seat by the coachman.

"Are we there?" he asked in Greek.

"We have arrived at a village, but I am not certain it is the one we seek."

The wagon reached the children, who made way for it, standing at the side of the road.

"Young man," said the coachman to the oldest boy in Aramaic, trying to win his trust with a simple compliment, "we are looking for Judah, son of Matityahu. We have brought him a letter from his friend Eupolemus."

The children exchanged rapid glances that gave away their familiarity with Judah, but said nothing. The oldest boy glanced at one of the other children and he ran at once up the path towards the village.

"We will take you to the village and then we will see," he replied to the man. Together with the other children he began to walk by the side of the wagon, keeping a safe distance from it.

"They are behaving like little soldiers," said the coachman in Greek to the older man by his side, and the two laughed lightly.

Matityahu recognized Kratos from afar. He maintained a frozen expression, trying to push the possibility of additional bad news out of his mind. Ever since Menelaus had seized power, the traditional Jewish villagers lived in constant fear of the developments in Jerusalem, or of new taxes they would be subjected to. He stared at the ground and waited for the wagon to approach him. Rebecca was in the house. The boys were not around. He lifted his eyes in concern, but Kratos' smiling expression soothed his worries.

"Welcome, Kratos. What brings you to us? I hope that this is good news for a change…."

"Greetings, Matityahu. I received a letter from Eupolemus, your son's friend, and he asked that I bring it to you."

Matityahu sent the children that had accompanied the wagon to collect all the members of the family from the fields. He knew that the news would soon attract everyone in the village, not merely his family. A letter from a faraway country was a very special event in such a small and quiet village as Modi'in. Meanwhile, Rebecca brought some fruits, bread, goat cheese, and olives, and then a pitcher with water for the guests. Matityahu invited Kratos and his coachman to sit in the shade of the house.

Word of the arrival of the guests and the letter they carried soon spread, and men, women, and children began to cluster around Matityahu's home. Matityahu held the letter, which was covered in dense writing. Everyone who arrived and asked about the letter was jokingly reprimanded by Matityahu to wait patiently for the arrival of Judah, who was, after all, the recipient.

In the meantime, Kratos filled in Matityahu and his audience with the situation in Jerusalem and the kingdom:

"Rumors from Antioch speak of war brewing between Egypt and the Seleucid Kingdom. At the moment all that is taking place is provocations and localized border skirmishes, but it is only a matter of time before a true battle takes place. Both sides have sent missions to Rome accusing the other of perfidy, hoping to acquire the support of the Roman Senate.

In Jerusalem, since Menelaus has been appointed, ahh, I understand that things have developed not so well for people like you, as you surely know," ended Kratos with an uncomfortable smile.

"No, no, tell us what is new, say what you know," the crowd eagerly called.

Kratos continued, "Well, Menelaus and those of your people who support full adoption of the Hellenic customs, the Hellenizers as you call them, have completed transforming Jerusalem into a Hellene Polis for all intents and purposes. Several new temples to the Greek gods have been established, the Sabbath is no longer observed, and barely any traditional Jews remain in the city—they have all fled to the neighboring villages. At the same time, a harsh and cruel process of enslavement of those traditional Jews who can no longer keep up with the tax burden has taken place.

The tax collectors are meeting difficulties in keeping up with the quotas Menelaus has committed to, and matters have grown so severe that Menelaus and the royal tax overseer have been summoned to Antioch next month for an inquiry. It is said that Menelaus has no additional sources of taxation he can draw upon."

Most of the villagers had now gathered, filling the shaded area under the shed. Some stood in the sun and listened from without. Kratos' news was of such interest to the crowd that even the children fell silent and permitted the elders to hear what was spoken.

Judah arrived and was excited to see Kratos. They embraced each other for a long moment while everyone around smiled, moved by Judah's expression of emotion. Then Kratos told Judah he had with him a letter from Eupolemus.

"Father, this is a personal letter, why did you gather everyone together?!" said Judah lightly.

"Child, in these difficult days, such a letter is a public asset. Thank us for waiting for you to show up," Matityahu told him to the laughter of the assembled crowd. "But before you get started on reading it to us, I would be interested to hear what you, Kratos, think of all these developments in Jerusalem."

Kratos cleared his throat, locked his gaze with Matityahu and spoke deliberately, "There is much beauty in the Hellene culture my people brought to Asia. However, Alexander the Great also believed that there were many beautiful and useful things in the cultures of the East and he sought to merge and take the best of both. Your people, in contrast, have kept your traditions unsullied to this day. You know, Matityahu, that I greatly admire your traditions and the wisdom of your sacred teachings. There are many others like me in the world. However, like Alexander the Great, I believe that the proper way is to integrate and merge the cultures. It may be that your faith in a single, all-powerful god is wiser and truer than faith in a multitude of gods with human characteristics and appearance. Still, the Hellene concept of all people being potential Polis citizens with rights that no man, not even the king, can transgress is incredibly wise. I believe that your prior High Priest was closer to finding the proper way to incorporate your traditions and sacred wisdom to the Hellenic culture. I fear that your current High Priest has simply given in to the pressures of special interests at the cost of abolishing and destroying all that is true and right in your customs...."

A heavy silence fell on the assembly once Kratos concluded. Kratos, as a disinterested observer, summed up the situation in such a clear-eyed manner that any further discussion seemed superfluous

A few moments later, Judah opened the letter and began reading aloud:

"Dear Kratos,

Greetings. I hope that you are doing well in training more cheeky youths like we once were. I write to you, to my family, and to Judah in a single letter sent from the farthest edges of the Roman Dominion. The mail in the lands ruled by Rome is amazingly efficient, but I doubt this is so in the lands between Rome and my home. Should this letter reach you, I ask that you bring it to the hands of my family, and then to Judah in Modi'in.

I arrived with the Roman Legions in Iberia, a distant land whose name I had never heard in Judea. I have done well, and I am now an officer commanding two squads, each twelve warriors strong. This is a special unit unlike any in the entire Roman Army, and I am honored to have had the chance to influence its establishment and determine its methods of operation. Yes, you heard it right. It seems to be that a suggestion Eupolemus from little Judea made following an ambush me and my comrades survived has influenced the combat theory and training of my legion. That ended with me being placed directly under the commander of the Legion and my men are the finest unit in the entire Fifth Legion. Our specialty is that we have made espionage into a professional specialization, which incorporates an ability to strike deep behind enemy lines. However, aside from the activity of my own unit and local skirmishes, our Legion has not participated in any real fighting since we arrived. Scuffles between Hellenizer and traditional teenagers in Jerusalem are more dangerous than anything we have experienced here to date…."

A wave of laughter passed through the crowd and Judah used it to take a brief break.

"He is enjoying himself there and we are suffering here. This is where a real war is being fought," someone cried out.

Cries of agreement rose from the crowd. Judah continued reading:

"As a soldier, one desires to fight. Word is coming in of events on the Eastern front in the war between Rome and Macedon. The Macedonian army has experienced success after success, whereas Rome has suffered repeated defeats. We are pretty frustrated here, and hope our Legion will be sent to Macedon to participate in the fighting. So far, only a limited number of our officers have been so lucky.

I hope Phidias is still in shape. I miss my training with him and Judah. I am sure he has won great achievements for Jason's team, and hope that he is well and that his health is sound.

Father, I have not forgotten the customs of our people and I observe them as far as I am able. My commanders and comrades respect this and make it possible for me to observe the Shabbat, except, of course, when we are in action. We even instituted a special dinner on Friday evening, which reminds me of the feeling of holiness on this occasion back home. Please send my love to all of my family.

Judah, you would shine here. The men of Rome are brave and wise in the arts of war, but you would have surpassed them all.

I hope that you are well, that Jerusalem and Judea are peaceful and prosperous. I love and miss you.

Eupolemus."

The next day, Kratos continued on his journey, leaving the land of the Jews behind him for all time.

A few weeks passed. Dreary routine seemed to have returned to Modi'in. One day, a company of soldiers was seen galloping in the distance, headed eastwards. Throughout the day, the men tried to guess what affair the company was involved in, but only late the next evening did the situation become clear. A group of people from the villages around Jerusalem arrived in Modi'in. Some were injured. They updated the men of the village on developments in Jerusalem over the past few days: Menelaus had been summoned for an inquiry in Antioch for failing to meet the tax quotas he had committed to achieve for the king. He had left his brother Lysichamus in charge of the city in his absence. This man turned out to be a criminal, who robbed the Temple treasury. Rumor of this spread throughout the city and its environs. Hundreds of people gathered around the Temple, and thousands more streamed into Jerusalem from the neighboring settlements. Moderate Hellenizers, as well as traditional Jews, all felt cheated and betrayed. The unrest frightened Lysichamus. He sent in the garrison and his loyalists amongst the radical Hellenizers to break the crowd up. The city was consumed by riots. The garrison, which was unprepared for an event of this magnitude, withdrew into the fortress and called for additional forces to aid them. The outraged crowd captured Lysichamus and executed him. Within a single day the garrison commander was able to bring in reinforcements and regain control of the city. Many were wounded or were killed during the riots.

The men of Modi'in feared for the safety of the people of Jerusalem and its environs, and decided to send a mission to Jerusalem. This mission included Matityahu's sons Yohanan, Simon, and Judah.

A week later the mission returned to the village with grave news. The riots had died down. However, when Menelaus had reached Antioch, he had met there Andronicus, the representative of the king, for the king had left the city to deal with other urgent business of the kingdom. In the meantime, Hunio, the exiled High Priest, revealed that Menelaus had removed gold and silver vessels from the Temple and sold them on his way to Antioch in order to meet the tax quota. The Jewish community in Antioch was outraged and demanded Menelaus be punished, but he was able to bribe Andronicus and win his support. Hunio was murdered in his home, and although the authorities claimed it was but a robbery, an accusing finger was directed at Menelaus and Andronicus. The death of the final legitimate High Priest, the scion of the House of Zadok, distracted the Jews of Antioch from the theft of the Temple treasury and led the Jews of Antioch to sink into a deep grief.

The members of the committee could not say any more, but over the next week additional news came in. it turned out that Andronicus had taken advantage of the absence of the king from Antioch in order to eliminate the king's nephew, who had supposedly shared rule with him over the past five years. Many believed that Andronicus was acting on the king's orders, but the king, who was summoned back to the capital, protested his innocence to the queen and had Andronicus executed.

In the meantime, Menelaus, who had heard of the riots in Jerusalem and the death of his brother, rushed back to Tyre, where he petitioned the governor of Coele Syria, Strategos Ptolemy, for aid. In parallel, the council of traditionalist Jewish Elders sent a mission of three dignitaries to the Strategos, to complain of the actions of Menelaus and his brother, and to petition that Menelaus be punished. Surprisingly, the king himself arrived in Tyre. However, much to the disappointment of the Jews of the city, who sided with the Judean representatives, he ruled in favor of Menelaus. In his rage at the Jews who had rebelled against Menelaus and his brother in Jerusalem, the king executed the three elders from Judea, expressing his refusal to recognize the traditional Jewish elder assembly in contrast to the Polis Citizens' Council. The king reconfirmed the appointment of Menelaus as High Priest and ruler of Judea. He further ordered Ptolemy to equip Menelaus with a reinforcement of soldiers and provide him with any help he might require in order to collect the tax quota he had undertaken to meet.

169 BCE—Emissary of Rome

Dramatis Personae
Bold = main character
* = historical figure

- *More-Tzedek*—A priest and traditionalist leader, a Zadokite loyalist*
- *Jason*—Last Zadokite High Priest, served as High Priest between 175 and 171 BCE*
- *Menelaus*—Current High Priest, appointed in 175 BCE by Antiochus IV*
- *Hunio IV*—Son of the Zadokite Hunio III*
- *Mithridates (Antiochus IV) *—King of the Seleucid Kingdom from 175 BCE onwards. Also titled Antiochus Epiphanes—Divine Antiochus*
- *Gaius Popillius Laenas*—A Roman envoy*
- *Matityahu*—The father of Judah and his brothers, village priest of Modi'in*

More-Tzedek and Jason had agreed to meet on the banks of the Jordan River, opposite Jericho, at the site where, according to tradition, the Children of Israel crossed the river before entering the Land of Israel. Jason emerged from the East Bank accompanied by armed horsemen. More-Tzedek awaited him, alone, on the West Bank. When

Jason arrived, More-Tzedek removed his tunic and swam across.

The two shook hands. They did not embrace. There was no affection lost between them.

"Tell me about developments in Jerusalem," said Jason.

"It is getting worse every day. Menelaus has betrayed the laws of our People and turned aside from our path. In the first year of his rule I yet hoped that he would cleave to the true path. After all, he is a priest. I wrote him a letter summarizing the central pillars of the Torah, hoping he would at least uphold these most sacred of laws. But he is steeped in evil. He has surrounded himself with despoilers, and extorts and pillages our brother Jews in order to meet the tax quota he has promised the king. Ever since the murder of Hunio and the opposition of the elder council to him, he has forbidden its members from gathering in the Temple and avoids visiting it. As far as he is concerned, only the Polis Citizen Council exists and has status now. He does not maintain the duties of the High Priest, and the work of the Temple is performed by a small number of loyalist priests."

"I am in contact with my nephew Hunio IV. He has been received in Egypt with great honor and has received the blessing of Egypt's king to establish a new temple. He will not return to Judea!"

Jason watched More-Tzedek closely for his reaction to this news. He expected that news of young Hunio establishing a temple and remaining in Egypt for all time would shock him. It meant that Jason would remain as the sole legal Zadokite candidate for the high priesthood, regardless of his responsibility for the chain of events leading to the current situation.

"I have heard of this and have written to him," responded More-Tzedek. "He is the rightful High Priest. He will have to return to Judea when the time comes."

"War will soon begin. Ever since the death of Queen Cleopatra, the king of Egypt has plotted to restore Coele-Syria to his rule. When that happens, it will be I who returns to Jerusalem."

More-Tzedek was silent, but Jason could tell by his expression what he thought. "I know that you are still angry at me. I promise you that things will be different this time. I will make things right for our people and amend the mistakes of the past. Tell our people to hold on."

More-Tzedek looked right through him, his eyes blank. For some time now, he had been hearing voices. Thoughts and ideas which simply could not be his own flowed through him. He too was a scion of the house of Zadok and enjoyed the support of Hunio III prior to his death. If young Hunio had settled down in Egypt and Jason was unworthy... "We will hold on. God is with us." He turned around and slowly entered the river, headed to the other bank.

***

War broke out in early spring. Mithridates, also called Antiochus Epiphanes, passed through Judea at the head of the Seleucid army on his way to Egypt. Word of the strength of the army and its size spread throughout the land. Eye witnesses who saw the army pass wondered at the size of the mighty elephants, the cavalry, and the phalanx formations and their long Sarissas. The armies assembled for a fateful battle by the fort of Pelusium, at the eastern edge of the great Nile Delta. The battle ended in a crushing Egyptian defeat, with thousands of them falling captive.

Although the war was far from lost and the fort of Pelusium still stood, the advisors of the king of Egypt, Ptolemy VI, chose to smuggle him away by boat. However, the fleet of Mithridates dominated the sea and took the young king of Egypt captive. With the king of Egypt in his hands, Mithridates purchased the heart of the Egyptian army and its commanders by releasing the thousands of Egyptian soldiers he had taken captive unharmed. He informed the leaders of the Egyptian Army that there was no reason left to fight and that he had no intention of conquering Egypt, but only of spreading his protection over Ptolemy VI so that he would be able to continue to rule. Pelusium soon surrendered without a fight. The Seleucid army rapidly took over all of Lower Egypt, with the exception of Alexandria, the capital, whose garrison refused to surrender. The Alexandrians furthermore crowned Ptolemy's younger brother, only twelve years old, and prepared for a long siege.

Mithridates crowned himself Pharaoh and claimed to be protecting Ptolemy VI from the rebels in Alexandria and that he intended to restore the proper king to power. Although his army lacked siege engines and was unprepared to capture a large and fortified city, he nonetheless besieged Alexandria. The Alexandrians, in the meantime, sent a mission to Rome requesting aid.

Rome was mired at the time in Macedonian muck. Its legions had been defeated repeatedly by Macedon's mighty phalanx army. The siege of Alexandria, the chief port of Egypt, disrupted the grain supply to Rome, leading to a rise in the price of bread in the city. The Roman Senate sent an emissary to Egypt to meet with Mithridates and work to remove the siege from Alexandria.

Mithridates received the Roman emissary in his tent, seated on a raised chair, his chief officers and advisers at his side. A king receiving an emissary for an interview. He felt on top of the world. The conquest of Egypt was an achievement which overshadowed even those of his father. His army has proven its strength and he had proven his greatness. Rome, whom he had so feared, had proven itself incapable of dealing with the army of Macedon, which Mithridates judged to be weaker than his own.

"Gaius Popillius Laenas, Emissary of Rome, brings you the greetings of the Senate," the ambassador said officially, icily staring at Mithridates.

"Welcome, Emissary of Rome. What brings you here to us?" Mithridates responded, ignoring the customary pleasantries in the face of this patronizing and tough man. He knew well the mindset of these Romans, who thought of themselves as the lords of the entire world.

Gaius was a solid and relatively short man. He had a very simple, one-dimensional worldview: Rome and her allies were good, and everyone else was either a barbarian or a pathetic attempt by barbarians to mimic the civilized Romans, who held the most advanced Republican government in the entire world. As was the case with many Romans, his attitude towards the Greeks was conflicted. On the one hand, Rome had copied the Greeks in many fields. But on the other hand, Rome did everything much better than they ever could, the proof of it being that Rome was the mightiest power in the World, while the Greek city states were now its protectorates and clients. The Macedonians were not considered by him to be worthy even of such respect as he was prepared to extend the Greeks, nor were the kingdoms founded by the Macedonian generals in Egypt and Asia. Towards Mithridates, a man of Macedonian origins who had spent much of his youth as a hostage in Rome, Gaius felt deep repugnance.

"The Senate is concerned with disruptions to the grain supply to Rome and holds you responsible for it! I hereby inform you that the Senate will not be pleased should you attack Alexandria," Gaius said sternly.

"The Senate will not be pleased?!" Mithridates raised his voice, striking a frightened pose but smiling at his men, who replied with mocking grins at the Roman emissaries. "But is this not the same Senate whose armies are defeated by the armies of Macedon?! May I remind you that I am ruler of the Seleucid Empire, ruler of Egypt, Syria, Medea, and Babylon."

Gaius felt rage rise within him. He knew that he could not return from his mission with a negative response. The city of Rome had too many mouths to feed, and it could not bear a rise in the price of bread. However, given the quagmire in Macedon, Rome could not at this time act against the Seleucid army. He must therefore sway Mithridates into ending the siege of Alexandria.

"The Senate will… be pleased if you end the siege of Alexandria," Gaius responded with the most diplomatic tone he could manage, his hatred for Mithridates nearly choking the words in his mouth.

"Now that sounds better," replied Mithridates, "I am a friend of the Senate. I will carefully consider your **requests**."

"I must return to the Senate with an answer. I will be grateful if you provide me with one."

Mithridates knew that his army was not prepared for the long siege required for the conquest of Alexandria. Furthermore, winter was coming, and the Nile River might overflow its banks, which would make waging war difficult and even put his army at risk. The Senate was not asking him to loosen his grip on Egypt after all, only to remove the siege on Alexandria, in order to avoid harming the grain supply to Rome. This wouldn't stop him from returning the next summer, properly prepared, and taking Alexandria by storm.

"You may inform the Senate that Antiochus Epiphanes is concerned by the difficulties of his friends and is responsive to them. The siege of Alexandria will end. I ask that you emphasize to the Senate that, as far as I am concerned, the treaty of Apamea which Rome forced my father to sign—and in particular the limitations imposed on the military of my father—is null and void. I am withdrawing from Alexandria as a gesture to Rome as a friend of the Senate."

Gaius nodded lightly, a gesture which was more of a confirmation of having heard Antiochus' words than an expression of thanks. He spun on his heels and rapidly withdrew from the tent.

Mithridates left Ptolemy VI in Pelusium and removed most of his army from Egypt, which was left in a state of uncertainty. Ptolemy VI supposedly ruled most of Egypt as a puppet king under the protection of Antiochus, while his brother ruled in Alexandria. The grain supply to Rome was renewed.

The Seleucid army passed through the Land of Israel on its way back to Syria. Mithridates decided to take advantage of the opportunity to visit the Polis of Jerusalem. An announcement that the king was arriving at the head of part of the army was transferred to Menelaus.

In Jerusalem, the leaders of the Polis convened for an emergency session. Menelaus understood that the king was not making a courtesy call. The taxes collected from Judea had not reached the quota he had committed to, and he feared that the king was arriving to collect the bill. He made clear to the citizens of the Polis that they would all have to share the burden.

The next day, at noon, the convoy of the king was expected to reach Jerusalem. At dawn, Menelaus published a decree forbidding traditionalists from approaching the Temple and the space between it and the garrison fortress. He also instructed the garrison and his own mercenaries to spread throughout the city and ensure that the decree be fully applied. He could not permit anyone to take advantage of the situation to raise complaints against him before the king.

Menelaus and the dignitaries of the Polis emerged to receive the king's convoy outside the city gates. Towards noon they noticed a dust cloud rapidly approaching the city from afar. Several dozen flag-bearers rode ahead of the main force. The manes and tails of the horses fluttered in the wind as they galloped towards them.

The horsemen did not slow down as they approached, leading Menelaus to fear that they intended to trample him. The dust cloud covered him and his escorts, when the leading horseman suddenly halted in front of him, displaying almost unbelievable control of his horse. The other horsemen halted similarly, in a formation which flanked them on both sides.

"King Antiochus Epiphanes is arriving!" thundered the leading horseman towards them, "Who are you?"

"I am Menelaus, High Priest and leader of the Polis...."

"Prepare to greet your king," the horseman shouted at him, and passed him by, ordering his men as he went. Some of the horsemen now entered through the gates, seizing the dominant positions that would secure the entry of the king into the city.

King Antiochus Epiphanes approached the city at the head of a massive column of cavalry.

Menelaus could feel his legs shake and his throat dry out in trepidation.

The king halted before him and stared at him in mockery and scorn from the heights of his mount.

Menelaus kneeled and gestured at his men to do the same. "Your Highness... the citizens of the Polis of Jerusalem are delighted at the honor... which has befallen us in hosting you in our city," he said as he kneeled before the king, his voice trembling with fear.

Mithridates nodded without responding. He lifted his eyes to the walls of the city and the mountains surrounding it. He liked the place. He glanced again at the High Priest before him and his entourage. "High Priest Menelaus, you promised me much but failed to deliver. In the past you excused your failure by the traditionalists' lack of cooperation. I provided you with more soldiers...."

Menelaus paled. This is my end, he thought. He will remove me from office. He tried hard to suppress his panic. "Your Majesty, I am making every effort, and we have very nearly reached the quota. I told all of the citizens that they would have to contribute more...."

"I was told that your Temple holds treasure," the king cut him off, "Lead us there!"

He does not mean to punish me, thought Menelaus with relief. But what is there to take from the Temple? The sacrilege at the entry of the king into the Temple did not even cross his mind.

Accompanied by Menelaus and feeling like a god, Antiochus Epiphanes penetrated the depths of the Jewish Temple. No one dared stand in his way. Since Menelaus was made High Priest, the status of the Temple had deteriorated. Traditional Jews had ceased to deposit their savings there. The heavy tax burden had led many of them to withdraw those accounts which they had previously deposited in the Temple. When Antiochus realized that the Temple treasury was nearly empty he was overcome with a fit of rage. He shoved Menelaus off and roared that if he could not meet his tax quota he would have to make up the shortfall by reducing his people to slavery. In the meantime, the king ordered his men to strip the Temple of everything of value—the golden menorah, all the golden and silver vessels, the silk fabrics and the golden threaded cloth. It was all looted, while violating the most sacred site to the Jewish People.

Once word of the desecration spread, Jews throughout the world grieved. In the Land of Israel, and particularly in Judea, traditionalists took it particularly hard. Every holiday and celebration, even weddings, began in keening and with mourning. Throughout the land, apocalyptic prophets who declared that God had abandoned the Temple and his chosen people with it roamed across the land. Feelings of loss, apocalyptic catastrophe, and destruction led to despair amongst many.

In Modi'in, Matityahu was shocked to his core when word of the sacrilege arrived. He called together everyone in the village, men and women, elders and babes.

"This is the true test of our faith and loyalty to the God of Israel. At such a time, the only thing we can do is draw strength from our faith and from our history. The Temple was already destroyed once, and our spirit did not weaken. On the contrary, it is precisely when a cataclysm strikes that we are at our best, that we purify our spirits and grow stronger in the observation of our faith. The destruction of the First Temple did not break us, nor did exile, and we will not give up now," swore Matityahu to his audience.

There were other local leaders who, like Matityahu, displayed leadership and succored their people in their time of need. Groups of faithful believers drew together into devout communities, and, given the situation, grew more radical in their religious observances, seeking to maintain a strict religious life-style. Rumors spread throughout the land about a community of mystic hermits in the wilderness of Judea, on the shores of the Dead Sea, who devoutly upheld the Mitzvot and remained loyal to the House of Zadok. A priest by the name of More-Tzedek was said to lead them and serve as a source of religious authority and a spiritual anchor. These men shared their property, marked their days by the ancient Jewish sacred solar calendar, and maintained a life based on ritual purity and upholding the commandments of the Torah. In spite of their limited number, they saw themselves as a beacon of faith, and believed that they were preserving the traditions of the Jewish People in their most pure form. This dedication was, for them, a means of dealing with the horrors of that fateful period in which traditional Jews lost their spiritual leadership and sacred symbol—the High Priest and the Temple.

*Note to reader—you may now watch a movie relevant to the chapter you have just finished by either clicking the code or scanning it in an appropriate application. Alternatively, click on the following link: https://youtu.be/hoMTlQVADp8

168 BCE—The Tables Turn

> Dramatis Personae
> **Bold** = main character
> * = historical figure

- *Eupolemus*—*Childhood friend of Judah, son of Yohanan ben Hakotz*
- *Marcius Porcius Cato*—*Also known as Cato the elder, a Roman Patrician who filled various senior positions in the Roman administration*
- *Glitarius—The Roman friend of Judah and Eupolemus*
- *Cassandra—The sister of Glitarius*
- *Aemilius Paulus*—*A Roman Consul*
- *Fabius Maximus*—*The eldest son of Aemilius Paulus*
- *Marcus*—*The son of Cato*
- *Aulus Antonius*—*Tribune (one of the senior commanders) in Aemilius Paulus' legion*
- *Gaius Popillius Laenas*—*Roman envoy*
- *Mithridates* (*Antiochus IV*)*—*King of the Seleucid kingdom from 175 BCE onwards. Also titled Antiochus Epiphanes—Antiochus the Divine*
- *Yosef ben Hyrcanus*—*Jewish ruler of an estate in the Gilead, in the Transjordan*
- *Jason*—*Was appointed in 175 BCE to serve as High Priest, replacing his brother Hunio III, by King Antiochus*

- *Menelaus*—The current High Priest in Jerusalem. Was appointed by Antiochus IV in 171 BCE to replace Jason*
- *More-Tzedek*—The leader of a community of Zadokite loyalists in Kumaran, by the Dead Sea*
- *Flavius, Rango, Caesarius & Elaius—Eupolemus' comrades from the Fifth Legion*

E upolemus and five warriors who had served under his command returned to Rome following their discharge from the Legion. Eupolemus sent a messenger to Cato informing him of his return to Rome and asking to meet with him. He then bid farewell to his comrades from the legion and made his way to Glitarius' home.

In the time that had passed while Eupolemus was in the Legion, Glitarius had lost the remaining traces of his boyhood and had become a man. He did not seek to advance himself in the public hierarchy and hence chose not to seek a commission in the army, joining his father's business instead. He had not yet married and still lived in his parent's home. When he saw Eupolemus, he retained his Roman reserve despite his joy at being reunited with his friend. Eupolemus, who was used to the sternness and restraint that Romans held in such high esteem from his years of service in the legion, did the same. Glitarius' parents greeted him with much kindness and extended their hospitality, inviting him to once again stay at their home during his time in Rome. No sooner did he settle in than a messenger arrived at Glitarius' home and invited Eupolemus to a meeting with Cato.

The venerable senator met him for a private audience in his habitation in Rome.

"So, now that you have undergone the training of a soldier

and commander in the finest army in the world, where are you headed?" Cato asked Eupolemus after he spoke with him briefly about his experiences in the Legion.

Eupolemus noted tension in Cato's voice. "I intend to return to my homeland," he answered hesitantly, "I have heard that King Antiochus…."

"You have nothing to worry about regarding him," Cato cut him off abruptly. "We have kicked him out of Egypt and we will give him a final reckoning in due time. It is Rome that now needs good soldiers. We have been reaping disgrace and ridicule in this miserable war against Perseus the Macedonian for three years now. People are beginning to think that Rome has declined from greatness. Given this situation, many concerned citizens have called upon the General Lucius Aemilius Paullus to accept the Consulship. Aemilius is establishing a new legion in these very days. All the soldiers and officers being recruited to it are experienced men. This legion will join the forces already in the field and bring this pathetic war to a decisive end."

Cato concluded his impromptu speech and expectantly awaited Eupolemus' response. He was truly proud, both in his own person and in his perception of his status as the premier spokesman and representative of Rome, to explicitly ask Eupolemus to enlist in the new Legion.

Eupolemus knew that he owed much to Cato. He also liked the idea of finally participating in a real war. Many of the soldiers of the Fifth Legion had hoped to be called to Macedon to participate in this war, of which they had heard from afar as they were stationed in semi-indolence on the other side of the empire. He raised his eyes to meet Cato's blue eyes. They were icy cold.

"Patron, if the honored Consul will agree to accept me, I will be honored to join the Legion."

Cato's blue eyes blinked and were once again the smiling eyes of the grandfatherly elder statesman.

"A number of soldiers who served with me accompanied me in my return to Rome," continued Eupolemus, "and they too will be glad to join this new Legion."

"Aemilius' eldest son, Quintus Fabius Maximus, who is eighteen, as well as his younger seventeen-year old brother, Publius Cornelius Scipio, have joined this Legion."

Cato noted Eupolemus' surprise. "So, you noted that their names are different than their father's? Good, it shows you have learned the customs of Rome. Aemilius has four sons—too many for a father who must support and fund his heirs in cursus honorum[20]. That is why he handed them over for adoption to the esteemed houses of Fabius and Cornelius. In honor of his ancestral home they were granted a fourth name, Aemilius, which they will not pass on to their children. You understand, to the Patricians the name of the game is power and influence, and these come with the house. You can achieve stature as a new man through skill at war, but if you wish to guarantee your offspring a future, you need to marry into a high-stature house or get a notable from such a house to adopt you as his son."

Eupolemus nodded, but said nothing. He was not sure if Cato was hinting something about his own future prospects, or criticizing Aemilius or even the customs of Rome.

---

20 Meaning "course of offices"—a sequential order of public offices held by aspiring politicians in the Roman Republic. The cursus honorum comprised a mixture of military and political administration posts. Each office had a minimum age and wealth for election.

Once Cato realized Eupolemus was not intending to speak, he continued, "In any event, my own son Marcus is enlisting as well. You and your men will fight at their side. Bear in mind that you will not receive the position of a Centurion; Quintus may have promoted you to this rank, but that was because you commanded a special and unusual unit. You cannot command a true eighty-soldier Century."

Eupolemus nodded in agreement. His forehead crinkled with a newly risen thought. "Patron, don't you think it may be a good idea to form an intelligence and raiding unit like that formed in the Fifth Legion?"

"I will make sure that Aemilius hears of the idea."

Eupolemus nodded in thanks and then paused, considering. "You mentioned earlier that Rome had expelled Antiochus from Egypt?"

"The Seleucid army defeated the Ptolemy army and was about to conquer their last stronghold in Alexandria last year. The Senate sent Gaius Popillius Laenas to put affairs in order. Antiochus understood that he would not be wise to irritate Rome and left Egypt with his tail between his legs. Once we finish with the Macedonian affair, and this is only a matter of time, we will have the leisure to handle this Egyptian-Seleucid affair in order as well. The land you come from is right between the warring parties, is it not?"

"It is, and they have struggled for control over it more than once."

"Stick with us and I dare say you will not be sorry. A Roman Citizenship is the finest prize any man can ask for in this world. But first we must put paid to these Macedonians."

Eupolemus had arrived at Cato's home in a chariot driven by one of Glitarius' house slaves. On their way back, he noted that the carriage seemed to be taking a different path back than the one it took when he had arrived. The carriage pulled into a luxurious district of the city and halted by a home that seemed somehow unpretentious in comparison to the surrounding villas. The coachman gestured at him to descend. The gate of the villa was open, and a slave-girl stood within, holding a lantern in her hand.

"The Lady Cassandra invites you in, my lord," said the slave. Eupolemus leaned back in surprise. In the short time he had managed to spend with Glitarius prior to meeting Cato, his friend had updated him about his sister's fate. It turned out that Cassandra had married a patrician from a respected family two years previously and left her parent's home. Her husband had died in the Macedonian war only a few months after their wedding. She lived in a small home that her husband had left to her with a small number of slaves and servants. As the widow of an officer who fell in the line of duty she was entitled to a state pension for her entire life that was sufficient to enable her to live comfortably, if modestly.

"My lord, my mistress awaits you," the slave girl prodded him.

Eupolemus overcame his surprise and entered the dwelling, following her.

Cassandra was waiting for him in the parlor, lying drowsily on one of the reclining couches. Despite the late hour, she roused herself swiftly and had the house staff prepare and serve food and beverages to her guest. Eupolemus sat on one of the couches in silence and waited as slaves rushed to the room with platters of refreshments and flagons of beverages. In the meantime, he shamelessly looked at Cassandra, who stood in the center of the room and managed affairs. When he had last seen her, she was a beautiful girl, but with a somewhat boyish figure. She had since filled out, and as far as he was concerned, the changes to her figures were in exactly the right places and perfectly proportioned. Her long raven hair was partially upswept, with rebellious strands left loose to fall on her bare shoulders. Her eyes were precisely made up, emphasizing her green eyes and striking features.

When they were alone, Cassandra smiled and sat on a couch near the one he had selected.

"Did I surprise you?" she asked, smiling.

"A pleasant surprise. The years have treated you well. How are you doing?"

"As you can see, and as you have no doubt heard, I managed to get married, leave my parents' home, be widowed, and become the owner of my own home, property, and slaves. Not a bad set of accomplishments for a woman my age."

"I was sorry to hear of your loss."

"We had not had the time to have any children. Julius was a patrician through and through, and as such aspired to a public career which would entitle his descendants to hang his mask amongst his revered ancestors[21]. War is a rare opportunity for such a man to stand out and win renown. It is a shame; I truly did love him, and he loved me."

The shadow of sorrow stole across her face. She shook off a rebellious hair curl from her forehead, as if she were brushing off the thought of her late husband.

"You have a good-hearted look to your eyes. You always did. It is frequently smiling, even naughty, and sometimes shows

---

21   The Patrician households of Rome commonly displayed the death masks of those patriarchs of the clan who made great public or military achievements.

arrogance verging on presumption, but it is always touched by good that makes others wish to be with you. Have you ever been told that?"

Eupolemus blushed slightly. Cassandra rose from the couch and sat by his side, a light whiff of perfume travelling with her. She placed her hand on his arm and stroked it softly.

"Have you come to... comfort me?"

"Yes, I am a renowned widow-comforter," he replied with a smile.

"Some comfort you are. Aren't you leaving to the same war that killed my husband with Aemilius Paulus?"

His expression stiffened. He had just left Cato's home. How did she know what they had spoken about?

She smiled at his surprise, and, as if reading his mind, continued, "Cato and the other elder statesmen of the Republic are worried. They are concerned that something might burst the bubble of Rome's successes. They live in constant fear of the next Hannibal, who will defeat Rome's army in the field and then won't hesitate before moving in for the kill as Hannibal did. They are doing everything they can to support Aemilius, recruiting for him the finest soldiers and officers, seeking to help him build an invincible Legion. As soon as I heard about your meeting with Cato, I knew that he would recruit you. Was I right?"

Eupolemus nodded. He gently took her small hand between both of his own rough calloused hands. Her own hand was as soft as only the hand of someone who had never worked for a living in her life could be. Her emerald green eyes mesmerized him, inviting him to dive deep into their depths. He felt a fierce attraction for her, but there was something in her expression that led him to hesitate. A sort of focus that made clear that she was after something.

"Cassandra, you are a beautiful and special woman. Any man would desire you," he said quietly, thinking as he spoke. "I am a foreigner with no past or assured future in Rome. I can offer you some comfort, but it is clear that you want something beyond that. Why am I here?"

She smiled. Her hand brushed lightly up his arm, stroking shoulder. "You are all the same, with no idea what we want from you, aren't you? I want and will take what comfort you can offer, but I am offering you much more. Cato, who is at the peak of his power and influence, likes you. In the Macedonian War, you will serve at the side of the future generation of the leaders of Rome and serve under the beloved man of the hour. If you do well in the war and return to Rome, you will receive citizenship, and with me even a patrician rank. You will be a new man[22]. But with my connections, and those you form during the war, we can promote you further. As for me, I will win a handsome, strong, and .... good-hearted man."

The next morning, Eupolemus sought out the soldiers who had returned with him to Rome. He found Flavius groping a beautiful woman in a tavern near where he was staying.

"I thought that you had come to Rome to find a bride, not to waste all your money on working girls," he said, surprising him from behind.

"Commander, I came to seek love, not a bride. And has no one ever told you that it is rude to sneak up behind a man when he is with a woman?"

"Never mind that—I need you to locate the others. We are

---

22   That is how Romans called those who rose to greatness from lowly origins.

joining Aemilius Paullus' Legion and heading for Macedonia. We won't let this war elude us just because the Fifth Legion couldn't make it to the party."

Flavius leapt to his feet, almost dropping the woman in his lap.

"What happened to your plan to head home to your priestly family?"

"The plan will wait. I'll meet you here tomorrow at dawn."

He returned to Glitarius home to collect his belongings and say his farewells. As he was packing up his items in his room, Glitarius entered.

"I heard you spent your night in the home of another member of my family."

"Rumors travel swiftly in Rome," Eupolemus replied in kind.

"You have always taken an interest in my sister. Are you priests even permitted to marry foreign women? I thought that was forbidden to you."

Glitarius asked the question far too quickly, revealing his purpose. Cassandra wanted to make sure that she was not wasting her time on the wrong man, and Eupolemus appreciated her for her thoroughness.

"Marriage to foreign women is a very common phenomenon among us. All the patriarchs of our nation, and many of our kings, have done it. It is a well-known habit in my own family. In the distant past there were those who sought to disqualify us from serving in the Temple because of this."

Glitarius nodded slowly, seemingly satisfied, but was hardly done with his questions. "So, what do you think of my sister?"

"Any man would desire a woman like her. What I can't understand is what she sees in me," answered Eupolemus casually, returning to his belongings, but carefully attentive to Glitarius' response.

Glitarius fell right into his trap. "Well, she likes you, and that's no surprise. Besides, a new man, I mean a new citizen of Rome, is good for her. That way she can keep her independence and not become his property...."

Glitarius halted his words in midsentence, fearing he had said too much.

Eupolemus continued packing his belongings. "Cassandra is amazing. I have neither offered nor asked for any commitment from her. One cannot know what state I will be in when this war is over, or if I will even survive it. In any event, I intend to return to my homeland to visit my family once the war is done. I may then return to Rome, and then we will see. Perhaps you and I will then truly be family."

***

Flavius was able to locate three members of his unit—Rango, an Iberian-Ligurian half caste[23] who was courageous to the point of recklessness; Caesarius, a Faliscian[24] with an innocent and childish face and a gift for languages, disguise, and acting which was highly useful for espionage missions; Elaius, a true Roman who towered to enormous heights and could stun a bull with the blow of his hand; Flavius, also a true Roman, and unlike the others even a Patrician, though Flavius' family was not ranked highly amongst the mighty of Rome and lacked means, which led him to enlist in the infantry rather than the more prestigious and aristocratic cavalry. None of them hesitated to answer

---

23   The Ligurians were a Celtic influenced tribe in Northwest Italy.

24   A Latin Tribe of Central Italy. Absorbed into Rome in the early expansion of the Republic.

Eupolemus' call. War was a chance to progress and achieve rewards which would otherwise be unattainable.

The next day the five of them met on the street corner. Each of them carried their personal military equipment. Eupolemus arrived with a large cart driven by one of the servants of Glitarius. They travelled together to the house of Cato, where they were greeted by Cato and his son Marcus. Marcus was accompanied by a slave, who would serve him in the campaign. From the house of Cato, the seven left to the Legion assembly area.

As Cato had stated, Eupolemus did not receive the position of a commander. Due to their arrival with Marcus, son of Cato, the five of them were considered his men and were attached as common soldiers to his Century, which numbered many Roman Patricians. And yet, from the moment training began, Eupolemus and his men stood out in comparison to all the other warriors. They demonstrated a higher skill level in personal combat than anyone else, and worked together without words thanks to their many years of service together. The four were alert to the smallest signal from Eupolemus and stood ready to carry out his commands, even though he was not officially considered to be their commander. They rapidly drew the attention of the commanders and won considerable esteem from their comrades in the century.

Two days before the legion left by ship for Macedonia the Tribune Aulus Antonius, one of the senior commanders, summoned Marcus and Eupolemus to him. It became clear that Cato had upheld his promise and told Aemilius of the special unit established by the Fifth Legion in Hispania. Selarius told Eupolemus that Aemilius liked the idea and had asked him to delve into the matter and interrogate Eupolemus for more details. The meeting lasted for hours, and Selarius grilled Eupolemus down to the smallest detail. He was impressed by the fluency of Eupolemus in many languages, among them Latin and even a few dialects of Greek. This could be highly significant if they were to establish an espionage unit, as the Macedonians spoke Greek.

The Roman army finally landed in Macedonia to join the Roman forces in the field. The Romans assembled themselves before the Macedonian fortifications, but Aemilius did not seem to be in any hurry. The idea of frontally assaulting the fortifications of the powerful and skilled Macedonian army in their strong line between mount Olympus and the Aegean sea did not appeal to him. The armies therefore faced each other without coming to blows. Experienced veterans laughed that two armed camps of this size had never maintained such pacific proximity.

Several days after the Roman army was established, Eupolemus was summoned to Aulus once more. The tent was filled with various senior commanders when he arrived.

"You have been given a once-in-a-lifetime opportunity," Aulus informed him. "Take your men and begin to scout the terrain. Aemilius wants you to find us a place to break through where we can penetrate the enemy defensive line."

Eupolemus and his friends assembled within a few hours to carry out the mission. They purchased a carriage filled with agricultural produce from a local farmer, as well as clothing and additional equipment, and brought them back to camp. Within an hour the wagon was outfitted with hidden compartments for their weapons. At their request, Aulus gave them four horses. Two were hitched to the front of the wagon, on which three of the crew would travel, and the other two were ridden by Eupolemus and Flavius. The entire team wore the clothes of local farmers, including hats, kerchiefs, and sandals. Their weapons were stowed within the wagon and they were armed with no more than knives they carried under their clothes. All their preparations were carried out on the outskirts of the camp in order to avoid excessive attention, but Aulus and a number of other officers arrived and watched them. When their organization was complete they looked like a group of local farmers. Aulus and his officers said nothing, but it was clear that they highly appreciated the professionalism Eupolemus and his team displayed.

Three days later, Eupolemus and his men were scouting the land to the North of the Roman encampment, having failed to identify a potential breakthrough point. Eupolemus was already deliberating on whether he should give up and return empty-handed, but was unable to do so. Finally, he led his squad straight up the mountains, until they reached a tall and remote pass fortified by an unimpressive wall flanked by two guard towers on both sides, with a small fortress nearby. Eupolemus and Flavius took point. Rango drove the wagon with Elaius by his side. Behind them, on the piled cauliflowers and sacks of flour, sat Caesarius, tense and prepared to draw his weapons if necessary.

"Who are you and where are you headed?" the guard in the watchtower shouted at them in Greek.

"We are laborers seeking employment in the interior land. Can we get there through here, commander?"

"Why did you come here?" insisted the sentinel.

"We arrived from Thessaly. We heard the Romans were occupying the coastal highway, so we decided to take the high road through the mountains."

The gates in the wall slowly opened and they passed through. A group of warriors armed with large axes stood behind the wall, prepared to embark on a mission. Their leader pierced the villagers with his gaze, his face a mask of cruelty. The area between the pass and the fortress held more soldiers, but they seemed bored and apathetic, and showed no interest in a group of seemingly common farm laborers making their way through the mountains.

After making their way from the fortress, Eupolemus halted and carried out a rapid debriefing to gather and process the information picked up by his squad.

Rango was unable to hold himself back. "Eupolemus, if we attack them by night ourselves, we will be able to inflict enormous casualties on them; perhaps we can raze the wall down and destroy the place."

"We will not!" replied Eupolemus calmly, but firmly.

"I actually think it can be done…." Caesarius began to say.

"You are correct, but our mission was just to find vulnerable spots where the legions can penetrate into the interior, and it is far more important that we report our intelligence than destroy the fort. Even if we are successful, it is enough for one man to escape our raid to render our exertions futile—and worse. The Macedonian army would immediately reinforce the pass."

"Did you notice the group which left when we entered?" asked Elaius.

"Thracians," replied Flavius, "they are part of the Macedonian army. But the fact that they left means that they may be a semi-independent gang, out to rob the neighboring villagers or gather supplies for the fortress."

"Or rob our supply dumps," said Eupolemus distractedly, for he was primarily focused on another matter. "The bottom line is that we must return as quickly as possible to the camp. Pay attention and be sure to notice as many details as you can when we pass through the fortress again."

After a few hours, as they made their way silently in the darkness through a wooded ravine, they noted the sparkles of a fire ahead of them. Eupolemus sent Rango to find out what it was about, and he returned reporting that these were the Thracian warriors who had already gathered for their night's rest.

"We need to walk down this route, and we cannot do this without being noticed by them," Eupolemus said to his men and added with a smile, "you wanted to fight so there you are. They outnumber us, but we will have the advantage of surprise."

They prepared for action wordlessly, everyone knowing what must be done. They moved their weapons to make them accessible and went down the dark path.

The Thracians heard them from afar but were unable to identify them because of the darkness. Since the path led from the Macedonian fortress, they did not fear that it was an enemy, but some of them still stood alertly, axes in hand, and struck a rather threatening countenance with their shadows flickering on the path and the trees by the firelight.

Caesarius hailed them. "We are only simple farmers. Please don't hurt us."

The seated Thracians burst out in wild laughter at the expense of their more cautious standing comrades. There were eight of them, massive muscular warriors armed with axes matching their size. Their leader, however, remained standing and waited until Eupolemus and his men drew near, gripping the axe on his right shoulder.

"Why did you return?" he asked with naked hostility. "You saw that we haven't lost yet, didn't you? You aren't really looking for work—you are seeking to loot the corpses of the fallen!"

Caesarius made a show of being surprised, which he was. He

raised his hands protectively and shouted back, his face a mask of fear, "No, we really weren't, we are just poor farmers. We were looking for work, but we fear the war...."

Throughout the exchange, Eupolemus and his friends continued to approach the Thracian campfire and were now no more than three steps away from the Thracian leader blocking their path.

Suddenly the Thracian raised his axe menacingly, approaching the horses pulling the wagon. His comrades around the campfire guffawed at the seemingly intimidated peasants.

"Halt!" commanded the Thracian. "Dismount and leave the wagon and the horses. They are ours now. You can continue afoot."

Caesarius lifted his hands up in protest, "We are innocent Thessalian farmers, you cannot...."

"Silence!" the Thracian cut him off, "One more word and we will put you on the slave block tomorrow."

The Thracian watched with satisfaction as the browbeaten farmers scurried to the trees to park their wagon and tie their horses, and turned back victoriously to the campfire, where he was greeted with uproarious laughter and congratulations.

Caesarius approached the Thracian chieftain as if he were pleading. Eupolemus had selected him because his acting skills and relatively small stature made him a very convincing and unthreatening peasant. The leering Thracian turned to him, leaving his axe on the ground. At that moment Eupolemus and Flavius, Rango, and Elaius charged the Thracians in unison. Their first four victims didn't even realize what hit them. But Caesarius failed to eliminate the Thracian leader with a knife stab. The man had animal instincts and dodged away at the last moment, suffering no more than a scratch. He somersaulted back, grabbed his axe and cleaved Caesarius when he tried to stab him again. The melee that followed was between evenly matched parties, four on four. All Thracians were now standing, and hewed at Eupolemus and his squad with abandon. Eupolemus and his men were armed with Roman short swords and were therefore at a disadvantage against the greater reach and heft of the Thracian axes. Still, precise strikes and coordinated teamwork carried the day, leaving the Thracian leader wrestling alone with gigantic Elaius for his axe, his comrades fallen around him. Eupolemus did not wait to see who would win and ended the battle with a sharp stab.

The four of them gathered around the body of Caesarius. Losing only one man in a battle against eight skilled warriors was a significant success—but that did little to dull the ache at the loss of their friend.

The next evening they returned to camp with the body of Caesarius and eight Thracian axes piled in the wagon. The information they brought about the mountain pass confirmed earlier information that had reached the commanders of the Roman army, and the very next day an eight thousand-strong Roman force was on the march, Fabius Maximus, son of Aemilius, and Eupolemus' squad among them, to conquer the place.

King Perseus of Macedon must have had his own spies, for he soon found out about the Roman maneuver and sent ten thousand mercenaries, buttressed by two thousand elite Macedonian veterans, to oppose the Romans at the pass. However, he was too late. The Romans overwhelmed the garrison at the pass and took it for themselves. When the Macedonian reinforcements arrived they sought to dislodge the Romans, but they fought at a topographic and morale disadvantage, and were flung back with heavy losses.

The conquest of the pass by the Romans was disastrous for Perseus. His line was outflanked, and he was forced to withdraw before the Romans could take advantage of his predicament. His army rapidly redeployed to the plain of Pydna, where Perseus knew the moment of truth had arrived. This would be the true test of strength for his army: Macedonians and their allies and mercenaries against the Roman Legions. No more hiding behind natural and manmade fortifications—it would be a set piece battle on the open field. He had one chance and one chance only to preserve his independence. Defeat in battle would mean annexation by Rome. He drew courage from his soldiers. They too understood that this battle would determine the fate of their homes and nation and were determined to defeat the Romans and preserve Macedonian independence.

On the night before the intended confrontation between the armies of Rome and Macedon, an eclipse of the moon occurred. The Roman camp was filled with the sound of beating drums and lit torches were flung heavenward, calling on the moon to rise once again. The commander of the Roman army, Aemilius Paullus, had some knowledge of the essentials of eclipses and calmed his men. Nonetheless, he was always careful to publicly honor the gods, both because he thought propitiating the gods could do no harm, even if it did little good, and to bolster the courage of the true believers. That was why he offered sacrifices to the gods and made several vows to them to ensure his victory. In the Macedonian camp, however, the eclipse was met with great fear, as many saw in it a sign of the impending fall of King Perseus.

At dawn, the armies assembled for battle. Aemilius Paullus took his time, permitting the sun to move to the Western hemisphere, to ensure that its rays would strike the back of the Romans and blind the Macedonians rather than his own men. This turned out to be a two-edged sword. The sight of the massive Macedonian phalanx, rank after rank of massive Sarissa armed troops creating a dense and impenetrable screen from horizon to horizon, amazed and shocked the Roman soldiers. Even Aemilius Paullus himself was shaken. Still, he rode before his men, cheering their spirits and bolstering their morale.

The battle, when it finally began, favored the Macedonians from its beginning. Even though the Romans displayed self-sacrificing courage and hurled themselves on the Macedonian ranks almost fanatically, the Romans could not penetrate the ranks of the phalanx and were crushed by its advance.

Aemilius, mounted at the rear of the Roman forces, felt his heart cringe at the site of Rome's finest, his son included, being pushed back. He had spent his entire life seeking to atone for the stain on his family's reputation left by another battle. His father was one of the two Consuls who led the Roman army to defeat at the hands of Hannibal and the army of Carthage at Cannae. Aemilius was only twelve when his father died in that battle, and the loss had been etched on his soul and accompanied him throughout his life. The terrible possibility that he might end his own career in a similar defeat passed through his mind. At that moment he noticed something which might have great importance to the outcome of the battle: as the Macedonians advanced and the beaten Romans fell back before them, gaps formed in the impenetrable Sarissa wall. This was the result of the uneven terrain, which was characterized by hills, valleys, and pits, as well as a result of the natural tendency of some portions of the phalanx to advance faster than others, depending on the resistance they encountered. An exciting idea dawned in Aemilius' mind. He began barking out orders at his men, instructing them to direct their efforts at the gaps in the phalanx.

The strength of the Macedonian phalanx was its weakness as well. A phalanx soldier holding a Sarissa in both hands was very nearly useless in close melee combat. As soon as the Romans penetrated the ranks of the phalanx, they enjoyed an overwhelming advantage over the Macedonians, and made the very best of it. They furiously charged the Macedonians exposed in the gaps between the phalanx formations, slashing at them with their Gladius blades from up close. All who stood in their way were mowed down like hay beneath a scythe.

During the battle, when the Romans at one point had to fall back in the face of the wall of Sarissas that the Macedonians deployed before them, Marcus lost his father's sword. He began running between the people around him, shouting at them that his family's honor was at stake. Within a few seconds his comrades bunched around him and charged the Macedonians with unparalleled courage, heedless of the injuries they acquired pushing them back. As some held the Macedonians back, Marcus and some of his other companions turned to seek the sword amongst the bodies and fallen weapons scattered around the battlefield. To their joy, Marcus soon found the sword, lifted it with a roar and, buoyed by their success, led his companions to charge the Macedonian ranks. They deepened the breach in the Macedonian ranks, as their comrades did elsewhere in the front, generating a general breakdown and rout.

The Macedonian soldiers realized what was happening and tossed their long and now useless Sarissas to the ground, turning tail and fleeing the field. Any gap in the phalanx formations became a conflagration consuming every Macedonian in its path. Fortunately for the Romans, many such gaps in the Macedonian phalanx formation were scattered across the Macedonian front. In short order the entire Macedonian army crumbled and collapsed.

Aemilius Paullus watched events from the top of his horse, his heart overflowing with satisfaction. With the burden of command relieved, he permitted himself to act as a proud father and seek out his son and his friends. For now, and forever more, he thought, this battle has transformed me into an eternal hero of Rome and assured the honor of my family. Father, we have finally atoned for Cannae.

***

Antiochus Epiphanes and his officers were enjoying a leisurely royal lunch served in the royal pavilion, relaxing in the breeze peacock feather fan waving servants were creating for them.

Nine months had passed since he had evacuated Egypt with his army, and he was now returning with all he needed to conquer Alexandria. In the interval, Antiochus had taken care to generously bribe many leading senators of Rome to ensure noninterference in his campaign, although given the difficulties Rome was facing in Macedonia he had begun to think that these payments were superfluous.

One of the king's counselors rapidly entered the royal pavilion, directly approached Antiochus, and whispered something in his ear. Antiochus' satisfied smirk vanished at once. He drew himself up, wiped his mouth with the back of his hand, and grew flustered. All his companions ceased their talk and stared at him in trepidation.

"Rome has conquered Macedon?!" he repeated the words of his counselor in shock. "Gaius Popillius Laenas is here?!"

"Yes, my king," the counselor confirmed. "He is at the entrance of the camp and demands you go to him at once."

"What?! Why does he not enter?" Fear was apparent on Antiochus's face when he turned to his officers, "Come with me, we will go to him."

As he made his way to the perimeter of the camp, Antiochus felt his stomach turn. This sudden visit by Gaius, during the campaign to conquer Egypt and after Rome had fully occupied Macedon, was inauspicious. That Gaius had demanded he come to him only raised his fears.

The Roman ambassador stood alone, hands at his hips, his expression dour and severe. He was enraged every time he contemplated his previous meeting with Antiochus. Now he felt free to settle the account. His companions stood behind him, weaponless. He was an ambassador of Rome—he required no weapons to ensure his safety. No man was born who would dare to attack a Roman ambassador, he thought proudly. Not today, at any rate.

Antiochus saw Gaius waiting for him and hastened his steps towards him, followed by his men. When he reached Gaius, he extended his hand and cried out, "What an honor, please, enter my camp..."

"Halt your men! Approach alone!" Gaius commanded him peremptorily in Latin.

Antiochus stopped on his tracks, frozen in surprise. His men halted as well, even though they did not understand Latin.

"Yes, yes, of course," murmured Antiochus in embarrassment, gesturing at his men to hold their position and advancing towards Gaius on his own.

He extended his hand to Gaius once again, but Gaius made a point of ignoring his gesture.

"You are to withdraw all of your soldiers from Egypt. Every

last one! At once!" Gaius immediately barked at him.

"What?! But, is this in the best interest of Rome? ... If I rule Alexandria I will put things in order... the prices of grain exported to Rome will be much lower...."

"What in what I just said was unclear?!" Gaius raised his voice in reprimand.

"Is this the opinion of all the Senators? I have excellent relations with...."

"Watch your tongue!" Gaius's tone was clearly threatening now. "This is the will of Rome. I await your response."

"I, well, will have to consider this... give me a while to consult with my men...."

At that moment something took place which would become the talk of every city in the classical world. Gaius raised a stick and marked a circle in the soft sand around the stunned Antiochus.

"I will have your answer before you leave this circle!" Gaius commanded the Seleucid king dismissively, and stared at him contemptuously.

***

Jason was dining with his host, Joseph ben Hyrcanus, in his Transjordanian estate on the Gilad when an urgent messenger arrived and interrupted their dinner. "Eminence, I bring important news. The Seleucid army is retreating from Egypt in haste."

Jason leapt to his feet in excitement. "Only one thing could have brought about this outcome," he cried out, "Antiochus is dead!"

"Indeed, my lord, that is what rumors are saying," the messenger confirmed.

Joseph was not so quick to jump to conclusions. "As long as we have not heard this from a reliable source, this is only a rumor, no more than a guess. We should not rush things."

"On the contrary my friend. We must move with haste to establish facts on the ground for whoever comes to power in Antioch to take into account. Antiochus got his just desserts. It is a shame your father did not live to see this day."

Joseph's face grew sorrowful for a moment. His father had been one of Hunio's supporters and had held close connections with the authorities in Egypt. Following Antiochus' rise to power, and following the unseating of Hunio by Jason—with the assistance of the Hellenizers—his father had committed suicide. Joseph initially blamed Jason for his father's death, but during the years Jason was High Priest the two had reconciled. Following the unseating of Jason, the bond between the two grew stronger, and Joseph provided Jason with sanctuary at his estate.

"Joseph, this is my time, our time. As soon as I seize back control you will return to the status your father held in Jerusalem in the day of my brother and father. We must act now!"

Joseph's dubious expression gave way to support. "What do you want me to do?"

"The men of the countryside will support my claim," Jason clenched his fists, his excitement infectious. "I am, at the end of the day, the rightful heir of the House of Zadok and they have had enough of Menelaus. But I will need warriors to advance my claim. Your men are armed and veteran fighters. With them I can get rid of Menelaus and his mercenaries and take my rightful place."

Word of Antiochus' death and the return of Jason spread like wildfire throughout Judea. The men of the villages around Jerusalem had suffered greatly from the Hellenizing revolution of the past years. Some of them were former residents of Jerusalem who had abandoned the city, whether willingly or by coercion. They felt nothing but hatred for the Hellenizer youth of the Polis and Menelaus' mercenaries. Thousands responded to Jason's call and made their way to Jerusalem, carrying improvised homemade weapons. This enabled Jason to arrive at the city on a wave of popular support which he had rarely enjoyed as high priest.

Menelaus had a host of mercenaries personally loyal to him, or at least to his purse. These were men he had hired to secure the tax collection mechanism of Judea and safeguard the stability of his rule. They were supported by the youth of the Polis who had been trained to fight in the ephebia and who were also loyal to him. The older citizens of the Polis, unlike the youths, were split between the supporters of Menelaus and those of Jason, but none of them were eager to take up arms and be drawn into a fratricidal war.

Jason had updated the garrison commander of Jerusalem on events and asked him to stay out of his fight with Menelaus, claiming that this was an internal affair between the Jews. The garrison commander decided to stay put and wait for clarification of the rumors regarding the death of the king, and ordered his soldiers to cloister themselves in the fortress.

Fights broke out across the city. The villagers fought Menelaus' loyalists with bitter hatred, seeking revenge and unleashing their frustration and outrage at all that had occurred over the past few years on Menelaus and his men. Hundreds were killed and thousands injured on both sides. Given the refusal of the garrison to intervene, Jason's forces proved the stronger. As evening fell, Menelaus fled the city and Jason assumed control.

The following noon, the chief priests and those sages who succeeded in reaching Jerusalem gathered in the Chamber of Hewn Stone. Now that Jason had rightfully seized rule of Jerusalem based on the support of the traditional Jews, they demanded he set in place a balanced and just regime which would cancel the privileges of the Polis citizens over their fellow Jews. More-Tzedek and the priests were willing to live with Jason rather than Hunio IV assuming the High Priesthood, but they demanded that the ancient Hebrew sacred calendar be returned to use in Judea. The attendants spoke heatedly; Jason had a hard time managing an orderly deliberation, and at the end of the meeting no agreed-upon decisions were reached.

From the Chamber of Hewn Stone, Jason turned to a meeting with the garrison commander, with whom he agreed upon temporary measures to be taken until spirits settled down. He then proceeded to an assembly of the Polis citizens' council. Fearing for his safety, Jason was accompanied by a guard of armed soldiers. This meeting also broke down in stormy acrimony, as some of those present whose family were slain or wounded in the fighting held Jason responsible for this outcome. The concluding remarks were not much different from the conclusion of the Chamber of Hewn Stone conference: an agreement to disagree. Jerusalem seethed, unstable and torn by mutual hatred between traditionalist and Hellenizer.

***

Antiochus rode at the head of the long column, surrounded by his officers. His head was bowed down in humiliation, greater than he had ever known. Tears welled up in his eyes every time he ran his meeting with Gaius through his mind's eye. His mind simply could not process how the Roman envoy had evicted him from Egypt with but a few preemptory sentences.

Someone called for his attention on his left. Antiochus ignored it.

"Your majesty!" called out his personal secretary from the ground. Antiochus lifted his head. Several mounted officers stood nearby and were watching him intently.

"What is it?" he asked resignedly.

"Your majesty, it is the Jews. They have rebelled. The former High Priest whom you had unseated has reclaimed power. The rightful High Priest has fled to Samaria…."

Antiochus remained detached as he heard the report, as if he were sleepwalking. He stared at his secretary and officers indifferently. But then he saw the expression of his officers. They exchanged pitying glances, as if they were sure he was finished. All at once Antiochus roused himself, his senses sharpening like a trapped predator.

His secretary noted the sudden change in his king and smiled in understanding. "My king, our people await your commands."

***

Jason awoke to the sound of screams outside his chambers. Within seconds More-Tzedek burst into the room, followed by others.

"You are a false prophet," More-Tzedek roared at him, "It is because of you that our brothers have been led astray, to build a futile city and a congregation built on a lie. All of your work shall be in vain for the law of the King will consign you to the fire…."

"What the blazes is he talking about?" Jason asked the others, understanding he would be unlikely to get a clear answer from the agitated More-Tzedek.

"King Antiochus is coming. Our men report that his army has advanced all night. They are but a short distance from the city and will soon storm it."

More-Tzedek continued to rain fire and brimstone on Jason, "False works, both in establishing the Polis and in your current lie that the king is dead, you have led them through a lie, it is because of you that the elect of God were condemned and persecuted…."

Jason did not hesitate, not even for a moment. He, better than anyone in the room, understood the meaning of what was said. While More-Tzedek and his agitated companions spoke out at once, filling his room with an ungodly din, and additional people rushed panicked into his chambers, Jason hurriedly collected his personal belongings and prepared to leave. At the doorway he turned around and spoke firmly. "Collect the men and wait. I will go to the king and assume all responsibility."

He left at a run, not giving them any chance to stall him with questions. He did not, of course, have any intention of sacrificing himself for his supporters, let alone his opponents, nor did he believe that the king would be satisfied with his head—it was his own head he was thinking of, and the only thing he sought to save from this fiasco.

Antiochus, humiliated at his expulsion for Egypt, unleashed his wrath on the Jews of the city and its environs. Jerusalem was crushed and the traditional Jews in the city and the environs, who were considered to be supporters of Jason and rebels, were harshly persecuted. Hundreds were killed or injured. Thousands, women and children included, were carried away into slavery. Menelaus was returned to power as a royal appointee, supported by a far more extensive garrison than in the past, making him more powerful than ever.

Rumors spread in Judea that Jason, the last of the line of Zadok to serve as High Priest in the Temple, had fled to Greece, finding sanctuary in Sparta, some of whose people believed themselves to be distantly descended from Abraham, the ancestor of the Jewish nation. He would never return to Judea.

Winter 167 BCE—Matityahu

> Dramatis Personae
> **Bold** = main character
> * = historical figure

- **Menelaus***—*The current High Priest, appointed in 171 BCE by Antiochus IV*
- **Mithridates (Antiochus IV)***—*King of the Seleucid Kingdom since 175 BCE; also titled Antiochus Epiphanes*
- **Matityahu***—*Father of Judah and his brothers, village priest of Modi'in*
- *Afles*—Representative of the Seleucid regime*
- *Elianus—A Hellenizer*
- **Yohanan***, **Simon***, **Judah***, **Hannah***, **Eleazar*** **and Jonathan***—*The children of Matityahu and Rebecca by age*
- **Eupolemus***—*A friend of Judah, son of Yohanan ben Hakotz*
- **Cassandra**—*A Roman lady*
- **Flavius**—*A Roman legionary*
- *Elijah—Leader of Alexandria's Jewish community*
- *Hanoch—Alexandrian Jewish warrior and former officer in the army of Egypt*
- **Miriam**—*Old flame of Judah from his youth in Jerusalem*
- *Joseph*—Matityahu's brother*

- *Philipus the Phrygian*—Current Seleucid garrison commander in Jerusalem*
- *Joseph ben Zacharia*—Rebel warrior, one of Matityahu and Judah's men*

The traditional Jews in Jerusalem and its environs sought to survive and recover under the harsh revenge of the king. Many of them found it hard to bear the heavy taxes Menelaus once again subjected them to, which only led Menelaus to bear down twice as hard, which in turn ensured he had to contend with constant unrest and rebelliousness.

When the king was informed of this, he concluded that the obdurate faith of the Jews in their one god was the source of their constant unrest and rebelliousness. He sent his minister of taxes to Jerusalem accompanied by a veritable army, ordered to take draconian action—those who failed to pay their taxes were enslaved, their sale in the slave markets of Syria, both filling the treasury and thinning the traditional Jewish population of Judea, particularly the area surrounding Jerusalem. The minister razed the homes of traditional Jews, destroyed the walls of Jerusalem, looted whatever his men could lay their hands on, took thousands of men, women, and children captive, and led them to Antioch for sale as slaves. Following these actions, almost no observant Jews were left in Jerusalem.

By order of the king, the Akra was built in Jerusalem. A vast fortress towering over the Temple, capable of housing not only a sizable garrison but also the leading Hellenizers. Unprecedented taxes, amounting to a third of all grain harvested from the fields and half of any fruits harvested from the orchards and the vines of Judea, were levied on the oppressed population. Traditionalist Jews had become no more than serfs on their own lands and lived from hand to mouth.

Several months later, King Antiochus unleashed his final, most terrible blow against the Jews. It was a decree, unprecedented in either the Hellenist kingdom or any other land in the known world. In it the king forbade the Jews to carry out their traditions and the commandments of their faith. A royal decree issued in Antioch explicitly forbade the Jews to worship the God of Israel. A flesh and blood king had declared war on the formless, immaterial god.

In Judea, the king's men, accompanied by soldiers and extremist Hellenizers, went forth to enforce the decree on the horrified traditional population. These expeditions sought to ensure that the king's decree was being followed, and that the rural of Judea ended the circumcision of their sons, ate swine flesh, worked on the Sabbath, sacrificed to the Greek gods, and ceased to perform the various other commandments of the banned Jewish religion. People who refused to obey the decree of the king were tortured by the soldiers, some of them to death. They were force fed pork and their infant children were stripped to determine whether they were circumcised. The parents of circumcised children, and the children themselves, were publicly flogged, and the lives of traditionalist Jews were forfeit.

All the residents of Modi'in gathered in the village square, where Matityahu, his back straight and unbowed, was exchanging words with Afles, the Seleucid clerk who headed the regime's expedition.

"You are the village headsman. It is you who must make a public example for your people to follow. You must offer a sacrifice to Zeus. That is how you will win the king's good graces and save your people. This is what the community leaders of every village have done," declared Afles in arrogant Greek.

Behind Afles stood his companions, a group of extreme Hellenizers. With the exception of a single man who seemed to be in his forties, all of them looked like the young products of the Polis educational institutions, completely cut off from the ancient traditions of their people. Amongst them the sons of Matityahu recognized a familiar face from their time in Jerusalem. Elianus, amongst the worst and most extreme of the Hellenizers, was arrogantly smirking at them. He also recognized Judah, and his inferior status filled him with satisfaction.

The Hellenizers were surrounded by a score of armed and mounted Seleucid soldiers. They gazed at the scene in amusement. They had already witnessed and participated in several such scenes in the villages the expedition had previously passed through. Each village they visited showed decreasing resistance to the decree, as rumors and horror stories about the fate of those who dared to resist spread throughout the land.

Matityahu visualized the spirit of his father Yohanan in his mind's eye. Father, I hope you understand my actions, he thought. Rage, accumulated over far too long and tinged with frustration and despair, flooded him. In a voice trembling with excitement, which carried throughout the village, he replied, "Even if all the nations that live under the king's rule obey him and have chosen to follow his orders, departing from their ancestral religion, my sons and brothers and I will continue to live according to our ancestors' covenant. We will never abandon the Law and its commands! We won't obey the king's orders by turning aside from our religion to either the right or the left."

Afles seethed with fury. Even before the older Hellenizer finished translating Matityahu's words from Aramaic to Greek, he fully understood Matityahu's meaning by his body language and tone. He angrily pushed the interpreter toward the mobile sacrificial altar the expedition had brought with it. The interpreter grinned in comprehension and lifted the plump suckling piglet to the altar.

The men of the village held their breath. Many were struck by terror. The stories from other villages made clear what was about to happen. They would not allow anyone to strike or harm Matityahu, their leader. Should he give the sign, they would charge the Hellenes as one. If even a single soldier should try to harm him—the same.

Judah could sense the turbulent emotions of his father and how he steeled himself for action. He gestured at his brothers to draw closer and approached his father, brushing against him, to let him know they were prepared to act on his behalf.

Matityahu was not a man who would send others to do his work. A strange serenity, like the calm before the storm, filled him. He stepped forward and placed his hand forcefully on the hand of the sword with which the Hellenizer intended to slaughter the piglet. The Hellenizer flinched back, surprised, but did not let go of the sword. Matityahu shook his head from side to side, asking the Hellenizer without words not to perform the deed. His gaze was stern, but it also held a spark of hope, a silent plea. He did not hate that man, he just wanted to stop him.

The villagers could not believe their eyes. It seemed to them that Matityahu was giving up and had decided to slaughter the piglet instead of the Hellenizer. Only after a long moment passed did both they and Afles understand that Matityahu had never even considered that possibility. Afles roared a reprimand at the Hellenizer. The Hellenizer pulled his hand back, trying to free it from Matityahu's firm grip. He finally freed himself, taking a step back but leaving the sword on the altar. Afles continued to shout and was approaching them. The Hellenizer stepped towards Matityahu, hands thrust out to push him away from the altar. For just a moment the Hellenizer's eyes widened in terror and shock before the sword Matityahu had picked up from the altar pierced his heart. Matityahu looked right through the man he had slain. His lips murmured "Hear, O Israel! The LORD is our God, the LORD is one!"

For a moment, silence fell across the village. All of creation seemed to hold its breath. And then all hell broke loose. Afles charged Matityahu in rage, throttling him with both hands. The soldiers drew their blades and charged forward, only to be met by the united mass of the villagers, led by the sons of Matityahu. Some of the villagers gripped tools or crude weapons, but others charged the armed and armored soldiers with their bare hands. At first it was by no means clear who would be victorious in the ensuing scuffle.

It all ended almost as soon as it began. Every member of the king's expedition, both soldiers and Hellenizers, were on the ground either wounded and injured or dead.

Matityahu looked around, trying to come to terms with what had just happened. In his hand he still held the sacrificial blade, now red with the blood of Afles, whose body lay at his feet by that of the Hellenizer.

Judah carefully approached his stunned father and gently removed the blade from his hands. His mind was feverishly analyzing the situation and considering options, and he quickly concluded that he, his family, and all Modi'in had crossed a one-way bridge. The Seleucid soldiers would soon arrive to avenge the deaths of their comrades. None of the men of Modi'in would survive. Indeed, it seemed likely that the neighboring villages would also be razed by the furious soldiers.

"Father, we must go. Now!"

Matityahu's eyes turned slowly towards his son. He sighed and nodded, grateful to his son for taking command of the situation.

The villagers rapidly organized for the flight from their homes. Messengers were sent out to warn the surrounding villages of what had happened and to invite them to join them or flee elsewhere. Judah led them all to the mountains of Gophna, a remote wilderness in northern Judea, in the debatable borderlands with the Meridarchy of Samaria.

***

Following the decisive victory in Pydna, Aemilius Paulus became governor over Macedonia on behalf of Rome and implemented new administrative measures which permitted the Macedonian cities to live according to their own customary law, subject to municipal councils. While he subjected the Macedonians to a yearly tribute of one hundred talents of gold, this sum was more than tenfold lower than the taxes they had previously paid to their own kings.

As his army recovered and rested in its camps, and after he had put Macedonian affairs in order, he left on a tour of the venerable Polis of Greece. His two sons joined him, but the other patrician scions were released from duty to return to Rome should they so desire. Eupolemus and Flavius took advantage of the opportunity to return with Marcus to Rome. Rango and Elaius on the other hand, chose to remain with the army, hoping to receive a share of the spoils, and perhaps a land grant, when the army was demobilized.

Upon their return from the war, Eupolemus and Flavius found that being members of the circle of friends of Marcus, son of Cato the Censor, opened up many doors. Marcus arranged a spacious rent-free apartment in a villa of one of his father's friends for them, which by chance was not far from Cassandra's home. Since the primary hero of the war, the Consul Aemilius Paulus, had yet to return to Rome, the noblemen's sons who participated in the war and returned served as a sort of substitute, and were repeatedly required to quench the thirst of the citizens of Rome with stories about the war. That was how Eupolemus and Flavius frequently found themselves to be supporting cast in Marcus' heroic tales, and sometimes took center stage when they shared their own heroic tales.

As for Cassandra, Eupolemus met with her frequently. She loved the aura of victory which clung to Eupolemus, and liked his association with Marcus and the sons of Aemilius Paullus, who had been adopted into the leading houses of Rome. One night, as they lay entwined in her bedchambers, she moved to advance her plans.

"My dear, I enjoy hearing you recapitulate your battlefield tales, but I hope you realize this martial aura is a temporary thing. It is not as if you have a military career behind you or held high rank …."

"Yes, I know. Although it seems to me Marcus is relying on this war as a political springboard…."

"Marcus is set up nice and tidy, make no mistake," Cassandra said softly, "Cato and Aemilius have already settled on Marcus wedding Aemilius' daughter. Marcus' marriage will be political, just as Cato's was. That is how one ascends the ladder to a higher station."

"So are you advising me to marry Aemilius' other daughter?" Eupolemus laughed.

"Arrogant barbarian! No serious house would give their

daughter to you. Be grateful that I grant you my favors," Cassandra replied in mock anger, releasing herself from his embrace and sitting on him, pinning his hands beneath her thighs. "Now you are my prisoner."

"Very well, mistress, how can I satisfy your desires?" He replied to her in the same coin, his smile and expression well revealing the types of desires he had in mind.

"Forget about that now! You will neither receive nor grant any such favors until you give me clear answers. I, too, need to look after my interests. I want to know what your plans are and what place I have in them. Seriously now."

He grew serious and drew into thought for a few moments. Then he slid beneath her, freeing his hands, and sat behind her in an embrace.

"This is not simple for me. I love you more than I ever believed I could love anyone. But I am the eldest son of my father and am supposed to lead the family. I owe them at least a return visit, an explanation, and a proper farewell. I will travel to my land and to my father's home. I had planned to do this even before the Macedonian war, but I did not know then if I would return. It is now clear to me that I want to return. Return to you," he ended huskily, burying his face in her soft hair and kissing the back of her neck.

They sat in silence for a long while, she calculating in her mind, with him fearing her response.

"Very well, I understand. I do not like it, but I understand. In fact, I respect you for your loyalty to your father and family. When do you intend to go?"

"Soon. I have considered waiting for Aemilius to return to participate in his triumph, but he seems to be delayed in Greece, and Marcus and Cato say that there is considerable opposition in the Senate—they may even forbid a triumph. I will sail to Alexandria and from there I will make my way home. Flavius will accompany me as far as Alexandria; he has decided to try his luck as a sword for hire in Egypt."

***

The men of Modi'in were not the only ones forced to flee their homes in fear of the king's soldiers and the Hellenizers. Many other Jews throughout Judea and beyond were forced to do the same, fleeing into the wilderness to live lives where they would be free to worship their god and uphold the commandments of the Torah. It was the Modi'in group, however, which soon became the symbol of the struggle against the persecutions of Antiochus IV, and the bearer of the torch of Jewish rebellion. In part this renown was derived from the tale of Matityahu's slaying of the Hellenizer and the king's emissary, and the defeat of the Seleucid soldiers who had accompanied them, a story which spread like wildfire throughout Judea. But how they conducted themselves once they had fled into the mountains was what caused the legend to grow. Unlike other groups who were content to hide way from the Seleucid regime, the men of Modi'in were proactive. Under the leadership of Matityahu, they raided the surrounding countryside, often striking at the Hellenizer collaborators with the regime. They roused the traditionalist Jews throughout Judea and destroyed the alters and idols of the Hellenist gods, while enabling traditionalist Jews to perform their religious rites, including the circumcision of their sons.

In every such visit the men of Modi'in were received with great honor and were supplied with equipment and food by the local population—and often with new recruits as well.

Proud, erect, and armed, the rebels gave the rural Jews of Judea who had been robbed of their spiritual and political center in Jerusalem, and whose daily life was under constant assault by the persecutions of Antiochus, a reason to feel pride, and even a glimmer of hope.

After only a few months of activity, the Seleucid authorities and the people of Judea had come to believe that thousands of rebel warriors had taken control of the Judean Mountains to the North of Jerusalem.

***

Eupolemus woke up from a restless sleep in the belly of the ship. He was unable to sleep well in the dense, foul air of the hold. Flavius was nowhere to be seen. Making his way to the deck, he realized why he had been left below alone. The great lighthouse of the port of Alexandria could be seen on the horizon, and all the passengers on the ship had gathered at the bow of the ship to gaze upon it. It was a massive structure that rose high into the air, and which could be seen from afar. At day, the lighthouse was marked by thick white smoke which rose to the heavens, and at night a vast fire burned at the top of the tower.

Flavius left the knot of passengers at the bow and joined him. "I did not want to wake you up; it took you so long to fall asleep. Care for a look?"

Eupolemus shook his head, his eyes still heavy with cobwebs. "In a bit. I'm hungry. How about you?"

The two made their way to the stern and crouched by the rails.

"We will be in port in a few hours. Is anybody waiting for you?" asked Flavius.

"No one knows I am coming and I know no one in the city," admitted Eupolemus. "We will make our way to the Jewish quarter and take it from there. When a visitor arrives, the members of the community take care of him. I am sure that among them we will also be able to find people who can help put you together with those to whom you can offer your services as a warrior."

The port of Alexandria was huge, even greater than Rome's port of Ostia. It offered a breathtaking view from the sea. Hundreds of ships and boats of all shapes and sizes were docked at the port or making their way to and from it. A massive Egyptian warship, with several boats tethered to it, was anchored at the entrance to the port. Other boats made their way to and from the ship. These boats were those of the port administration, which boarded all ships making their way to the port. Their job was to record the type of cargo—passengers, goods, or both—to coordinate the entry into the port, and to direct each ship to the proper pier. The walls of the port and the towers surrounding it held relatively calm armed soldiers; their small number indicated that this was a secure port which feared no external danger. Hundreds of ships were docked within the port itself, and the docks between them were crowded with thousands of people, donkeys, and wagons, who were loading and unloading goods, transporting them to and from the port. The din of the port could be heard from afar, as if its sounds floated on the water.

Eupolemus had heard so many tales about Alexandria that it seemed to him that he was returning to a place he had visited in the past. This would be his final stop before he returned to his homeland, and a completion of a long tour between the three great capitals of the ancient world—Antioch, Rome, and Alexandria.

Flavius and Eupolemus disembarked from the ship, each of them carrying a large sack with all of their personal belongings. Eupolemus wore an unadorned tunic, fastened to his waist with a simple rope, to all appearances a common traveler. Flavius on the other hand was bedecked with the arms and armor of a Roman Legionary. On the crowded piers, and even after they left the port to the wide streets of the crowded city, Flavius' outfit and bearing proved to offer a considerable advantage, leading the crowds to swiftly and respectfully part before him.

Eupolemus questioned a passerby in Greek, asking him where he could find the Jewish Quarter. The man smiled in understanding and, much to Eupolemus' surprise, replied in Aramaic.

"Have you fled Judea? More and more refugees are arriving every day. I can recognize our people from afar usually, but I wasn't sure about you, not until I heard you speak." The man looked over him with interest. He noted the tall Roman soldier at Eupolemus' side and his forehead crinkled in interest.

Eupolemus was concerned at the man's casual reference to refugees from Judea. "I am Eupolemus, son of the priest Yohanan ben Hakotz. Yes, I am indeed from Judea, though I have been absent from my homeland for many years. This is my friend, Flavius, and we have just arrived from Rome. Tell me, why are our brothers fleeing Judea?"

"Rome?! I did not know our people lived in Rome. I am Yehezkel Hierolimus."

Yehezkel arced his hand to the left. "You will find Jews all over this area of the city. Are you looking for someone in particular, or just a place to stay for a few days?"

"You said many are coming from Judea. Why?" insisted Eupolemus.

"Don't you know?! Do the Jews of Rome have no contact with the holy land? King Antiochus has passed decrees amounting to the mandated destruction of our people and our religion. Upholding the commandments, observing the Sabbath, circumcising infants, or any form of worship of God is forbidden. Observant Jews are persecuted and even executed, sometimes by horrific torture. The Temple has been profaned with swine sacrifices to the Greek idols—it is now an idolater temple!"

Eupolemus felt dizzy and almost staggered at the news.

Yehezkel noted his amazement and quietly added, "I am sorry to inform you of things in this manner. In any event, this is why so many are fleeing Judea and ending up in Alexandria. These persecutions theoretically apply to all Jewish subjects of the Seleucid Kingdom, but are enforced, for now, primarily in Judea."

"So, where do they go?"

"Those with family or friends go to them of course. All the rest go to the great synagogue, in the center of the Jewish Quarter." Yehezkel pointed at a narrow street leading southward, "the community has mobilized to provide aid for the refugees. Anyone who arrives is provided with lodgings, food, and even with employment later on."

The news of the arrival of one of the sons of the priest Yohanan ben Hakotz swiftly spread throughout the Jewish quarter of Alexandria. Hundreds of Jews streamed towards the chief synagogue of the quarter, assuming that he had been sent by his father to carry out some purpose or another. Eupolemus was astounded when the questions of the crowd surrounding him inadvertently revealed that his old friend Judah and his family were the leaders of a Jewish rebellion against Antiochus and his persecutions.

Eupolemus was shortly thereafter summoned by the leaders of the Jewish community in Alexandria. The meeting was held in another, smaller synagogue. This synagogue was only active on the Sabbath, and hence was isolated from the prying eyes and din of the crowd. Several priests and notables who had recently arrived from Judea had also arrived at the meeting. Once they realized he had not been in Judea over the past few years, they began to share with him what they knew. This was the first organized and coherent account he was given of everything that had occurred in his homeland since he had left. He had a hard time believing his ears when he was told that Judah's father had killed the emissary of the king, and that this had been the spark that lit the rebellion against Seleucid rule.

Once spirits had calmed, Eupolemus began asking questions. He wished to hear everything people knew about the condition of the rebels, the manner in which the rebellion was conducted, the armaments of the rebels, and the response of the Seleucid military and authorities to the rebellion. Without ever consciously making a decision, it had become clear to him that from this moment forth his thoughts and deeds would be dedicated to the success of the rebellion. He would have to use all the skills, knowledge, and experience he had gained during his sojourn in Rome to aid Judah and his people—and Alexandria was the best place to recruit the aid they needed to succeed.

The Jewish community in Egypt was the largest and most secure and affluent Jewish community in the world. Many of the sons of the Jewish community had served in the army of the Ptolemys for generations and made up a significant portion of its manpower in the present day. Until now, the Jews of Egypt had contented themselves with aiding the refugees who had fled the persecutions of Antioch in Judea. Now, however, he must find a way to recruit them into open support of the struggle against the Seleucid tyrant. He must convince them to donate money, equipment, armaments and even recruits—anything to aid the prosecution of a long and bitter campaign against what was still the foremost power in the Eastern Mediterranean.

When Eupolemus finally stood and began to speak, his appearance and behavior, as well as his words, captivated the hearts of his audience. He shared with his surprised audience his experiences over his years in Rome, and then moved on to speak of events in the Land of Israel. He spoke as if he had personally witnessed each outrage in Judea and, although he did not explicitly state this, as if he had indeed been sent by his father to secure the aid of the Jewish community of Alexandria for the struggle against Antiochus.

"Antiochus has pushed us into a corner. This is a sign that we can no longer tolerate the presence of the idolaters in the Holy Land. Our brothers are refusing to violate the commandments of the Torah and are sanctifying God through their martyrdom... the sons of Matityahu are fighting for their faith—I too will join them. This is, however, a war not of a single man or of a single family, but a war of all the children of Israel. We need your help. The hand of God has guided you to live in Egypt at this hour of need so that you may aid your kin in Judea. You shall be for us what Joseph was for his brothers, the Sons of Jacob. Egypt is an enemy of Antiochus, and its leaders will look in favor upon our struggle. It lies within your power to determine the outcome of this struggle. We must all work together towards a common purpose, which is no more than winning the right to quietly worship our God as we and our ancestors always have."

His audience stared at him with eyes glittering with excitement, some of them nodding in agreement when he spoke. He felt he had won their heart. But then a debate broke out and the elders, whom Eupolemus thought supported him, expressed their reservations. Yes, they liked his confidence, but they were concerned that his family might actually be in the Hellenizer camp and Menelaus loyalists. They also doubted the ability of the rebels to defeat the mighty Seleucid army, which had defeated the Egyptian army only two years previously, and sought to cool his enthusiasm and expectations.

An impressive-looking elder called Elijah, whose words were attentively followed by the others, indicating his stature, turned to him. "Fire-breathing speeches are all well and good, but you must realistically assess the military power of our Judean brothers. To defeat an army, what is needed is an army. The Jews of Alexandria and Egypt will mobilize to provide what assistance we can, have no doubt of this. But before the kings of Egypt permit us to act openly, and perhaps even intervene on their own, they will want to know that this struggle has a chance of success. The Judeans will have to prove themselves, display some indication of success, and then the support will grow accordingly," cautioned Elijah, ending his words with a prophetic overtone.

Upon his return to the central synagogue, Eupolemus found Flavius awaiting him by their packed personal belongings. Dozens of people were present in the hall, and many of them glanced at him and exchanged whispers with each other when he entered. He felt a need for some time by himself to organize his thoughts and make plans. He sat in the corner, leaned his head backwards, and closed his eyes.

He had never felt as homesick as he did at that moment. He repeatedly visualized all of the events he heard about over the past few hours in his mind's eye. Homes in Jerusalem torched and Seleucid soldiers beating and killing traditionalists throughout the streets of the city and throughout the land; Matityahu, the father of Judah, slaying a Hellenizer and the king's emissary. He wondered what side of the conflict his family truly was on, and whether they were safe. He shivered when he thought about the possibility that something might have happened to his father.

He opened his eyes. Flavius was still seated opposite him. He was bedecked in Legion garb as before, and openly wore his weapons, but something in his expression had changed. A sense of danger roused Eupolemus' senses. He looked around him. He glanced at Flavius, who raised his chin at a group of young men on the other side of the synagogue. Eupolemus immediately understood the reason for Flavius's tenseness. Those men were soldiers. True, they did not wear a uniform or openly bear arms, but years in a Roman Legion made their military bearing unmistakable to him.

As one, the young men rose and advanced on him. Their lockstep pace indicated clearly that they were used to working together as a team. Flavius casually moved to stand in their path. His bulk and the uniform of a Roman soldier were enough to give pause to any maliciously intentioned individual. The group paused where they were, but showed no trepidation with Flavius. Eupolemus casually advanced, cautiously standing side by side with Flavius. He was somewhat reassured by the newcomers' bearing, however. They were too calm for people up to malicious intentions.

"Greetings. We are sons of Israel, like you," said the leader of the group, a man in his late twenties. "My name is Hanoch. I have served as an officer in a Jewish battalion of the Ptolemy army. The men beside me are some of those who have served under my command. All of us have extensive combat experience, including against the army of Antiochus. We have heard that you are returning to the homeland to join the rebels. We would like to join you—we can offer much assistance."

Eupolemus exhaled with relief, gladdened after the cold welcome his ideas had received from the elders of Alexandria only a short time ago. Nonetheless, he did not want to fall prey to misguided hopes, and so sought confirmation from Hanoch, "Will King Ptolemy permit his soldiers to intervene in Judea? Isn't he frightened of Antiochus?"

"Both Ptolemy brother-kings detest Antiochus, as does their sister-queen Cleopatra II. In spite of Rome's protection of Egypt, they will be very cautious not to provide Antiochus with any pretext to take arms against them once again. They will never dare to openly interfere directly in Antiochus's internal affairs, but we believe they will have no objections if we offer aid to our brothers."

"Welcome, then. How many men can you bring with you?"

The young men guffawed, a spark of excitement in their eyes. Eupolemus found himself liking them more and more. "Did I say something funny?"

"We can organize an entire army," answered Hanoch. "Hundreds of young men like us will be delighted to volunteer. The elders are not happy about it, but we aren't asking them. The question is what is really happening in the Land of Israel. So far, all we have heard is rumors and stories, particularly about the sons of Matityahu…."

"Truth be told, I haven't been in Judea for several years, and I know no more than you do. I was on my way back home after serving several years in the Roman Legion with my companion Flavius, and only when we got here did we hear what had happened in Judea—but I intend to arrive in Judea as quickly as possible to find out what is going on."

"The Roman isn't with you?" asked Hanoch, and nodded at Flavius.

Eupolemus slapped his friend's shoulder affectionately. "That is not entirely clear. He was looking for employment here in Egypt as a mercenary, but perhaps I can persuade him to join me."

Flavius understood the spirit of the exchange, though it was spoken in a foreign language. "Will this little war of yours have any money in it?"

"I doubt it, but it will certainly have much more action than here," Eupolemus replied, knowing that Flavius had already made up his mind.

"So it is as we feared. We have no real idea what is happening in Judea, or who is leading the struggle," said Hanoch, returning to the issue at hand

"That's right, but I do know Matityahu and his sons personally. I can understand how they ended up heading the rebellion. In fact, I can think of no people more suited to this than them, but they surely need funds and equipment."

"Then I suggest only I accompany you," Hanoch said, turning serious. "We will scout out the land together and get an impression of the situation. The others will remain here for now and help organize recruits and raise contributions."

Eupolemus smiled and reached out his hand to Hanoch in agreement. Hanoch shook the proffered hand, and a moment later found himself pulled into an excited embrace.

Hanoch's optimism regarding the attitude of the Ptolemys towards aid by the Jewish community in Egypt to the rebellion turned out to be misplaced. The leaders of the Jewish community were given an unambiguous message not to do anything yet that might upset the tense peace between the two kingdoms.

But Hanoch was also right in saying that the kings would be happy to see the fall of Antiochus and would be pleased to receive information about the rebellion. His fact-finding mission to Judea received the blessing of both the leaders of the community and the duly notified royal court.

Hanoch insisted on making their way to Judea by horse rather than by ship. Eupolemus and Flavius tried to persuade him that this was a long and difficult desert journey but were unsuccessful. Hanoch feared that the Seleucid navy would board their ship on the way, or else be waiting to arrest them when they disembarked at a harbor. In the Jewish community of Alexandria, thirsty for stories of heroism from the Holy Land, the stories of the struggle of Matityahu were exaggerated by the wishful thinking of the narrator and his listeners. Hanoch accordingly feared that the ships of the Seleucid fleet were patrolling the coast to isolate the rebels. He did not realize that the impact of the Judean rebels, for all of their courage, had not yet spread beyond the limited confines of the northern Judean Mountains. No one in Antioch had yet heard of Matityahu or his sons.

Before they left Alexandria, Eupolemus received a letter from one of the community's dignitaries urging him to visit her. Intrigued, he met with the lady, and then recognized Miriam, who was the first love of his friend Judah when they were boys. She was now a married woman and a mother of five. She was still lovely, but very different from the beautiful girl he remembered. The image of Cassandra rose in his mind, and he felt his heart ache for a moment in yearning.

Miriam promised to help, both in her own name and in the name of her husband. Throughout their conversation she maintained the detachment and restraint one would expect of a married woman. However, her eyes spoke a hidden message, even if her lips did not dare utter it. Only when they parted did she break down; when he offered his hand to bid her farewell, she collapsed into his arms instead, burying her head in his chest. He had the feeling she was imagining Judah there instead of him. When she recovered, she rose on her toes and whispered in his ear, "look after Judah for me," and walked away rapidly inside the house without looking back.

***

The long ride in the parched and hot desert had drained the riders of any desire to converse. Flavius and Hanoch could not understand each other in any event. Flavius knew no language but Latin, whereas Hanoch could speak only Greek and some Aramaic. Eupolemus, who could speak all three languages, and as the son of a priest even the ancient Hebrew, was deep in thought and did not converse much with either of them. On the third day they reached a verdant and shady oasis where two merchant caravans were encamped. One caravan had arrived from the deserts of Arabia and was headed towards Gaza. It carried valuable merchandise, spices, perfumes, and incense. The other caravan originated from Jerusalem and was headed to Alexandria, containing, among other things, young male and female slaves.

The slave traders were primarily Nabataeans, and their leader was a tough-looking brawler with numerous scars bearing mute testimony to a violent life. His human merchandise were roped together to keep them from escaping, though given the desert surrounding them this seemed entirely superfluous—there was nowhere to run to.

Eupolemus and Hanoch were moved by the realization that

the caravan came from Jerusalem, and suspected that the slaves were Jews. They introduced Flavius as a Roman emissary making his way from Alexandria to Antioch, and themselves as Egyptians serving as his guides and interpreters. The presence of the supposed Roman envoy led the usually taciturn slave trader to loosen his tongue in an attempt to impress and gain the favor of the representative of Rome. He revealed that the slaves were the children of Jewish families from the environs of Jerusalem, who had fallen into debt due to the excessive taxes placed on traditionalist Jews. The leader of the Jews appointed by the king, a priest called Menelaus, was responsible for collecting the king's tax quota. Finding it too difficult to collect the taxes from the villagers far from Jerusalem, in which bandit gangs roamed, he and his men had placed the entirety of the tax burden on the residents of the villages proximate to Jerusalem, where his rule was more stable. The families from which the youths were taken believed that they were being sent to Syria for a few years to work off their families' debts, while in practice they were being sold into slavery at full price. The Nabatean ordered a boy and girl to be brought before his guests to be displayed, stripped the girl savagely, and offered to sell them to the Roman emissary for a special price.

The girl wept silently, murmuring again and again in Aramaic, "Help me God, please, God...." while she covered her mouth with one hand and with the other tried to cover her small, firm breasts that jiggled in tempo with her sobs. The boy besides her looked younger. He did not utter a word and seemed overwhelmed by fatigue and despair.

The Nabatean laughed cruelly and pulled her hand away, displaying her nudity to the prospective buyers. "She is about sixteen, ripe and fruitful. She can only speak Aramaic, but will learn Latin fast enough. They are a bit filthy with the dust of our journey but you can see her beauty—would you like to have them washed up for you?"

Flavius felt ill at ease. Eupolemus, whose role required him to interpret the Nabatean's words into Latin, maintained a blank expression, but Flavius knew him well enough to sense how hard this scene was on him. For fear that Eupolemus might act rashly, Flavius thanked the Nabatean, refused his offer with restrained politeness, and excused himself as quickly as possible.

"There are nine of them," said Flavius sharply as they walked away. "These are not innocent merchants, these are men used to skirting the edge of the underworld."

"What will we do?" asked Hanoch.

Eupolemus swiftly considered their options and reached an unpalatable conclusion. "We mount our horses and move on," he said, finding the bitter words hard to spit out. "Saving a group of children won't help our people. If we attack them, some of the Nabateans may escape and expose us. One or more of us may be injured or killed in the fight. And then we would have to travel with a pack of children, which would limit and risk both them and us. This infuriates me, but it is the right thing to do."

Eupolemus had repeated his words in Latin for Flavius. Hanoch did not respond. He looked at the caravan, whose men had begun to prepare for their journey to Alexandria. His spirit revolted at the thought of abandoning the children to their fate, but he understood they had no choice.

Over the next few hours they rode in heavy silence, each immersed in his thoughts.

***

Matityahu had nurtured an intelligence network from the very first days of the rebellion. His agents included priests, headmen of villages near Jerusalem, and several moderate Hellenizers who maintained their loyalty to the Jewish tradition in secret. Phidias, the pankration trainer from Jerusalem, was another member of the network, risking being denounced as a traitor and executed for the cause of a foreign people.

The information this network provided enabled Matityahu to develop a fairly accurate assessment of the situation. He understood that the new garrison commander in Jerusalem, Philipus the Phrygian, lacked the resources or inclination to conduct a prolonged campaign in the hill country against the rebels. The soldiers of the garrison were not trained, experienced, or motivated to conduct such operations, and were too few to be successful at it. The primary task of Philipus was to ensure law and order in Jerusalem, in the main settlements and in the main highways. On the other hand, Matityahu understood that he could not push the Seleucid authorities too far and render Judea completely ungovernable—that would certainly provoke external intervention. Accordingly, Matityahu established a pattern of low intensity warfare from the hill country, focusing on the outlying villages. His military operations were based on rapid movement, raids and ambush, and destruction of the idolater altars. In the spirit of this policy, Matityahu encouraged the Jews of the villages outside the effective control of the Jerusalem collaborator government to continue to pay their taxes—but only to the extent that they were able. In this matter, just as in his military operations, Matityahu understood that reduced tax payment was something the regime might be prepared to swallow, whereas an all-out tax revolt would be certain to provoke a response he preferred to avoid at this point.

Matityahu's policy bore fruit, and Philipus, a career soldier whose primary concern was to ensure he would be rotated out of this trouble spot without too many complications, also worked to lower tensions from his end. Accordingly, he carried out the king's decrees in a pro-forma manner. Formally, the harsh decrees remained in force, but in practice he ceased enforcing them outside the walls of Jerusalem, and even in Jerusalem he ceased executing those caught practicing and upholding the Jewish traditions, merely flogging them.

The sun had begun to set. Within an hour darkness would fall upon the mountains and the cold would seep into the bones of those on its slopes. A few children still sat on the mountainside and were competing at stone throwing when they noticed three riders approaching from afar.

"We need to run warn the grownups," said one of the children, Matityahu ben Yohanan by name.

"They don't look too dangerous," replied his cousin, Matityahu ben Simon.

They were both six years and a few months old. Both had been named after their grandfather, Matityahu, the rebel leader.

"They could be angels," said another boy, "like the three angels who came to our forefather Abraham in the Torah."

"What are you talking about? Angels indeed," said the first Matityahu. "I'm telling you, we need to let the grownups know."

"Hey, nippers! What are you doing outside at this hour?" a cry rose behind them. One of the older boys had been sent outside to collect the younger ones. "Get back inside immediately!"

"I told you we should have told everyone. Now we will get in trouble," whined Matityahu ben Yohanan.

The youth who was sent out to call the children to their

families noticed the three riders and jumped back into the cave. A few seconds later, a young man, followed by several youths armed with bow and arrows, daggers, and swords, erupted from the cave and ran to the children. Two other boys rapidly ran at the ravine, calling the men. At the cave entrance several women and elders gathered, watching in trepidation as events unfolded.

The riders were still several hundred paces away but they soon noticed the panic that they had spread throughout the camp and halted. One of them drew erect in his saddle and called out from afar in Aramaic, "Peace be upon you; we are Jews. There is no cause for alarm."

The youths took position before the children, continuing to hold their weapons threateningly. Jonathan, the youngest of Matityahu's sons who happened to be in the cave when the event occurred and so led the youth, shouted firmly, "Who are you and what are you looking for here?!"

"Son of Modi'in," the stranger called out, astonishing all the youth, "I hope it is not your mother who taught you to be cheeky to the Hakotz priests, is it?"

The voice of the stranger echoed across the hilltops. The stranger removed a kerchief he had worn for protection against the sun and waved it in greeting.

"Eupolemus!" cried out Jonathan and, turning back, he shouted and waved with excitement to the people at the cave entrance, "It is Eupolemus! He has returned!"

A great bonfire was lit at the entrance to the cave, in blatant violation of every single precaution the rebels had put in place since the establishment of the camp. Several lambs were promptly slaughtered and spit over the fire. The inhabitants of the camp, women and men, babes and elders, gathered to gaze upon Eupolemus and listen to his stories. It seemed as if his mere presence in the camp, together with a representative from the Jewish community in Alexandria, instilled so much confidence in all of them to the point that their fear of the king's soldiers dwindled. Flavius also excited great attention, and the men stared at him in awe as if he were an important Roman leader. The two young Matityahus walked amongst all those assembled and bragged to anyone who was prepared to listen, and quite a few who were not, about how they were the first to see their guests. Several people held musical instruments in their hands, and the camp was soon making merry in song and dance in an explosive display of joy and relief.

The next morning, Matityahu summoned Eupolemus, Hanoch, and Judah to him.

"So, you ruffian, what brought you back to us?" Matityahu asked Eupolemus jokingly.

"I wish to one day write a story about the heroes of Judea, and I thought I could spare you a single chapter," Eupolemus answered in mock seriousness.

"Oh, I will shave my beard the day that you write a book," laughed Matityahu. "But jokes aside, you simply cannot stay here with us."

"What?! But I must stay here with you, I served and fought in the strongest army in the world, I can help in ways you can't even imagine...."

"Listen calmly. I have another task for you, one which would enable you to contribute much more."

Eupolemus fell silent, irritated, but his curiosity was kindled.

"Your father may have left Jerusalem, but he remains a respected member of the Polis. No one suspects, but he is feeding us information and influences decisions in our favor from within the Hellenizer power structure. Stay with us, and your father and family will suffer retaliation. You are young, energetic, sharp tongued, and now also surrounded by the aura of one who has visited far off lands. The Hellenizer youth will listen to your words. You will help us a great deal more by rejoining your father."

Eupolemus' heart told him to remain, but his head could not deny the logic of Matityahu's words. "I see your point. Let me stay for a week and share with you my knowledge of how the Roman army trains, manages supplies, and fights."

"Fine, but no more than a week. Do it with Judah and his brothers, and teach them as much as you can."

"Also, you met my Roman comrade in arms, Flavius. He served under my command and fought besides me. He is a true warrior. He came here in search of war, and to be honest he expected to be paid for it. He will have no interest in cooling his heels in Jerusalem with me. I don't know how long he will remain if you do not pay him, but I'm sure he will prefer to stay with you here and assist in your training. Judah told me he remembers some Latin, I think it would be very useful for him to communicate with Flavius."

"Great idea. We can pay him for his expertise—perhaps not at the same rate he would receive in the Hellenist armies, but he will be compensated for his troubles," Matityahu stated firmly, and turned to Hanoch. "What can we expect from our brethren in Egypt?"

Matityahu spoke no Greek, and so Judah had to translate the words of his father from Aramaic. Hanoch explained the position of the kings of Egypt and the leadership of the Jewish community in Alexandria, and spoke of the willingness of the Jewish veterans to join the rebellion.

"I will have to think on this," replied Matityahu. "In the

meantime I will be glad if you join Eupolemus and the Roman and assist us in training. Judah and his brothers did good work, but none of them have experience in a regular army or any idea how to fight one."

Following the arrival of Hanoch from Egypt, Matityahu gathered his officers to discuss the future conduct of the rebellion. Given the non-confrontational attitude of the authorities towards the rebels, and despite the potential possibilities of aid from Egypt, Matityahu saw no need for the arrival of volunteer battalions from Egypt at that point. Hanoch, who was hoping to lead a volunteer army in a holy war against the Seleucids, was initially disappointed, but he turned out to be practical and quick to adapt to the new situation and offer alternate initiatives. As a citizen of the Polis of Alexandria and a speaker of fluent Greek, he could travel throughout Judea in relative freedom. He therefore proposed to become part of the intelligence network, riding to Jerusalem and other settlements delivering messages and collecting information and helping to set up the foundations for the rebel army.

Judah had indeed long been concerned about the inferior skills of his warriors, who had almost no familiarity with melee weapons such as spears and swords, and who simply had no concept of fighting as a unit. He feared the day they would have to meet professional units of the royal army in pitched battle. The rebels' firm belief in divine providence only made things worse as far as he was concerned, and he was determined to remedy the situation, assembling his warriors and sternly addressing them.

"Brothers, a true hand to hand battle is neither a game nor an encounter decided by a miracle from heaven. It is an ugly, cruel, and painful thing. Those participating in it can suffer severe injuries, be crippled, and even die. To be prepared for battle we must train, train… and train some more. Prior to any cunning tactic, fighting spirit, leadership, courage, and divine intervention, all of which are always welcome, the basis for war is."

"That God is with us!" shouted one of the men, Joseph ben Zachariah by name. The response of many of the warriors showed that they shared his faith.

Judah felt that he was not getting through to them. He had to shock them if he wished to punch through their excessive confidence. "Joseph, please rise!"

The man stood up, grinning in satisfaction.

"Take with you two men and bring here twenty-two sticks, branches, boards, anything you can find with which we can train in fighting that is not an actual weapon," Judah ordered him.

Judah then approached Eupolemus and Flavius and quietly explained his plan to them.

A short time later, when the three returned with the sticks, Judah invited those who considered themselves to be the best fighters to rise. His two younger brothers, Elazar and Jonathan, immediately stood up, but he signaled them to sit back down. He chose twenty warriors, including Joseph, and ordered them to arm themselves with sticks and face the others. Eupolemus and Flavius then each picked up a stick and took position thirty paces away from the score of rebels Judah had selected.

"Pay attention, Jews," shouted Judah, who remained standing in the middle of the arena, at the warriors and the audience facing him, "Eupolemus and the Roman are now your enemies. In a moment they will attack you. You must defend yourselves and seek to overcome them. This is no game—whoever does not strike will be struck down."

To the surprise of the score of rebel fighters, Eupolemus and

Flavius immediately charged them. When the charging pair reached within ten paces of the befuddled group, five of the more daring rebels countercharged them, yelling and flailing their sticks.

To the audience watching the spectacle it seemed as if Eupolemus and Flavius mowed through them as if they were papyrus reeds. Within moments the five were lying on the ground bruised, stunned and groaning in pain. Eupolemus and Flavius didn't even slow down, charging through their downed foes and reaping the remaining rebels as if they were no more than wheat in the field. Their wooden "swords" struck repeatedly with blurring speed as the two bobbed and weaved through their bewildered opponents, slamming into them with their fists, elbows, and knees, kicking feet and the "hilts" and "blades" of their wooden "swords". The entire fight lasted no more than a few moments, and at its conclusion most of the score-strong rebel band was scattered on the ground, battered and bruised, except for a few who were wise enough to toss their sticks to the ground and give up without a fight.

"Well, as I was saying...." continued Judah as if nothing had happened, "The basis for victory in battle is a trained army! People who understand what they are in for, know what they must do, and are prepared to do it. This is true of pankration in the ring, just as true for single combat to the death, and doubly true for coordinated unit action in the battle of one army against another. There are exceptional cases, in which brave citizen soldiers were able to overcome trained professionals, but they always had some edge which enabled them to do so."

"Like I said, God is with us," insisted Joseph, groaning with pain from where he lay battered on the ground, having taken quite a knocking about from Eupolemus' wooden "sword".

Judah had a hard time concealing his amusement at Joseph's seemingly stubborn belief. "I do not doubt it—you have just proved as much." Then Judah grew serious and continued, "I will always pray to God for success, but I have never heard of a battle whose outcome could not be attributed to a rational reason. Within the fury of the field, the causes of victory and defeat are not always apparent; but later, when one analyzes and studies the battle, a logical explanation always emerges. **The important thing is that we do not want to rely on luck or on miracles**. We must be prepared and trained for combat. If the demonstration you had just seen had been real combat with real weapons… then all these men would now be dead," said Judah, pointing with his stick at the bruised warriors strewn about the "battlefield".

A week later Eupolemus and Hanoch left the camp, Hanoch heading straight to Jerusalem and Eupolemus to visit his father's house, intending upon settling in Jerusalem thereafter.

Later that night, Matityahu called Judah to him. Judah found him lying on his pallet, his eyes closed. Assuming his father had fallen asleep, Judah began to turn away.

"Do not go. I am awake," Matityahu said quietly. He rose to recline on his elbow and gestured Judah to sit besides him.

"Father, are you well? You seem to be in pain."

"I am well enough," smiled Matityahu and stroked Judah's face with his hand. "But yes, I suffer from pains. I do not know what it is. It is hard to find a good doctor up here in the mountains…."

The two of them smiled, but Judah seemed worried. "How serious is it?"

"Pretty serious, apparently. I will most likely not live as long as your grandfather of blessed memory did. But I will die happy, amongst all my children, and in the company of free and proud men."

"I am sure that we can somehow secure a doctor! If need be we will send for one from Alexandria...."

"Peace, Judah. We have our own doctors, and they are good enough. But sometimes there is nothing to be done."

They sat together in silence for a time and then Matityahu spoke out. "Something is troubling you, Judah. I can see it in your eyes. Ever since Eupolemus arrived. What is it?"

Judah told his father about the Nabatean caravan and the children sold by Menelaus to slavery. "Eupolemus told me about it. I cannot get the girl he described out of my head. As if I was there myself. I imagine her looking at me, crying out for my help, and then she just looks at me in silence, as if she is feeling sorry for me, pitying me for my cowardice. We are doing nothing to save our people from terrible and cruel slavery, for supposedly logical reasons—for expediency. I am ashamed of myself, father. Nothing can justify abandoning children in this manner."

"Only angels do not err, my son. Men make mistakes. I have nightmares often. I dream about the Hellenizer I slew in Modi'in. I do not know if my hand was guided by God or not. I want to believe that it is God that made me take a step from which there would be no turning back. As for the girl, things are even worse than what you think. I am responsible for the fate of these children. Menelaus must meet his tax quotas. The policy I promoted in the outlying regions has led people to reduce their taxes to what they can bear—which is less than what Menelaus requires to meet his quotas. I thought this would lead him to tax the rich Hellenizer citizens of the Polis. It turns out that I was mistaken."

"What will we do now, father? Where do we go from here? How long can we hide out in the mountains and make do with harassing the Hellenizers? Sooner or later we will have to face down the Seleucid army."

Matityahu's eyes glittered in the light thrown by the torches on the cave walls.

"I know, you are right. You must prepare our people, Judah. You must make an army of them. The day is not far in which it will be time to move to the next stage in our struggle. You were also right when you told our men that we were not ready. As you have proven the other day to all doubters."

Matityahu lay back on his bed, closed his eyes, and added with a smile, "There was simply no one to make us ready. I am a priest, a village headman, not a general. It was you who were born for battle, you who are the right man for the job...."

Judah examined his father's face. He noted the many new wrinkles in his face. In the torchlight his father seemed older than his age. Judah placed his hands softly on his father's stomach, who fondly patted him on his hand. He rose to leave, but his father's whisper halted him.

"One more thing, son. Be very careful about doubting the possibility of divine aid. We have a diverse group here. Some of our people believe God is involved in every aspect of our lives. Others fully believe in his existence but doubt his involvement in our life. Some perhaps do not believe at all..."

"I believe!"

"I know, I know. What I am saying is that right now we need a unifying leader, who will be followed and supported by all factions. The priests of Zadok lost their birthright by their own hands, but they still hold great influence amongst the people. They will see you as a threat because you are a priest who is not of their line. For centuries, they have nourished a tradition according to which the descendants of the priest Zadok are the only ones entitled to the High Priesthood. But Zadok received this birthright from man, not from God[25]. They fear the more ancient tradition according to which the priest Pinchas was promised the priesthood by God, on account of his loyalty and zealous faith in God[26]. The tradition of Pinchas is the more correct one, and one that favors our leadership, for as priests we are just as much his descendants as the line of Zadok. However, at this point the support of the Zadok priests is essential. Be careful and do not speak to any particular audience. Be respectful of the Zadokite priests, and do not question the involvement of God in our lives or our struggle. Try to maintain consensus and emphasize that which unites us as a people—common goals, a shared past, and our values."

"I just don't want them to bank on miracles and expect God to do all of our work for us."

Matityahu's eyes glittered in amusement. "Too bad; that would have been nice, just this once...."

---

25 The high priesthood was promised to the line of Zadok by King Solomon. Kings 1, chapter 2, verses 26-27 and 35.

26 Numbers, chapter 25, verses 11-13.

End of summer 167 BCE— Friendship and Loyalty

Dramatis Personae
Bold = main character
* = historical figure

- *Menelaus*—The current High Priest. Appointed in 171 BCE by Antiochus IV*
- *Mithridates (Antiochus IV)*—King of the Seleucid Kingdom since 175 BCE, also titled Antiochus Epiphanes*
- *Matityahu*—Father of Judah and his brothers, village priest of Modi'in*
- *Yohanan*, Simon*, Judah*, Hannah*, Eleazar* and Jonathan*—The children of Matityahu and Rebecca by age*
- *Eupolemus*—A friend of Judah, son of Yohanan ben Hakotz*
- *Flavius—Roman legionary*
- *Hanoch—Alexandrian Jewish warrior and former officer in the army of Egypt*
- *Joseph*—Matityahu's brother*
- *Elnatan—Devout Jewish leader*
- *Phidias—Pankration trainer*
- *Philipus the Phrygian*—Current Seleucid garrison commander in Jerusalem*

- *Misa—The Jewish slave girl of Phidias*
- *Malalas—A slave trader*
- *Hadad—The personal servant of Malalas*
- *Sika—Malalas' bodyguard*

The group that had gathered in the big cave numbered fifty men. Matityahu and his five sons, Joseph, his brother, and two of his elder sons, and the patriarchs of other families from Modi'in and some of their sons, and a few other patriarchs from the villages adjacent to Modi'in. These were the men who had joined Matityahu and who made up the nucleus of the uprising. They silently listened to the voices from outside the cave, where one of the leaders of a group of faithful read verses from the Torah scrolls to his men. The words that penetrated into the cave echoed off the walls, on which the lights of the small fire that burned in the middle of the cave flickered.

"If you hear in one of your cities, which the LORD your God is giving you to live in, anyone saying that some worthless men have gone out from among you and have seduced the inhabitants of their city, saying, 'Let us go and serve other gods' whom you have not known, then you shall investigate and search out and inquire thoroughly. If it is true and the matter established that this abomination has been done among you, you shall surely strike the inhabitants of that city with the edge of the sword, utterly destroying it and all that is in it and its cattle with the edge of the sword. In order that the LORD may turn from His burning anger and show mercy to you, and have compassion on you and make you increase, just as He has sworn to your fathers, if you will listen to the voice of the LORD your God, keeping all His commandments which I am commanding you today, and doing what is right in the sight of the LORD your God."

Matityahu sighed at the sound of the sonorous chant of the verses from the scroll of Deuteronomy[27]. The dark and endless desert had always filled those who resided within it with mystical feelings, he thought. The religious fanatics who had recently joined them were pulling their group in an overly extreme direction. Elnatan, their leader, had lost his father and three brothers a few months ago. They were murdered by Antiochus' soldiers together with hundreds of others, including elders, women, and children. They were traditionalist Jews who desired nothing more than the freedom to live by the traditions and faith of their ancestors. They had fled into the hill country between Jerusalem and Bethlehem and lived there in caves and tents. When the soldiers first pursued them there, they drove them away with a barrage of stones they flung at them from the mountain heights. The soldiers returned on Saturday in greater numbers and determination. The Jews remained seated and prayed, refusing to violate the Sabbath, even when the soldiers began to slaughter them. Only a single elder had survived, and that only because the Seleucid commander responsible for the slaughter desired the tale to spread throughout Judea as an object lesson. The elder did indeed spread the tale, and added that the soldiers were accompanied by Hellenizers and that it was they who advised the soldiers to arrive on the Sabbath, knowing that traditionalists would not fight at that time.

Elnatan was not in the camp at the time. When he heard what had happened to his family, he swore to avenge himself upon the Hellenizers. Jewish men, both hot headed youths and mature men who had lost their families to the soldiers, gathered around him. They were all filled with faith and extreme religious

---

27   Deuteronomy, Chapter 13, verses 14-29.

passion, which won them the title "Hassidim." They travelled between the villages, told the villagers what the soldiers and Hellenizers had done, and further enflamed hatred against the Hellenizers.

In contrast to the legend that arose around him, Matityahu's opinions regarding the Hellenizers were far from extreme. Unlike Elnatan and his followers, he did not view them as enemies. He realized that the Hellenizers, just like the traditionalists, were divided into different factions, some moderate, some less so, and that some Hellenizers adopted the outer customs of the Greeks without renouncing the Jewish traditions. He felt that the decisions that would be reached in the cave this night would have far-ranging effects on the future.

The recitation from the scroll of Deuteronomy ended and Elnatan and three of his followers entered the cave and joined the assembly. Matityahu nodded at him and spoke, carefully considering his words.

"Simon the Righteous, of blessed memory, led Judea for forty years. He was the Patriarch of the House of Zadok as well as High Priest, and the founder of the Council of Elders. Simon the Righteous determined that the President of the Council would not be a priest, and instead appointed Antigonus of Sokho to this position. This was a very clear and very brave statement. He handed the leadership of the body to a man with a Greek name, the scion of a Hellenizer family, who spoke the language and knew the customs of the Hellenes. Antigonus of blessed memory was the student of Simon the Righteous and followed in his footsteps, and that seems to have been the most important factor in his decision. We also all know the good work of the priest Yohanan ben Hakotz, who lobbied Antiochus the father and won great concessions from him, which enabled Jerusalem to recover and flourish. He too was a Hellenizer."

Elnatan and his men moved in discomfort, clearly disquieted by Matityahu's words.

"Honorable Matityahu," responded Elnatan, "I do not think that at the time you mention anyone would have expected Hellenizers to instruct soldiers on how to murder observant Jews on the Sabbath, and support a king who forbade us to uphold the commandments of the Torah. The situation has changed—and the Hellenizers are the enemy!"

Matityahu nodded soothingly, well aware of the tension Elnatan and his followers were in.

"When we are young, we tend to see life in black and white. Everything is clear. I am completely right, and the other side is completely wrong. My long years have given me a different perspective, and I know that it is not so. Who are we to presume to interpret and explain the intentions of the Creator? We must fight where we have to fight, and whom we have to fight. We must fight so that **we will be able to uphold the commandments of the Torah, not to force others to uphold them**. We must never place ourselves above or disqualify our fellow Jews, nor strike out against them merely for not thinking or acting as we do. Who is to determine which Jew is pure and which is profane?"

"You want us to greet the traitors in peace?!" Elnatan's voice quivered in barely suppressed outrage.

"Elnatan, in your place I too would seek revenge. I am not trying to diminish for a moment your terrible loss. The evildoers who murdered your family hurt us, all of us, as well. They have murdered our people, our kin, and we will have our revenge, you have my word on that. But the revenge must be tightly focused against the people who hurt us, and them alone, and not against all Hellenizers. We will pursue and bring the traitors who participated in this terrible crime to justice, our justice; perhaps even get our hands on the Hellene who commanded the action. We will also fight those extreme Hellenizers who are collaborating with the king and encouraging him to oppress us. Whoever raises his hands against our people, Greek or Syrian, Hellenizer or traditionalist, whether on the weekday **or on the Sabbath**—he shall perish by the sword. We are a peaceful people, but we will know how to fight in this hour of need. The tyrant has wakened a sleeping lion and his men will soon feel its fangs."

Cries of assent echoed throughout the cave. The words of Matityahu filled the listeners with enthusiasm.

Matityahu continued speaking, his voice soft and authoritative, "Three decisions will be made on this night. The first: death to traitors. A Hellenizer who murders or assists in the murder of our fellow people shall be slain by the sword. The second is that we have no quarrel with Hellenizers merely because they are Hellenizers; they are flesh of our flesh, an inseparable part of our people. The third is that should our enemies seek to exploit the Sabbath against us once more, we shall meet them in battle."

Silence fell across the cave. Most of those present agreed with Matityahu, and waited to see how Elnatan would respond. They were determined to fight for their freedom, but did not wish to be dragged into a bitter and fratricidal war by hatred and lust for vengeance.

Elnatan took a deep breath and considered Matityahu's words. The men of Modi'in were proud and brave. They were the first to raise the standard of rebellion and the first to fight back. Where would he and his men go if he broke ranks with them? He sat in silence for a while, and then drew erect and concurred.

"I will be content to take revenge on those who murdered

my family. Honored Matityahu, I will be honored to follow your footsteps and heed your words. It is no longer right to consider me the commander of those who came with me. We are all your soldiers now."

***

Over the past months, Phidias and Judah had met in secret outside Jerusalem on several occasions. Phidias had acquired a Jewish slave girl named Misa a year ago. He rapidly fell in love and freed her. She remained with him as a free woman, and as his companion, though they never married. Because of her, as time passed he felt closer to the traditionalists than to the citizens of the Polis. One day he decided he was tired of training the Hellenizer youth to fight the people he loved. He quit his job in the gymnasium, and left Jerusalem without anyone but a worried Misa knowing where he was headed.

A few days later, he unexpectedly showed up at the entrance of the rebel camp. Judah tried to talk him into returning to Jerusalem where he would be safe, but to no avail. Phidias immediately fit into the rebel training regimen, cooperating and in a funny way even competing with Flavius the Roman. He felt more satisfaction and joy in his life than he had known in years. The skills the brave rebels had achieved within such a short time under Judah's leadership astounded him. Phidias was proud of himself for training Judah as a youth. Their friendship, kindled years ago in the gymnasium, grew into total loyalty.

After two weeks of intense training, Phidias forced himself to part from Judah and his men, promising to soon return. He intended to sell his property in Jerusalem, join his woman, Misa, and relocate with her to the rebel camp permanently.

That evening he made his way back to Jerusalem. He walked the streets of the city alone, towards his home, a large backpack on his back. He did not know that in his absence the soldiers of Philipus, the garrison commander, had kidnapped Misa and imprisoned her in the dungeons of the Akra. Philipus, who had his own intelligence network, had been suspicious of Phidias for some time now. When he found out that Phidias had left the city, he ordered his agents to capture his woman and to wring every last bit of information about Phidias's comings and goings from her. In spite of her great love for Phidias, Misa could not withstand the torture. She broke down and told the torturers everything she knew. Philipus was careful not to persecute the Jews too harshly in order to avoid driving more of them into the ranks of the rebellion, or the rebels into acts of desperation, but he was determined to forcefully punish any treason in the Hellene ranks.

Phidias sensed he was under surveillance a city block before he reached his house. His heart shrank with fear for Misa. He took off his pack and straightened and stretched as if he required rest. He then rummaged through his pack, stealthily pulling out a knife and hiding it under his clothes, noticing two men who seemed to be following him at about twenty paces. He was angry at himself for not noticing them earlier.

The moment he turned onto the street his home was on, he noticed four soldiers standing guard the entrance to his home. He made a quick decision, and turned around, marching straight at the two agents following him.

The agents hesitated. They exchanged glances, wondering whether they should seize him or wait. The orders they had were to trail him and help the soldiers capture him if need be, but not to try to capture him themselves. Phidias may have been discharged from the garrison several years ago, and may have been unfamiliar to the new soldiers, who had not served with him, but they all knew of his achievements as the pankration trainer and former fighter.

Phidias recognized their hesitation, and had already begun to hope he would be able to pass them, lead them scampering at his heels to an out-of-the-way alley, and there personally introduce them to Hades, God of the Underworld and ruler of the dead. Three steps before he arrived, one of the agents made his decision. Phidias could see it in his eyes. The man reached out to Phidias, who twisted aside, pulling the outstretched arm with him and forcing his assailant to stumble, unbalanced. He immediately twisted back and stabbed his assailant with the dagger he had unsheathed beneath his cloak. The eyes and mouth of the agent opened widely, and he dropped to the ground unconscious. The other agent had no chance to realize what hit his friend. He tried to grab Phidias, who pre-empted him with a roundhouse blow to his chin with the hilt of his knife. The agents head was slammed aside, a second blow slammed immediately thereafter into his solar plexus, emptying his lungs from air, and then darkness descended upon him, with another blow to the back of his neck knocking him unconscious.

Phidias rushed away from the site of the brief scuffle, trying to leave the area before the passersby understood what had happened. His heart beat with hope. He knew that as soon as he got past the walls of the city the darkness of night would shield him from pursuit. Once he made it to the rebel camp he and Judah would figure out how to free Misa. Then he heard shouting behind him. Glancing over his shoulder, he saw the four soldiers who had been standing guard in front of his house running at him, their swords drawn. They were accompanied by another man, who Phidias recognized as a man who had walked before him earlier on his way to his home. Phidias belatedly realized he was another plainclothes agent and that he had called the soldiers as soon as Phidias neutralized his comrades who had shadowed him from the rear.

Phidias threw his pack at the soldiers and began to flee at a run. He heard loud shouting behind him, but he did not glance back again. He turned sharply into a dark, narrow alley without slowing down for a moment. After running for a good long while through a maze of twisting and interweaving alleys, the sounds of pursuit fell away—he had evaded his pursuers. He entered a narrow trail between the homes flanking the alley and hid away in the inner courtyard of one of the houses, catching his breath.

After recovering, Phidias carefully blended into the crowds and made his way to the gates of the city. Having reassured himself that the gate guards were showing no more signs of activity than usual, he pulled his cloak around him, hiding his features, and began making his way towards it, jostling with other wayfarers making their way out of the city. When he reached ten paces from the gate he realized that he was captured. Four soldiers began walking towards him with drawn blades. From the other direction another squad of soldiers approached him, and through the gate Phidias saw yet another squad prepared to intercept any attempt at a breakout. Understanding that the situation was hopeless, he decided to sell his life dearly, drawing his dagger and charging forward at the soldiers. They reacted as one with deadly force. They may have been ordered to capture Phidias alive, but none were prepared to risk their lives subduing an armed man.

Phidias was deprived of any burial. His body was tossed into the ravine outside the city walls, where it was devoured by wild animals. His property was formally confiscated, including Misa, who remained a prisoner in the Akra.

Word of Phidias' death reached the rebel camp within a week. Everyone knew that Phidias was worried about Misa and had returned to Jerusalem on her account, but did not know what had happened to her. Many in the camp, including Judah, felt obligated to honor Phidias' memory, and were prepared to take the risk of infiltrating Jerusalem to rescue her.

Matityahu disapproved. "That is tantamount to entering the lion's den. We have avoided undertaking any operations in Jerusalem up to this point. It is simply too dangerous."

Matityahu met Judah's determined gaze. He knew that expression all too well.

"Father, I owe this much to Phidias. We all do. We must at least try, in the name of friendship and loyalty. I give you my word that we won't try anything too crazy...."

"Going there is crazy!" Joseph, his uncle, cut in, "And if you think this is necessary, why risk yourself? Send Eupolemus to find out what happened to her. Chances are that she was reduced back to slavery and that he will be able to buy her."

"We can't risk exposing Eupolemus," Matityahu stepped in decisively. "His role is too important to link him to us in any way."

"Then send Hanoch and Flavius. No one knows them. You, on the other hand, could be identified."

"Hanoch and Flavius don't know the city like I do. I know every alley of it. They speak different languages, Greek and Latin. I can communicate with both. Together we are the team that can pull this off."

Judah stared at his father in supplication. It was clear to both of them that he would not take no for an answer and was only requesting his father's permission out of politeness. Matityahu traded glances with Judah's brothers, deliberating on whether he should explain, but then nodded in confirmation silently.

Infiltrating Jerusalem proved easier than they had feared. They arrived at the city from the West, mounted on horses. Hanoch took the van, dressed as a respectable Hellene, Judah and Flavius preceding him, playing the role of servants. Their path crossed the terraced hills covered with the homes built outside the walls.

They stabled their horses in the public stables near the gate in the walls of the city and made their way through the streets of the city on foot. Judah gradually noticed traditionalist Jews: beggars and panhandlers, peddlers at the street corners, beaten and humiliated men. Judah never imagined the situation had deteriorated so badly. But nothing could prepare him for the site of the Temple. Hanoch and he were drawn there, as if by an invisible force. Judah's heart ached with every step as he saw the statues of Zeus placed at the entry to the courtyard, saw and could not believe. They entered the court and witnessed with their own eyes that the Temple, the Jews' most holy site, had been transformed into a temple of Zeus.

They stumbled out. Judah noticed the tavern which, years ago, had been owned by a Cypriot officer. At that time, the owner had been respectful to his Jewish neighbors. They entered and sat at a side table. A waiter approached them, and Hanoch asked him who the current proprietor was. The waiter pointed his chin at a fat man sitting by the bar and conversing loudly with two other men. He had not been the proprietor at the time Judah had lived in Jerusalem as a young man. Hanoch asked the waiter to summon the proprietor and ordered food and a flagon of wine.

A few minutes later the owners turned to them. "Welcome, I believe I have never seen you before. Are you new in town?" he asked Hanoch, ignoring the other two, whom he treated as servants.

"This is not my first visit, but I have yet to have had the pleasure of being hosted by you," answered Hanoch.

"Are you seeking a place to stay? I have comfortable rooms. I can also give a room to your servants, or we can have them sleep in the stables. Where are you from?"

"From Alexandria, thank you. The city has changed from the time I last saw it. It seems that its Jews are all gone?"

"Well, not completely gone. But the king has given them a harsh blow and that's the truth. Their religion is forbidden by royal decree. There was a time we had quite a few entertainments around this issue. Jews were bound to the whipping posts," he pointed with his chin to the plaza outside the tavern, "and forced to declare their faith in Zeus and eat the flesh of swine. Those brave few who refused were whipped, sometimes to death. Many of them left the city, and others, those who adopted our customs, are citizens like any other. Are you one of them?"

"Me?! No, I'm not," answered Hanoch in fluent Greek. "Tell me, when I was last here I saw a pankration tournament in the gymnasium. I am a great fan of the pankration and I was pleasantly surprised. They said that there was a Hellene trainer, who was once an Olympic contestant, who established a high-level school here."

The tavern-keeper's eyes narrowed in suspicion. He was clearly hesitant to speak. "Do you know this trainer?" he asked cautiously.

"No, I never met him. I was active in pankration in my day,

and if there are demonstration or tournament fights occurring presently I would be happy to see them," Hanoch answered calmly, trying to soothe the tavern proprietor's suspicions.

"It seems there will be no pankration fights anytime soon. I did, in fact, know the trainer you mentioned," The innkeeper leaned forward and lowered his voice to a whisper. "He would come here occasionally. It turned out that he was training the rebels living in the mountains. The fool fell for a woman. He left a Jewish slave girl, whom he had made his wife, but when the garrison commander got his hands on her she sang like a canary. Now he trains the pankration only to the snakes of Hades."

"So, his wife sold him out?"

"Look, she didn't really sell him out. They forced the information from her. They say she loved him. The soldiers took their pleasure with her later, saved them the coppers they would have paid the whores. I know that straight from them; they frequently patronize my establishment."

"What happened to her? Do they still have her?"

"No, after her man was killed while resisting arrest, she became a total wreck and was sold to Malalas, the slave trader," the tavern-owner said and rose ponderously from the table.

Hanoch silently nodded. He recalled the slave girl he had seen on the Nabatean caravan.

Malalas maintained a large fortified compound on the outskirts of Jerusalem, outside the walls. It was not his permanent residence, for he was the owner of a vast estate in Syria. However, his business in the slave trade forced him to maintain many compounds throughout the kingdom. He had connections in the royal palace in Antioch, which was how he was able to secure a royal franchise for the slave trade in several cities in the kingdom.

The bell which hung over the main gate rang. It was a late hour for unplanned visits. Malalas wondered what business his unexpected visitors were on. His personal servant, Hadad, peeked from the doorway with a querying expression. Malalas shook his head slowly, indicating his ignorance, and rose towards the yard. It is too late for a visit, he thought, and remained standing on the porch. Sika, his personal guard, joined him, casually wielding a broadsword in his right hand. Hadad advanced toward the gate.

"Wait!" cried out Malalas. He decided not to take a risk. He would not be the first slave trader to be ambushed and robbed— or worse. He gestured at Sika, his guard, who immediately understood his desires and withdrew into the darkness. Malalas kept a group of thugs to guard the slaves. They were usually cruel men, whose attitude suited breaking the spirit of fresh slaves. Malalas entered the house quickly and returned after a short moment, a sword under his tunic. He then ordered Hadad to approach the gate.

Hadad spoke softly with someone in the street, then closed the gate and approached Malalas.

"Three people, master. A Greek master and two servants. He is going through the city and early tomorrow morning he must leave. He has expressed a certain interest in a particular slave girl. He did not say who specifically he was interested in…."

Malalas silenced Hadad with a hand wave. The whole matter seemed suspicious to him. He sought Sika, who had yet to return. "Tell them to come back tomorrow. But during the daytime."

"Sir, he apologized for coming so late and said he is willing to pay double."

Sika signaled at him from the other side of the courtyard that he and the other guards were ready.

Malalas' greed got the better of him. "Oh, very well," he grumbled. "Let's see how high he is prepared to go."

Judah entered first, Hanoch and Flavius at his heels. He and Hanoch had changed roles this time, with Judah playing the Hellene gentleman. "Greetings, master. May the blessings of the gods be upon you," he welcomed Malalas in Greek, smiling kindly.

Malalas was solid and well-built, in excellent shape for a fifty-year-old man. He had many years of active military service behind him, including commanding and carrying out missions of which the less told the better. His son had taken his place in the royal guard following his discharge, and he had devoted himself to enriching himself through the slave trade. It was a business in which reading people based on their behavior, gait, expression, and breath was essential. It was important in trade, and particularly important in selecting and sorting slaves. Now his senses told him that he was facing a man determined to get what he came for.

"Welcome, stranger. What brings you to my home at this time?"

"I beg your forgiveness concerning the late hour. I must leave early tomorrow morning. A few years ago, I met a man who helped me immensely. In fact, I owe him a grave personal debt. I was sorrowful to hear that he was killed and that his woman wound up in your possession. I feel obligated towards my old friend to redeem her, and would be prepared to pay you generously for the woman."

Malalas knew the story of the slave girl whom the garrison commander had handed over to him a few days ago. She belonged to a traitor who had been killed after being accused of aiding the rebels. If the story regarding her master was correct, then his uninvited guests were most likely associated with the rebels as well. She had come to him with no desire to live, and he feared she would be worthless. This could, therefore, be an opportunity to get rid of the slave girl and make a hefty profit on her as well.

"Come on in—but alone!"

Malalas signaled Sika and entered the residence, Judah following him closely. Sika and his four men advanced to the gate from the side of the courtyard, swords drawn. They stood menacingly in front of Flavius and Hanoch, ensuring they did not enter. Sika followed his master and Judah into the residence.

Malalas reclined on a couch in the parlor and invited Judah to join him, Hadad lighting the torches in the corners of the room. Sika remained standing at the end of the room, his sword in his hand.

"Bring the woman," Malalas ordered Hadad. "Before you think about doing anything stupid, my friend," Malalas told Judah, as he withdrew the dagger concealed under the folds of his tunic and placed it beside him, "I must warn you that I was an officer in the royal guard. This man here," he nodded at Sika, "served with me. Together, we killed more people than you have known in your entire life. Wait, wait, let me finish," he continued swiftly before Judah could interrupt him. "Your Greek is good, but not good enough. I know you are associated with the rebels. That does not bother me. On the contrary, I appreciate courage and loyalty. Your attempt to rescue this woman impresses me."

Hadad entered the room, pushing before him a young, scrawny, and debilitated woman. She swayed, unbalanced and weak. She looked across the men seated in the room, eyes filled with despair, and then dropped her gaze.

Judah understood that his cover was blown. He stood up and

turned to the girl, speaking in Aramaic, "Misa, I am a friend of Phidias. Don't lose hope…."

"Silence!" commanded Malalas, who did not understand Aramaic. "I did not say you could speak to her. This slave girl is still mine!"

"How much?" asked Judah, laconically. He assumed that the slave trader would ask for a high price, now that they were exposed.

"Relax, fellow. I like you. I need to think this through. Letting you have this girl might create serious problems for me with the garrison commander, Philipus. I might even have to make as if you liberated her by stealth."

"If that's what you want, we can do just that," said Judah.

Malalas responded with an outburst of laughter. "That's what I like about you, brimming with self-confidence. Look, for me this is just business. I will sell her to you for a talent of silver."

Judah was expecting a high price, but the sum named by Malalas was absurd. "I will pay twice the price of a regular slave," he said, his voice restrained. "That is a fair price. I cannot go higher."

The face of the slave trader grew dark in anger. "Get him out of here!"

Sika advanced, sword pointed at Judah's chest, nearly picking his skin. Judah began to compliantly turn right, towards the exit portal, casually deflecting the sword aside with his left hand without looking at Sika, but then spun back rapidly, launching an open-handed blow at Sika's throat, followed by a crushing kick to Sika's kneecap. Sika dropped the sword and fell, choking, grasping at his throat with one hand and at his shattered knee with the other. His eyes bulged with hate and pain, but he was out of the fight.

Malalas froze for a moment in place and then charged,

swinging his sword down at Judah. Judah sprung backwards and grabbed Malalas wrist, twisting in the direction of the sword swing, and then reversing course to the opposite direction, nearly snapping Malalas' wrist. Malalas choked in pain, dropped the sword, and tried to punch Judah with his off hand, but Judah dodged the blow, twisted Malalas' sword arm behind his back and pushed him forcefully forward, slamming his head hard against the wall, and then again for good measure.

Hadad hurled a large vase at Judah's head from the back and fled the room, calling out for the guards. Judah noticed the incoming object from the corner of his eye and was able to slightly shift his head, so that the heavy vase only bruised his shoulder. The distraction, however, led him to release Malalas for a moment, who took the opportunity to leap with a roar on Judah. He throttled Judah's throat with both hands, ignoring the pain he felt in his wrist.

Judah responded swiftly, chopping his palm down on Malalas' throat yet again who, stunned, let go of Judah's throat. Two powerful punches to the chin of the slave trader put him out of the fight completely.

Judah lifted Malalas' sword and led Misa outside. Flavius and Hanoch stood in the entrance to the house. The four guards lay on the ground, severely injured. Hadad, Malalas' servant, crouched in the corner of the yard, shivering in fear.

"Thanks for coming to my aid inside!" Judah said, looking at Flavius.

"What?! We had four of them to take care of...." protested Flavius until he noticed Judah's laughing eyes.

They remounted the horses, Misa holding on to Judah, and galloped into the night, rapidly leaving the city.

Made in the USA
Columbia, SC
28 December 2024

50808049R00176